# Enter the Moon

A Warriors of Luna Novel

Jennifer Fisch-Ferguson

No part of this publication may be reproduced in whole or in part, by any means, without written permission of the author.

Copyright © 2013 Jennifer Fisch-Ferguson

All rights reserved.

ISBN-13: 978-0-9911088-9-3

# DEDICATION

To Don, my mate and creative sounding board. To Alexander and Grayson who are amazing and insightful. To Pam- who knew editing could be such an amazing journey! Thanks to the rest of my friends and family who encouraged me.

# CONTENTS

CHAPTER One ................................................................................. 5

CHAPTER Two ................................................................................ 19

CHAPTER Three ............................................................................. 34

CHAPTER Four ............................................................................... 60

CHAPTER Five ................................................................................ 78

CHAPTER Six .................................................................................. 96

CHAPTER Seven ........................................................................... 110

CHAPTER Eight ............................................................................. 125

CHAPTER Nine ............................................................................. 136

CHAPTER Ten ............................................................................... 152

CHAPTER Eleven .......................................................................... 167

CHAPTER Twelve .......................................................................... 183

CHAPTER Thirteen ....................................................................... 197

CHAPTER Fourteen ...................................................................... 214

CHAPTER Fifteen .......................................................................... 231

CHAPTER Sixteen ......................................................................... 247

ABOUT THE AUTHOR ................................................................. 264

# PROLOGUE

Hot breath caressed her neck in an overly bold and too familiar touch which scared her; only because it caused her to shudder with desire. With a push against the hard body she launched herself to her feet and began to run. Branches and brambles tore at her clothes and hair with vicious yanks as she fought to make her way into the clearing. Heavy in its fullness, the Harvest moon hung suspended above her, and sat just above the horizon like a balloon ready to burst. It spilled precious light down and illuminated the unstable path she had to take. A long howl sounded close by and spurned her on faster than before. Fear slammed through her body as her breath left her lungs in a sharp exhale, and not paying enough attention she tripped and fell to the hard packed earth.

Tears coursed down her face making muddy trails as she looked behind her. Nothing yet, but she knew it was just a matter of time before he came to claim her; body and soul. She knew He wouldn't settle for anything less, and the terrifying thought made her scramble to her feet, ripping her long skirt to tatters in the process. It didn't matter and she began her run again. Soon her lungs burned and throbbed in her chest as her flight forced her to take shallow breaths leaving her need for oxygen unsatisfied. Her eyes filled with unshed tears as her hair fell from its careful chignon into her eyes.

She could hear his mating howl again, but this time she could also hear the soft canter of his steps as he ran towards her. She could sense his masculinity even though she didn't know his name. He pursued her with an untiring relentlessness, chilling her to the bone and pushing her forward in its intensity. Pressing forward she ignored the burning stitch in her side that threatened to bring her to her knees and consume her with its fiery intensity. Her lacerated arms stung as if millions of sharp teeth had scored her as she attempted to escape, had ended up being a futile effort and led her to wonder if she really had tried.

He caught her and pulled her up against his chest. His hot breath against her neck caused the small hairs on the nape of her neck to rise up in a field of despair. He sniffed her hair with deep satisfaction; the long, sharp teeth grazed her ear sending shivers of not quite pain and something else down her spine, which melded against him as if it fit there. He turned her to face him, the silky smooth motion enraptured her completely and she never even saw his face as it descended. His lips captured hers in a mating dance, so primal that it shook her to the core.

"Mine."

He growled the words against her lips, daring her to deny it. She couldn't voice the denial.

"Always mine."

White teeth gleamed in the dark, rearing back for a strike; she closed her eyes, pushed at him, and screamed. The struggle to move catapulted Kamaria into full awareness. Sweat trickled down the side of her face mixing with the flowing tears into a salty trail of terror. She kicked out of the twisted bedclothes that were cutting circulation off in her legs and she made it to the bathroom in time to vomit until stale bile soured her mouth. The cool porcelain diffused the flush from her face and when the sobs subsided, she walked back to her room where she once again slept uneasily.

# CHAPTER One

Kamaria DeKosse strutted down Rodeo Drive with all the confidence her privileged life gave her. Youth, beauty, and wealth were all hers and lent to the aura of confidence as she reveled in a self-assured walk down the busy street. She stood at five feet seven and some change, but she claimed five eight as most opera divas would. She had dusky caramel skin, bright brown eyes, and her naturally highlighted brown hair fell just past her shoulder blades. Despite knowing she fit into the "pretty" category, she could never be overly vain about it; her sisters had the true exotic looks in the family. Her sisters' beauty had never bothered her, considering she had all the talent in the family. Besides, being pretty was just fine with her.

She stopped at a boutique and with her lips curled in slight disdain looked over the clothes. Her air of belonging alerted the saleswomen and they billowed around her like a cape unfurling to call of commission. A half hour and eight hundred dollars later, Kama walked out of the boutique with new outfits and continued on her search for the perfect performance gown. Being from New York she wasn't a stranger to either Haute Couture or high fashion but her ability to find what she wanted failed her.

*Right, because I only have a week left and I can't find a thing. I refuse to take something off the rack for the most important performance season of my career. Oh wait, what is that?*

Kama stopped as a vibrant silver metallic shimmer caught her eye and like a fish on a line she went into another posh boutique. She finally felt relaxed and almost back to normal as she shopped; the nightmares had not made a reappearance to terrorize her in days and for the time being she enjoyed herself, as she had not been able to in the past months.

*The cure for nightmares is shopping. Who would have known? L.A. in the summer is just so alive and full of people. And super bonus, I get to meet up with Cynthia later. It has been ages since I have seen her. Who moves from New York to L.A their senior year? She broke up a perfectly good trio. I wonder if Gianna has forgiven her yet. Of course, I don't know that I have forgiven Gianna for going to Europe this summer. Good thing this trip to Los Angeles came along to keep me occupied.*

Everyone, from the L.A. natives to the tourists, sent a pulsing energy through the city and it had caught Kama up in its frenzy. Thus far, her whole vacation had proved to be a soothing balm to her nightmare jangled nerves and Cynthia had promised a great time later that evening. They had the attitudes exuding wealth, which translated into money to burn, and lithe bodies screaming sex. So there had been no question as to whether they could get admitted into the best night clubs Hollywood had to offer, but rather which ones they would choose to grace.

Kama returned, to the Beverly Wiltshire with her many packages, only two of which contained performance gowns. After giving her spoils to the bellhop to take to her room, she sat in the hotel bar nursing a glass of Chablis and made a battle plan for the next day.

*Okay, it's our senior year at Julliard and it will be my year for performances. I already have three concerts lined up and two more I can audition for. Not to mention the biggest audition of my life in September. So next on the list is finding the perfect dress for that audition. I have not spent the last three years setting my own fashion style to go with off-the-rack commonness now. Maybe my best choice is to find some really bold colors to highlight my skin tone.*

As the bar slowly filled, she found herself people watching instead of reading the romance novel she had brought with her. Kama didn't often have leisure time and she had a burning curiosity to know how the other half lived. She watched their interactions, for a moment she had a wistful longing to be one of the women meeting her boyfriend or husband there. Kama had made many sacrifices for her career: a childhood filled with practicing for hours every day, criticism and high-end expectations, and always being too busy to have a relationship were just the beginning of a long list. It had not mattered, but lately it seemed that everywhere she looked, people were paired up. She didn't have an attraction for anyone in particular at the moment, but she found herself thinking about relationships now.

*I do want someone for passion and companionship. I just have to get my career established first. After all, I can get married and live the romance novel version of life when I get everything on track. Sheesh. Am I really the only person in this bar who is alone?*

Kama drained the small amount of wine left in her glass, collected her wandering thoughts, and looked around again with a small sigh.

*No, there is one other. Wow, I can't even begin to imagine why he is here alone.*

The only other person alone in the bar looked so intently at his laptop that she couldn't tell the color of his eyes. But he had a perfectly shaped bald head, wide shoulders, and clothed in a finely tailored Armani suit. Something kept drawing her eyes back to him and she hoped there was a more valid reason than the fact that she found him incredibly attractive.

*Perhaps he is meeting mafia bosses to exchange bookie tickets, or maybe he might be a high end assassin waiting for his mark. Right, go ahead and throw your imagination into it. We are making a mystery out of the perfectly ordinary. Maybe we need to go on a date so we don't lose our minds. Next we will have him in some sort of covert group or something equally silly. Ah dammit, the royal we has snuck up on us.*

Kama watched him so intently she jumped none too discreetly when her PDA chimed quietly in her purse. It broke into her thoughts and upon checking it; she noted her dinner appointment reminder and turned off the chime. She put her novel back in her purse and looked for the best exit from the crowded bar. Because Kama had already started making up an intriguing history for him, she made a slight detour so she could walk by the small table where her mystery man sat. She caught a heady whiff of his musky scent, and let her imagination run into overdrive as she rode the elevator up to her room and the thoughts consumed her mind as she got ready.

A mere two hours later she emerged, hair curled and cascading down her back, and light makeup enhancing her natural beauty. She wore a stunning red cocktail dress with an empire waist and an asymmetrical skirt to show off her legs. Kama pulled a light silver evening shawl around her arms as she rode back down to the lobby. As the doors to the elevator opened, she almost walked into the bookie/assassin from the bar. He stared at her, and, unnerved she faltered in step and fell against him. She stood but was unable to do more as his steely olive green eyes caught and held her. She smiled at him as he held her elbow to help support her.

"Excuse me," she murmured in a sultry timbre.

Embarrassed as his light touch caressed her arm, she found herself unable to move away from him. She noted he didn't move either. Their eyes locked and after a few million heartbeats, he spoke.

"The fault is mine for not paying attention," he said.

His voice rumbled all the way down her spine and she continued to stare at him, until he looked away. She smiled as she noted that she certainly had his attention. Kama looked down as he released her elbow and the air caressed her skin. She moved past him into the foyer. As he walked by her into the elevator, she could have sworn he inhaled deeply but the action was so swift and subtle she convinced herself that she must have imagined it. After giving him what she considered to be her best alluring smile, she took a deep breath to steady her frenetic heart and then walked out of the hotel to where her car waited.

She had been invited to dinner with her parents and looked forward to their evening. There was much hugging, kissing and loud talking in their excitement. The conversation stayed light, as they caught up with the activities of each other's past few months. The delicious food reminded her lunch had been hours ago and she ate with great vigor and no shame about her appetite. As the night progressed, she tried her best to pay attention to what her parents said but failed and missed questions directed her way.

*Wow, I have spent a lot of time thinking about him. I don't even know his name; let alone anything about him other than he is very good looking. Oh, Mom is giving us a look. What important thing did we miss?*

"What, Mother?" she asked.

"I asked how your interview with the Mr. and Mrs. Zyniac went," her mother said.

"They were interested in hiring me for some business parties. And seemed suitably impressed when I offered them tickets to my recital and they promised to come if they were in New York," she said.

Her mother beamed at her answer and Kama didn't have the heart to tell her what a creep experience it had been. She had barely made it through the too long interview. Mr. Zyniac apparently had a yen for younger women. He kept looking at Kama like she was a prime piece of steak he wanted to chew on. She endured her interview with the creepy old man giving her lascivious looks and stroking her arm and all the while his wife ignoring anything indecent happening. After she had gotten them to commit to hiring her, she had gone back to the hotel where she quickly went to her room to scrub off the sleaze of his touch. She wanted to complain, but until she graduated from Julliard, she lived off of her parents' finances and good graces, so she sighed and continued to take interviews from people who knew her parents.

"That's wonderful," her mother said.

She knew her parents got her gigs with their friends out of love; they were only trying to move her career forward. Despite their good intentions, Kama longed to clarify to them that contemporary adult party music and opera were two different animals, but she appreciated their effort. She asked about their businesses and after lengthy answers, the topic changed from them to her upcoming year.

Kama smiled and launched into a glowing report on her schooling at Julliard. She relaxed into easy conversation and the quiet moment with her parents, since it didn't happen often and she enjoyed their company. She came from a large family, two brothers and two sisters; and having time to sit and really talk with her parents became increasingly rare as the years went on.

"How goes your dress hunt?" her father asked.

"I found two brilliant designs and have only one to go," she said. "I am hoping I will be able to find what I need here and not have some mad dash to find something back home."

"I'm sure they are spectacular," he said.

"Only because you are my father," she scoffed.

"No, Love, because I know as a DeKosse you accept no less than the best," he said.

"Yea, and I'm sure choking the death out of your credit cards is helping me find only the very best," she teased.

Her father looked properly aghast and then winked at her. The good natured teasing carried on throughout dinner and the loud laughter from their table drew smiles from those around them. Kama knew they would be looked at anyhow because of their family make-up. Her mother flaunted being a stereotypical Irish woman with flaming red hair and warm cinnamon colored eyes. Her father was a gorgeous mahogany color but had been born and raised in Italy. From this unique pairing had come five children, and Kama enjoyed being a beautiful mixture of the two.

*One would think in the 21st century an interracial family would be more the norm. Yet here we sit and still attract plenty of attention. Granted it's not as bad as it was when we were growing up, but still... Open your minds, people.*

While Kama loved both of her parents, she wore with pride the title of "Daddy's Girl." While she was growing up, they had shared the very special tradition of being night owls and many times she had fallen asleep in his lap as he read business reports. She did spend a fair amount of time with her mother, assisting in the catering kitchen, cooking up a storm and trying new recipes. Given the crazy schedule they currently all held, she enjoyed being able to spend some quality time with her parents.

The evening progressed in a light hearted fashion and she had a fantastic time... until her parents began making romantic eyes at each other.

*This is so my cue to leave.*

Kama tried to remind herself spouses were supposed to love each other, but as their youngest daughter she still became embarrassed from their displays of affection. Not that she minded her parents loving each other, and somewhere in the back of her mind she knew they must have an active love life, there were five children but she would deny the obvious and preserve her sanity as long as she could.

*I think they do it for my reaction. They know I don't want to see them do these things. Oh come on, not the hand holding and kissing of the wrist. For the love of cheese, I am still their child. I am out of here.*

She stood to excuse herself, as their not-so-secret looks were beginning to make her ill. Her imagination revved high and she knew soon it would produce images scarring to her psyche. Kama very politely and very quickly excused herself to do "something". Her parents' laughter followed her out of the restaurant and into her car. She managed to get into bed and asleep with no "can't be unseen" images plaguing her.

By the next afternoon, the horror of her parents making out had almost been forgotten through shopping therapy. Back on Rodeo Drive, the thoughts of finding a great dress buoyed her spirits and Kama knew the day would be wonderful. At a mere two in the afternoon, her day had been completely ruined by one stupid chit fouling her euphoric shoppers' haze more than she could believe. She walked down the street with her eyes cast down.

*I cannot believe she denied me my hard won appointment. She should understand I had another fitting. All stores run over for fittings. Stupid woman! How can she not understand that flying in for this appointment means they should bend a little? Or maybe I am expected to fly back from New York next week when the store has its next opening.*

"No big deal or anything. It only took me four months to even get an appointment," she muttered to no one. "Apparently thirty minutes late is a crime."

Kama had tried everything she knew: pleading, crying, and even a threat or two, but still they turned her away and told her to come back next week. She had tried to explain she would only there for a few more days but the manager didn't care. She "informed" Kama their store had clientele from all over the world and if she could not be on time, then apparently the fitting did not hold enough importance to her.

"Last time I shop at that rat hole," she said.

Kama found herself walking, with growing irritation, behind a man who meandered while he talked in low tones on his cell phone, oblivious to her and her foul mood. She just wanted him to be the one to move out of her way and not her having to walk around him. Her ire grew with each step as she followed behind him. He eventually stopped near a shop and she sidestepped to avoid walking into him and continued on to The Café for lunch.

*Okay, people don't have to worry so much about talking and driving so much as talking and walking. It is not hard to do.*

She looked back to find the man who had caused her so much irritation, and saw the object of her fascination from the night before. He wore another Armani suit and dark sunglasses, and looked just as good as she remembered. Facing forward again, she smiled widely.

*He is a lot taller than I remember. Hmmm, still good looking though, even if he can't walk and talk. I wonder what he is doing today. Maybe out on a secret mission?*

Her rumbling stomach made its presence known and she flushed with embarrassment. Her stomach had always been loud in demanding to be fed. So she moved with eager anticipation towards the enticing scent of food as she walked into the restaurant.

The Café bustled with people going in and out. The inside tables were so busy, she requested an outdoor table to have some quiet. She immediately realized her folly as all the foot traffic created just as much noise. All she wanted was to relax and regroup. She quickly ordered her food and drink and then sat back absently trying to figure out how to spend the rest of her afternoon.

*Okay, so I need to figure out how to get this shopping done before I go crazy. I wonder what his name is and what he does. I mean, he dressed well and all. Maybe he is a mob boss or something. Right, Kama, heat stroke has made us stupid. Drink some water and get back on track and stop obsessing over some guy we don't even know. Maybe I can find something orange or green for my first concert to work with this summer tan.*

As if summoned by her thoughts, the subject of her inner ramblings walked out onto the terrace and sat only one table away from her. Kama stared at him, and had to nod back in greeting, as once again he caught her staring at him. She was saved by the waitress flirting with him, which irritated her.

*Could she gooze at him any harder? My goodness, you would think he had just asked her out. Like he would ignore me and go after her. Whoa, Kama slow your roll. You just got all territorial over a man you don't know. Okay this is a clear sign of appointment missing induced stress. We need to go back to our room and relax.*

The waitress returned with iced water for the man at the other table and Kama's iced chai tea. To her credit didn't, she scream when the waitress apologized profusely for having lost her order. Kama reordered with a sigh and knew that she was going to starve before the food came.

"I cannot believe this day," Kama grumped.

"Don't worry. The food will come out quickly. I think she is new."

His table was to her left, so she turned to meet his gaze. She smiled at him; this time he had invited her to look. She turned up the wattage of her smile and tried not to sound nervous. Her imaginary roles for him made it a bit hard.

"Here is hoping. Today seems to be a test of patience for me," she said. "Then again, I don't think she cares for me and my grumpy attitude. She certainly seemed to like you well enough, though."

He smiled back at her, and Kama fixated on his olive green eyes and his muscular which build she appreciated. He had a deep, rough scar on his left cheek and a neatly trimmed mustache and goatee peppered with gray.

*I wonder if his moustache would tickle if we were kissing. No, now stop. We cannot think like this with him sitting right across from us. Kama, get a grip. Goodness, no wonder you don't date; you act like a right idiot. Why did we mention her flirting with him?*

She found him incredibly sexy and found herself tapping her nails against the table, since her hands refused to be still and she had nothing else to do with them. Her gaze wandered but always returned back to him. More times than not, when she looked into his face, his eyes were pinned on her as well.

*I wonder if I should be talking to him more. He looks like he is waiting for me to carry on the conversation. Crap, what are we supposed to say to him after that whole flirting line? Damn, where is the waitress?*

The waitress, summoned by Kama's desperate thought, finally came and plunked their food down in front of them. Kama had to suffer in silence watching the waitress again smile at the man and then, as an afterthought, ask Kama if she wanted anything else while sashaying back inside.

"Yes, I need some Tabasco," Kama said at the waitress' retreating backside.

The man took the Tabasco sauce off his table and held it out to her. She smiled at him gratefully but couldn't tell if he meant for his touch on her hand to be a caress or if she was making more out it than she should as she took the bottle.

*Okay, so let's not jump to conclusions just because he is being nice to us. We know very well that we are horrible at reading people. He probably felt bad about our shoddy service and helped out. And Kama, what is with the royal we? There is only one of us.*

*Smile and say thank you, you twit.*

"Thanks," she said.

"It's that bland, huh?" he asked.

Kama noted how carefully he watched her cover her food with the sauce and shook his head at her. She gave him a saucy wink before she answered.

"I like a little spice in my life," she said.

Her previous thoughts of caution were tossed out the window. She held the bottle just a tad out of reach as she returned it to him. He leaned over with his hand was poised to reach towards her; his phone rang, jarring them back into the real world. She sighed as he answered it.

"Excuse me, I need to attend to some business," he said. "Twist here."

Kama nodded, placing the bottle back the table as he walked over to a secluded spot and turned his back to have his conversation.

*So my crap flirting got interrupted by a call. Hopefully he isn't going to turn this into one of those "help me there is a crazy person talking to me" calls. I guess I will find out, if he returns. Twist what?*

She ate her lunch, not really tasting it despite the hot sauce. As the hushed conversation grew to a loud whisper she stopped trying to be covert and looked towards him. Kama tried hard not to appear to be staring but as his eyes snapped up and captured hers; she knew she had been caught. The smile he gave her made her mouth go dry and her stomach flip over on itself.

*Wow, he looks upset. Are his eyes gold? No, don't be silly. We know full well they are green; we have stared at them often enough in the past 24 hours. Perhaps they change with his mood. Oh, he's returning.*

"So, spice it up enough?" he asked.

"Yes, but I had hoped she would come back and offer some dessert," she said.

"I honestly think we could walk out and they wouldn't notice," the man said with a grin. "Guess you will have to find another way to keep your strength up for more shopping."

She started to wonder how he knew what she had been doing, but he nodded towards the pile of packages settled near her chair and shrugged.

"It's much more exercise than most people think," she agreed. "Especially once you have to go in for fittings and the like. I swear they should have catering services on site so we don't faint away from hunger."

"Well then, I hope you will make it through the rest of your day," he said.

"I'm sure I will need to get my real sustenance at dinner," she said and patted her lean stomach with a grin. "With all the hardcore shopping I have done today, it will be an impressive event for the next waitress to keep up with."

"That is an event I should see," he said. "Most women refuse to do more than pick at their plates."

"Maybe you need to choose your company more carefully. You can't trust someone who doesn't eat," she said. "Enjoy the rest of your afternoon."

Kama looked at her watch, gathered her packages, and tossed a few bills on the table. She didn't bother to look over her shoulder as she walked away in what she hoped was a calm and collected manner, but she could feel his gaze burning over her body. She imagined she could feel the heat as his eyes took in each curve and firm shape. She tried hard to figure out just how this little game would turn out, and decided the next time she saw him she would just have to turn up the charm.

*Okay, so he stays in the same hotel as us. It shouldn't be too hard to meet up with him again. Maybe this time I'll actually remember to ask his name. I can't believe I am getting goose bumps just because I know he stays in the same hotel. Maybe I should just stick to the stage. This flirting this is a lot of work for someone I'm not even sure is interested in me.*

##

With her shopping completed for the day, she sat alone in the bar of the hotel. Kama nursed her pain in a small darkened corner having a chilled glass of wine. Her day had gone from foul to outright appalling in just a few short hours. After a perfect lunch, she called her best friend and after a flurry of words got directions to her house and hopped in a cab. Having one's BFF to gossip and giggle about this mystery man would be the start of their fun. Cynthia had promised to take her to Lucky's, the trendiest spa of the moment, and then to a hot dance club. It wasn't to happen though, since Kama walked in on a very romantic interlude between Cynthia and the gardener.

The disgustingly cliché porn show, caused Kama to flee back to the hotel. She ignored the repeated phone calls from Cynthia and decided to have a nice glass of wine to block the fleshy images and wet kissing noises out of her mind. She dressed down as she intended to hide in plain sight, in comfy jeans and a fitted tee shirt, pulled her hair into a pony tail and grabbed her favorite romance novel. Nothing like pirates and their damsels in distress to take her mind off the day.

She allowed herself to become wrapped up in the world of pirate ships being burned down by their vengeful mistresses, puling child wives, and rakish best friends. The misery of the day faded into lusty wenches and swashbuckling men, so much so that Kama didn't notice she had a guest until he cleared his throat.

"Would you mind some company?"

Kama looked up, and when she found her mystery man, smiled; she had forgotten all about her plan to try to meet him again.

"I would love some company," she said.

She gestured to the seat across from her, marking her book for later. Kama then prayed fervently she wouldn't need to pick it back up. Calling over the waiter, she ordered a bottle of wine and another glass. She added a plate of figs, cranberry cheese, and crackers to the order and waited for him to get settled. He took a healthy sip of the wine after it had been served; his eyebrows rose in obvious appreciation. She had chosen a full bodied red that left a crisp after taste on the tongue. Kama smiled and helped herself to some appetizers.

"Thank you," he said. "This is excellent."

"Thanks," she said. "You know, I don't even know your name despite having met you a few times now."

"Jack," he said.

His intense look and warm smile made heat course down her spine and flush through her body. Kama relaxed as he sat back and took a few more sips of the wine.

*Okay, so far he likes my choice in wine and he made it a point to find me. I wonder how he found me without knowing my name. Actually, I wonder how I am doing with this flirting thing. Too bad there isn't a way to ask. Sheesh, I really should have tried to do this before now. Worked it out at sixteen or something instead of waiting until... Oh hell, just enjoy it.*

Kama decided to follow this advice; after all she would go home in another five days and most likely wouldn't ever see him again. She put what she thought to be a sultry purr into her voice and extended her hand toward him.

"Nice to meet you, Jack Twist," she asked.

She wanted to giggle at the raise of his eyebrows as she said his full name, but with great restraint she resisted as she shook his hand.

*I bet he doesn't even remember how he answered the phone at The Café, but point to me for remembering and surprising him.*

"I think I should know the name of the lovely woman I am spending my time with," he said.

"Kamaria DeKosse," she said. "But please call me Kama."

He took her hand and kissed the back of it softly.

*It does tickle and in a very good way.*

Kama tried hard not to melt at the feel of his soft lips and made a point to not look away quickly as her heartbeat accelerated. Even though she could feel her pulse pound through her veins, she didn't pull her hand away when he rested it on the table and covered it with his own.

"Very well Kama," he said. "My pleasure to meet you."

She flushed and wondered what on earth they were going to talk about. She didn't have to worry long because Jack naturally led their conversations, moving off topics when she floundered and when the conversation turned towards wine, she relaxed.

*Thank God Grandpa Giovanni has an obsession with his vineyard. I can actually sound intelligent on the subject. At least Jack can't hear these inner ramblings; he would think I had lost my mind.*

Not only did Jack know about wines but he had traveled to many of the same vineyards in Italy she had. She suggested he should visit a small village south of Tuscany and trying some of her Grandfather's wine.

After repeated yawns began to punctuate her speech, she regretfully bid Jack a good night. She floated up to her room two hours later, happy with the way the conversation had gone but disappointed he didn't try to kiss her again.

*The movies certainly make flirting and romance look a lot easier than it is. I wonder what tomorrow will hold.*

# CHAPTER Two

Kama stood on the balcony of her room at the Beverly Wilshire. Haze covered most of the skyline, as it had every other morning she had been there. Even still, she woke with a smile on her face, happy to be in L.A. that morning. Her evening spent with Jack lingered in her mind and she really hoped they would have another encounter.

*Even better, he really seemed to like holding my hand. Unless he is the type of touchy feely person and yet somehow I really doubt he has a personality of hugs, kisses and fluffy bunnies. Okay, let's figure out our day; a good cup of coffee, finding that elusive gown and, well, since my stomach is not being subtle I think a huge breakfast is needed. I sure won't be able to focus without it.*

Kama's driving concern with her gowns, was someone else would duplicate her creative style and steal her thunder. She shivered at the slight breeze, pulled her robe closer to her body, and went inside to get dressed. She emerged from her room a scant twenty minutes later; she had picked a simple but fitted sundress, cute little strappy sandals, and made up her eyes to give them a deep mysterious hood. Kama knew she had dressed just in case she happened to see Jack. She grinned at no one in particular as she exited her room and made it toward the hotel restaurant. After her huge breakfast, she got ready to go out and shop. Despite her worry, she knew L.A. offered a beautiful array of gowns not found in New York and it eased her mind a bit.

Kama spotted Jack standing in the lobby of the hotel dressed in a charcoal suit fitted to his awesome physique. She watched him unobserved; reveling in the time they had spent together the night before.

*He really is one of the best looking men I have ever met in my life. Heck, he's the sexiest man I have ever seen in my life, with perfect smile. I'm beginning to think he can hear my thoughts. Every time I am near him and thinking about him, he always manages to find me staring at him.*

He turned and gave her a slight nod as he spoke on his phone and gave her a smile, which made her want to melt. She waved back, returning his greeting with a sunny smile. Despite wanting to walk to him and convince him to have coffee with her, she had goals to accomplish and those had nothing to do with flirting with him. Kama left before he finished up his call and got into her car. She figured she would shop until she found her gown. Her reward would be a relaxing meal, sitting by the pool and finally finishing her book.

Hours later, Kama sat by the pool and stared at her book without comprehending the words on the page. She had been reading the same romance book that she had all week; the bodice ripping one with the pirates. She had chosen it because it promised to be light and fluffy and should have helped to relax her mind. Thus far it failed miserably and she fought the urge to light it on fire.

*Right, you would be able relax if you hadn't proven to be such an ultimate failure for two days in a row. Two days of pinching and prodding all to find a gown and I still have to find the last one. I refuse to have to fly to Paris or Milan to find a stupid gown because L.A. is lacking. Something will turn up here. Isn't Los Angeles supposed to be filled with struggling fashion designers just waiting to make their mark? Where are they? I am so sick of shopping.*

She felt the hairs on her neck rise in concert with a shiver down her spine and looked up to see Jack staring at her with a heated smile. The soft light muted the color of his eyes, and again she had to wonder what color they really were. They fluxed from green to gold back to green and she decided it really didn't matter. She didn't know if the expression she returned resembled a smile but she hoped so.

"Good evening, Kama," he said.

"Good evening," she said.

"Just when I thought I had you figured out, I find you out here deep into the world of pirates. Didn't you have huge shopping plans on your list for today?" Jack teased.

"I had an absolutely miserable day, thus I drown my sorrows in lace and frippery. There is no better way to soothe jangled nerves like mystery,"

Kama said. "You cannot begin to imagine the hell it is trying to find a unique gown."

She still reeled from the comment of him trying to figure her out. Kama hoped it meant that he had some sort of interest in her. She reasoned he must, if he had hunted her down by the pool. Her position couldn't easily be seen from the door. She started to say more when her stomach rumbled loudly.

"Do you know of any good Italian restaurants around here?" she asked.

Impressed her voice never wavered, Kama tried to keep her calm facade; she thought she would die of embarrassment when her stomach announced its presence again in his company. At least it had proven her point of needing food. Jack seemed not to hear it, so she pretended it never happened and tried to focus on their conversation.

"I'm sure we could find someplace nice," he said.

"If you would like to join me, you can finally watch post-dress shopping eating," she said. "I would really like the company. We still have a discussion to finish up."

Kama eagerly tried flirting with him again. From what she could tell, the key lay in being subtle. She tried her best not to look over enthusiastic as she invited him to dinner. A thrill went up her spine as she realized she had just asked him on a date.

*Wow, he doesn't even seem offended that I asked him. I would have thought he would be a bit more old fashioned and would want to be the one to do the asking. I suppose I still have a lot to learn about him. Well, if he agrees I can pick his brains. Maybe not. Would it appear desperate? Oh wait, he said something…*

"I would love to have dinner with you," he said. "Though, if you will remember, your continuous yawning ended our evening early. I just couldn't bear to think I would be responsible for dark circles under those pretty eyes."

"Well, perhaps you are not as engaging as you think," she teased.

Kama grinned in triumph as he tried to look offended but failed, a smile creasing his lips. She stood and walked with him toward the lobby.

She ordered a car service and turned to face Jack again, wanting to tease him more, but he spoke first.

"I have been told I am quite the conversationalist," he said. "I think perhaps the problem might be, despite your claims, you don't truly understand wine."

"How can I not understand it? My grandfather…"

Her next words were cut off as a sleek dark town car pulled to the curb. Another dark car sat behind hers and she tried to appear not to rush as she walked toward their car. Relief flooded her as she got in and Jack closed the door behind her. Kama thought she might have seen someone.

*No matter. We will be on our way in just a moment. Okay, just look ahead and smile. It's not who we thought it might be. Stupid black cars. Just enough to make a person nervous. No one needs this kind of drama late in the day. Especially not before dinner. Like they would be out stalking me.*

Kama smiled as Jack leaned forward, and in a voice too quiet for her to hear, gave the driver some directions. Kama decided to play the temptress this time and see where it got her.

*Right, except I have no idea how a temptress should act. All the acting classes in Julliard to enhance my stage presence and I have no clue of what to do when I am around this man. Okay, the quiet is making me nervous. Fill it with something before I say something stupid.*

While she tried to figure out her plan of attack she leaned forward and adjusted the radio controls until she found a station she could live with and out of habit began to sing quietly along with the song. Solitude by Billie Holiday filled the car; one of her very favorites and she relaxed as she sang. Kama let herself get swept up in the song and almost forgot her surroundings. She came back to herself as the hairs on her arm rose to attention as she realized he watched her carefully as she gave him an impromptu concert without meaning to. The smile on his face said he had watched her truly enjoy the song, and she smiled, not even a hint of embarrassment.

"So where are we off to?" she asked.

"I know this little Italian place that I can vouch for, and then we can go see a group perform," he said.

Kama let him be mysterious. She only hoped it wouldn't be some fancy place that served portions more suited to toddlers than to grown people. She hummed along with the next few songs, watching the scenery turn from the gauche, harsh lights of the city into a soft delicate luminance. Thirty minutes later, she got her first case of nervousness.

*Should I really be alone with a man I just met and barely know? I don't even know where we are going. Okay. Calm down and quit acting stupid. The driver knows where we are, so if I go missing he can be a witness. Except he might work for Jack. Crap what have I gotten myself into? Kama, get a grip. You invited him to dinner, It's not like that nightmare is coming true. For the love of all that's green, talk to the man and enjoy our date.*

The driver pulled into a driveway and they rode at least another ten minutes. The driver pulled into the parking lot of an ornate large log cabin. Only the presence of at least a dozen cars kept her from thinking it might be a private residence. Kama waited and much as she expected he walked around to open her door. She gracefully took his extended hand, delighted that he carefully tucked her fingers into the crook of his arm and escorted her to the door.

She noted they were made of a dark wood with beautiful brass handles resembling crawling vines. The panels were exquisitely detailed and obviously hand crafted. There were beautiful floor-to-ceiling windows and a sitting area around a huge fireplace. A maître d' stood at the entrance to a small restaurant.

*This isn't going to be a run of the mill, Americanized Italian restaurant. Although I can't imagine it will be authentic either.*

Kama gave Jack a light smile as they walked in. She waited while he talked to the maître d'. Despite the place being gorgeous, Kama mentally sighed. She had really hoped for something with a bit of culture, and she didn't consider wealthy a cultural flavor. Jack brought her a glass of wine.

"Why thank thee, kind sir," she said.

She met his eyes and noticed the gold was back. While Kama sipped her wine, she figured that they were at a private club and had hope for the food quality. By the time she got done with her perusal, the maître d' stood before them.

"This way to the garden," the he said.

They followed him outside and Kama took note of the lovely sculptured flora that served as a barrier to the outside world. Comfortable with her flirting attempts, which were going well, she found she had Jack's complete attention.

*Right, so what to do with it? Part of the problem is being around him makes me feel like an idiot. Heck, half the time I even talk like an idiot and to myself. And of course my heart wants to hammer right out of my chest. The bigger problem is all I want to do is touch him. I understand what lust is, but, damn no one ever told me it could be so consuming. Now he is staring because we are sitting here mute. And we are out of wine.*

She hid behind her menu but didn't look at it. Kama thought of herself as a good judge of character, but there was something different about Jack. Every simple touch, caress, or glance had her yearning for more. And she was slightly disgusted that she might be acting like those she had previously scorned.

*What exactly about this man could turn me upside down and into a panting, hormone-driven ditz around him? I never thought I would be this childish.*

She physically shook her head at her mental dilemma and tried to focus on dinner. When the waiter appeared, he greeted them in Italian. Jack ordered for the two of them. His Italian had a very American accent and Kama smiled at his attempt.

The menu he chose impressed her; he had managed to pick out three of her favorite dishes. He started with *pinzimonio*, then a bowl of *carabaccia*. For the main course he ordered her favorite, pasta al *cartoccio*. Then asked for the ricotta *ubriaca* be served as dessert with some fresh coffee. Kama only interjected to ask for a bottle of *Chianti Colli Fiorentini* to be served with their appetizers.

"Not a bad menu at all," she said. "And here I expected to get some less than authentic food out of this place."

"How you could expect me to fail to satisfy your wants?" Jack asked.

Kama found herself armed with the best come back ever, but stopped as Jack's phone rang. He excused himself apologetically from the table and went off to have his conversation. Her own phone rang a few seconds later and she sighed. Cynthia, her erstwhile friend, had been trying to apologize all day. Kama answered and made quick plans to meet up the next day; perhaps they could get back to their normal friendship, to put all the weirdness behind them and stop the barrage of calls. She hung up and to her delight the waiter soon brought two glasses of ice water and a basket of fresh bread and cheese. She chatted in fluent Italian with him for a few moments and then, noticing Jack returning, added in a request for crostini di fegatini.

"Welcome back."

"I apologize, I had to take the call for business matters," he said with a slight air of embarrassment.

"No worries. It happens," she said.

The waiter returned with the appetizers and the wine. He opened the bottle, let Jack preview it, and poured two glasses.

"Salute," Kama said.

She raised her glass to Jack and, after his return toast, took a sip. She found the wine a delicious blend and knew it would complement the seafood dish. She would have to argue Jack's statement that she didn't know wine.

"So, about my not knowing wine," she said.

"I stand corrected," he said. "What went horribly wrong with your day? You did classify it as miserable, a rather intense description."

"Well, my objective is to find a gorgeous gown no one else will have," she said. "A good concert gown is a personal signature. I tend to choose bold colors, but lately bold colors and prints are the trend. Now I have to find something else to make me stand out. Bad news is, I missed my fitting yesterday and today everything looked like it either came off the rack or from last season."

"And here I wasted most of my day in a boardroom without working air conditioning," he said with a wry grin. "I never realized just how complicated shopping for a dress could be. It sounds like it rivals business negotiations."

"Despite your attempts at humor, I'm pretty sure you would fall over before I actually found a grown," Kama sighed. "It took me two days to find the last one, but at least I already have the accessories."

Kama relaxed and enjoyed the cuisine. It met her criteria for real Italian with simplistic taste and aromas. She kept up a steady stream of conversation with Jack; it ranged from wine, to music, to travel, and back to shopping. When dessert came, her eyes lit up and she reached for a decent portion while Jack teased her again.

"More energy for your next shopping marathon?" Jack asked.

"Absolutely," she said with no hint of apology. "Really, I know it sounds too dramatic to be true, but shopping for a gown just wears you thin. It's a constant popularity contest and I get tired of trying to prove a point."

"However, you would never be satisfied with common," he said.

"Yes. Who knows? Maybe the sky will blow up and I can get a miraculous fitting at Lobos tomorrow."

The waiter returned and poured fragrant coffee for them. After an appreciative sip, she led him into more small talk. They covered little bits of everything; even still, Kama felt that they learned relatively little about each other. Finally, they landed on the world of entertainment and it opened up a lively debate on the current music standards.

Kama told Jack, with no hidden disgust, those who chose to writhe on the floor, half naked and yowling like a cat in heat, did not display talent.

"Come on. It is sex for sale. All you need to do is look good, put out when asked, and gyrate for those who want you but can't touch you. These people cannot even pretend to have the talent of such musical greats as Pearl Bailey and Bessie Smith," she said.

"I agree. I like jazz and it's what I listen to," he said. "I honestly never found reason to listen to things I don't care for, no matter how naked and writing the performer."

Kama snorted and rolled her eyes at his mocking of her word choices. She found she really enjoyed her time with Jack, and even more because it gave her practice with her efforts at flirting.

*This isn't so bad, considering he is the first person I have ever really pursued. Granted, I am still going on the hit and miss thing, since I'm still not sure how to read his reactions. Although, he seems to appreciate me when I'm just being me. I hope he doesn't think I am putting on an act to get him. Then again, am I making any headway? I suppose I would know if I knew what reaction I expected from him.*

After their meal, they walked down the back steps, onto a private waterfront, and strolled along the beach.

"Thank you for the lovely dinner."

"My pleasure," he said. "Else I would not have gotten my new education about music."

They walked, hand in hand, silently enjoying the mild night for a few more yards before Kama's curiosity got the better of her. She could tell by the way he walked he had a destination in mind. The tiki-torches on the beach created many path options.

"So, where are we going now?" she asked.

"You'll see," he said.

"I don't know that I'm too terribly impressed with mystery," she said. "I mean, it's too dark for casual strolling, so the place must be near."

"It's not that dark," he said. "Don't you like surprises, Kama?"

"Sometimes," she answered.

She tried not to be offended when he laughed at her cautious answer. So far he had done nothing but behave like a perfect gentleman, and she made herself relax. They walked down a secluded stretch of beach and Kama looked toward the darkened sky. There were some stars visible, meaning they were quite a distance from the city burn of L.A., but she enjoyed the breathtaking view. Finally, the torch lit path led then to a small alcove. A small building nestled therein boasted a neon sign announcing it as Eight to the Bar.

"A jazz club, in the middle of nowhere," she said. "Nice."

Jack smiled at her and led her into the small building. Kama loved the atmosphere as soon as she entered the club. The music acted like a quiet accent to the conversations going on and her spine tingled. She always had strong reactions when the music was particularly good. She might have specialized in opera, but she loved music, not just artists. She nearly squealed with excitement when she found that her favorite duo of all time would be playing that night. She almost asked Jack if he knew, but tossed out the notion that he could know anything so personal about her.

"Do you dance?" he asked her.

"Yes," she said.

He led her onto the dance floor and proceeded to impress her with his skills. They didn't try to have a deep conversation as they danced. Instead, they focused on the tantalizing movements that brought them closer. Kama felt like her cheeks would split from smiling so wide. As the dance ended and the floor was cleared but she found no disappointment because the band would soon perform.

"So is this your favorite hangout?" she asked.

"One of the best jazz houses in the area," he said. "Where else would I take a chanteuse but to hear some fabulous music? Not to mention, Charlie and Rainbow Bird are some of the best musicians I have ever heard. I couldn't imagine missing them. They are doing a two-night gig and this is the last night."

Kama sat back as her favorite musicians took the stage and enthralled her for ninety minutes. She couldn't believe her date with Jack was turning out so perfect.

"I'm glad you are enjoying yourself, even if you did steal my thunder by asking me to dinner right before I had the chance to ask you."

Kama smiled at the realization that he would have asked her out if she hadn't beaten him to it. Maybe, just maybe, she had been reading him correctly.

"Someday I will have to return the favor," she said. "This has been amazing."

"You can return it now," he said.

Jack gestured to the stage where Charlie made the announcement that the band would be taking a break. He followed up by caressing the worn top of an old piano and encouraged people to indulge their passion for improvisation. One brave soul took the stage, but Kama shook her head as temptation and fear warred in her mind.

*No way in hell am I getting up there after Charlie.*

She shook her head vehemently to physically show her silent point. Kama noticed Jack watching her internal war with a grin. Again he urged her to go up on stage, but she demurred. She had no problem with her talent, but she didn't want any comparison to be drawn between her and her idol. Jack must have really wanted her to sing because he asked her a third time.

"I just want to spend a quiet evening with you. There is no need for me to get up there when we have perfectly good entertainment," she said.

"Are you really going to deny me the chance to hear your wonderful voice from the stage? Come on, you sang beautifully in the car. Let's hear what you can really do," Jack implored.

The gods of chance caused Charlie to walk by their table to at that very moment. Kama forgot to breathe as he smiled in their direction, and then turned to deny Jack once more.

"We're here to enjoy jazz greats Jack, not have me up there," she insisted.

"Well, Baby Girl, how do you think we got to be so great?" a bass voice rumbled up her spine. "Surely you can grace us with one small song."

Kama looked up into the darkest chocolate eyes she had ever seen and swallowed hard against her very dry throat. Charlie stood about three inches from her and extended a hand to her.

"I don't think I can," she whispered. "Not after you were up there."

"Baby Girl here needs our love," Charlie said to the crowd. "If she comes up here, Rainbow Bird and I will accompany her. What cha'll think?"

He gestured to the audience who burst into loud applause and cheers.

Jack raised an eyebrow and gave her a smile that might have made her melt, but she wasn't sure if she was felling anger or gratitude towards him. Finally convinced there would be no way she could get out of singing, Kama stood and accepted the hand Charlie still held out to her. She climbed the stairs leading to the stage and stood under the glare of the lights, reveling in the attention focused on her. A warm tickle coursed through her body and she enjoyed the pleasurable sensation pulsing through her when she stood on the stage.

"Okay, Baby Girl, what 'cha gonna sing?"

"Wild is the Wind," Kama said.

"Speak up, Baby Girl. I know I didn't jus' heah ya right," Charlie said.

"Nina Simone's Wild is the Wind," Kama said louder.

He shook his head and sat at the old, black piano and led the band into the smooth haunting melody. She dared not look at Jack, but she could feel his gaze on her. It all changed the second the lead-in chord sounded. Kama became the consummate professional; every mannerism, each motion, and her stance spoke of her years of training. She lost all inhibition and when she opened her mouth, liquid gold poured out as she sensuously slid her voice around the melancholy vocals. She sang only for Jack and used all the pent up emotion from earlier in the day in her performance.

Three and a half minutes later, the song ended and thunderous applause erupted. It shook her from her musical trance and Kama curtsied.

"I do believe ya duped me, Baby Girl," Charlie said.

He took her hand and led her off the stage. Kama faced him wide eyed hoping that her nervous rendition hadn't offended him somehow.

"How did I dupe you?" asked Kama.

"Well, you not wantin' to come on stage and all, I figured you were tryin' to spare us some screechin'," he said. "Apparently not the case, as you got pipes of gold deep in ya soul and the talent to steal the breath from ma lungs."

He winked at her and she gave him a big smile.

"I didn't want to get up there because I grew up listening to you and to be on stage with one's idol is a bit daunting," she explained.

"Try being an idol someday, Baby Girl," Charlie said. "Don't 'cha know, anyone who can perform hot enough to make every man want her and every woman want to be her, has the power to enthrall the world."

Instead of sitting, Kama led Jack back on to the dance floor. She received passing praise from other dancers, but being held close by Jack stopped a lot of the overly long prattle which was what she had counted on. The music moved in a soft pulse and as she got lost in his gaze she leaned forward and kissed him. Her feather-light touch explored his lips and then she drew away. She appreciated his letting her set the pace, but her nerves got the better of her. She feared doing something wrong and he would become disinterested; at the same time, the notion that he might move too quickly frightened her. Yet, he returned her kiss without becoming aggressive, so she grew bolder and kissed him once more swirling her tongue in his mouth, drinking in the taste of him and the sharp bite of scotch he had drunk.

'This is a hell of first kiss,' she thought.

She broke the kiss smiling against his lips. Her body pressed against his chest. The light dress she wore proved to be a lousy excuse for a barrier against the heat emanating from both of them. She stayed there for a moment to catch her breath and, after the eternity of a heartbeat, she resumed the dance.

The song ended and they made their way back to the table where they sat in silence for a few moments. Kama tried to think of something to converse about, but failed since all she wanted to do was kiss him again.

"So what are you plans when you go home?" Jack asked.

"Julliard is fairly demanding of my time. When it's not music it is very much the academic aspect I have to focus on; I can't afford to slip. This is the longest vacation I have had in a while," she said. "When are you returning?"

"My business here is almost done, though I will be here five days just to tie up loose ends and all," he said.

"Okay," she said.

They sat and listened to music for a while longer; Kama laid her head on his shoulder, content just to be with him. Charlie and Rainbow Bird wrapped up their set and came to say good-bye before leaving.

"See ya roun' Baby Girl," Charlie said. "I shuh would love for ya to give me a call an' maybe we can talk 'bout doin' a cover of your song theah."

Kama smiled widely and stuttered some kind of almost coherent affirmative answer. She took the card he held out and placed it in her purse for safe keeping. The excitement rolled off her and she decided to kiss Jack again to celebrate her fortuitous meeting. This time Jack took over the lead even though she initiated the kiss. She pressed into his embrace and was startled when a dim sound caught her attention. She stiffened in his arms as the chime sounded again from her purse.

"Oh god," she gasped.

"What?" Jack asked.

He had an amused look on his face, but Kama wondered just how long it would last.

"I need to go," she said.

"Now? It's almost one in the morning; you can't possibly have an appointment," he said.

Kama grabbed her purse and hurried to the door.

"Kama? Are you okay?" he asked.

"Really I am fine, but I do need to leave. Thank you for the lovely evening. I will see you tomorrow perhaps?"

She ran out of the jazz club and to the car they had come in. Somewhere her brain registered the driver knew where to pick them up, and her safety had never been in question. She demanded the driver take her back to the hotel. Ten minutes into the return trip, reality set in. She fought down her panic as she realized what she had done.

"Oh God, I just left Jack at the club," she moaned.

She put her face in her hands and sighed. She knew he would think her an absolute nut case, but she had no choice. The alarm had sounded and much like Cinderella at the ball, she had to leave. After exiting the car, she sent it back to get him.

*Yea, I'm sure he now thinks I am a psycho. Great.*

She made it to her room, closed the door, and breathed hard against it. Sweat trickled down her back and she couldn't wait to change out of her clothes. She didn't bother to shower, but instead put on her pajamas and climbed between the cool sheets.

*Hell, just how am I supposed to explain this to him? I cannot believe I just left him there.*

Despite the exciting night she had had, she fell asleep as soon as her head touched the pillow.

Kama woke up hours later, stretched luxuriously and then lay in bed smiling up at the ceiling. She recalled the events of the night before but pushed her faux pas to the back of her mind. Otherwise she knew it would ruin the good memories. Soon enough shopping would fill her day, as it had the days before. She realized because of her time with Jack, the constraints of her very busy and serious life in New York were temporarily gone. She could party, play and have fun like a normal girl and it wouldn't hurt her or her career in the least.

Before she could spiral too deep into her thoughts, her phone rang. She looked at the display a long minute before answering. Cynthia had tried to make good offering a treatment at Lucky's day spa to appease her. She had warned Kama, no fewer than six times, that Lucky's did not accept late appointments. Then, dropped the bomb that she already had plans for that evening but Kama could enjoy it alone. Kama accepted the peace offering and didn't mind that Cynthia wouldn't be there. She wondered if she might be able to convince Jack to join her.

*It would be a nice repayment for last night, as well as a good apology for leaving him stranded. Now just to convince him…*

Kama got out of bed and got ready for one more day of gown shopping.

# CHAPTER Three

Jack watched Kama run to the car and hop in. Her true intentions weren't realized until the car sped off.

"She just took my car," he said. "I can't believe she left me here."

He thought about the enigma named Kamaria DeKosse. It had been a whirlwind ever since she had made a point to saunter by him. Despite only having had one real date with her, he had learned to expect the unexpected with her. Jack smiled at the thought of her vivacity, and wondered what intrigued him so much.

*Probably the fact that she just took your car and stranded you or maybe it's that soul wise voice that comes out when she sings.*

He dialed the hotel and asked for a car service to come get him, and gave the name of the jazz club. He returned to his musing as he waited. Aside from her obvious beauty he couldn't pinpoint what made her stand out.

Jack had been in numerous relationships and thought he had a good handle on how women acted. He spent most of his time in the cab on the way back to the hotel wondering what had made her run like fire had lit up under her. He knew it wasn't some well contrived act. In fact she had to be the clumsiest flirt he had ever met, and she had no idea how to use a poker face. She wore her emotions as plain as day, and even though he responded to her efforts, she still tried as though he had missed the point.

*What kind of game is she playing? It is rather nice to have her pursue me; she is gorgeous enough to have her choice of men. Then again she doesn't act like she's a shark out for the kill. Maybe she's had a sheltered upbringing? It's possible she doesn't know her own allure, but I can't see why she wouldn't be aware. Maybe she just doesn't date a lot; she seems to flip from temptress to maiden in a second.*

His inner wolf snorted in agreement about the woman. The rest of the ride followed the same thought patterns and Jack shook his head. The woman drove him a bit crazy. His wolf snorted again like he was missing the big picture.

"Welcome back, Mr. Twist," the concierge said.

"I trust my car has been returned?" he stated.

"Yes, sir. Ms. DeKosse sent it back to you in a panic, but I assured her you had a car on its way for. She fled in contrite embarrassment."

Jack chuckled and walked to his room. Once there, he booted up his laptop and took out his files. He had been in Los Angeles for two weeks working tirelessly with Garra Shipping. They were a small company, only ten years old, but they had exclusively handled his shipping needs from the west coast for eight years. He wanted to buy into the company, definitely not welcome news to the Garra brothers, but a deal Jack planned to cement before he left. The problem stemmed from the brothers not wanting him to buy into the company no matter how small of a percentage, and had told him so quite clearly. Even so, he had scheduled one more meeting trying to convince them that his idea had the potential to be a great alliance.

His computer chimed, whirred, and finally completed its startup routine. He noticed his assistant Carla online and messaged her.

"You're in the office already?" he asked. "Did you actually go home last night?"

"We're still working on Garra Shipping. Of course I am here," she wrote back. "I image it's the same reason you are working at 2:30 am."

Jack grinned; he could hear the dry tone of her voice as he read her text. Carla embodied business, which explained why they worked so well together. He could imagine her reaction if he told her that the real reason he sat up at two in the morning was that he had gone on a date. All his business plans had been turned upside down by one Ms. Kamaria DeKosse. He thanked The Blessed Mother for Her gift and then tried to refocus his thoughts onto the upcoming business.

"I have a final meeting with them today, and I'm not sure if I should try to force their hand," he said.

"You have been playing nice all week," Carla said. "Perhaps you could entice them with financial incentives. If that fails, it's time to show them why most other companies think you are a bastard."

"I didn't come here to put them over a barrel, Carla."

"Right, but this merger isn't just business; you are trying to set up alliances," she said.

"But forcing them to let me in isn't the best way to get any sort of alliance," he said.

"Well figure out which is more important," she said.

"If we only ask for ten percent, would it give us enough of a foothold?" he asked.

"Twenty percent is the minimum, but Jack, you can force them into at least thirty-five percent shares. We own one of their lending companies; we could just take over."

"I would rather they let me in willingly; I don't want the hostility," he said. "Look. Email me some more specs. I've got to get a few hours of sleep. I can't go into these negotiations distracted."

"Okay. Well, make sure they understand this takeover is going to happen, either voluntarily or not," Carla said.

Jack shrugged and logged off. He hated the lack of progress so far, but he wanted an alliance with the Garra's not just a takeover. He supposed he should be happy the brothers had agreed to meet him at all again, considering the last few meetings had been crackling with tension. He had managed to arrange their meetings on the neutral ground of the hotel. He wasn't the type to bend and bow, but he did respect other's authority in their own territory. It just made it harder to be as aggressive as he wanted, but he didn't plan to leave until he had his alliance. His wolf sighed, preferring to show the Alpha side and just take over, but diplomacy won out. He drifted off to sleep wondering how Kama planned to spend her day.

"Focus, Twist," he grumbled to himself. "Business first. What the hell is wrong with you?"

Even berating himself into unconsciousness, he still dreamt of her. And upon waking, knew that he would rather spend the day with her, even if it meant gown shopping. He wanted the merger and alliance to be settled so he could move on. Frustrated, he got up and went back to his laptop to crunch the numbers Carla had sent him. Determined not to think about Kama until after the meeting.

The bar of the hotel made a near perfect meeting place; at two in the afternoon, only a scattering of people were present and thus, gave privacy for Jack and the leaders of Garra Shipping to conduct their final meeting. He stood as the two men approached the small table in the back where he sat. Marcos stood six feet tall and dressed impeccably in business formal wear. Carlos stood about a foot shorter than his brother and wore what most would consider gang member attire.

"Thank you for coming," Jack said.

"This can be short and sweet," Marcos said. "We are turning down your very generous offer to buy in."

Jack swallowed the disappointment he felt and tried to remain calm.

"Is there some reason Garra Shipping and Twist Enterprises shouldn't partner?" Jack asked.

"Mr. Twist," Carlos said. "We have successfully run Garra Shipping for a decade. Just because you are one of our bigger clients doesn't mean we should have to let you buy in."

"What my brother means, Mr. Twist, is that we are fine," Marcos said. "We enjoy our business relationship with you, but we are not ready to further it just yet. All this talk of alliances, reciprocal training, and even placement for the young who don't wish to stay in Los Angeles is very temping. However, some members are not certain you don't mean to use us for other purposes."

"Think about this, Señor Garra," Jack said. "I am not trying to take over your company. I am just trying to form a new kind of allegiance, not all about business, but about taking care of our own."

"Then why bother to buy in?" Carlos said.

Jack got ready to launch into a speech about what good could be done, when the waiter walked over with a tray of drinks. He handed them out and then gave a small piece of paper to Jack. His spine all but rippled as Kama's scent slammed into his nose. He calmed himself and tried to remain impassive as he read her message: You look like you needed this.

He looked around the bar and found her staring at him from a bar stool. She twisted the stem of her glass trying, to appear nonchalant and not looking at him; but as his gaze fell on her, she met his eyes, smiled, and then looked away as two more pair of scrutinizing eyes turned toward her. His heart thudded in his chest and he forced himself not to smile back. All of a sudden, the Garra brothers weren't the priority on his list. His siren had just called and he had to answer.

"I hoped you would reconsider," Jack said. "I am in town for the rest of the week; please contact me if you would like to talk about this further."

*Hell, I guess I'll just have Carla go ahead and start the takeover process. I can't believe I am walking away from them to go talk to this woman. A buyout of their lender will be easier anyhow; banks like to take my money.*

He walked away from the men with no further words. He could feel the surprise from them; he had been pursuing this merger/ alliance hardcore for almost two weeks. Jack mentally shrugged as he walked towards Kama. He heard her heart rate accelerate when she noticed him. He grinned as she turned her head back to the bar to cover up her blush and compose herself.

*Screw it. They don't want to merge and quite frankly I have better things to do with my time. I'm not successful in business because I worry about hurting people's feelings. Maybe the alliance won't happen, but I'll have my merger.*

He did look back at the men once; he saw them get up from the table and walk away. The weight of their steps highlighted their displeasure.

*They didn't want the merger or alliance. What the hell are they upset about?*

He stopped wondering as he got closer to the bar. He could smell the perfume on Kama's skin and goose bumps broke out over his arms. To Jack's amazement, he found he needed a moment to compose himself, so he looked at the poker machine she had been playing at. The scores were pretty awful.

"Been having fun?" he asked.

"I suppose so," she said. "I had to find something to do to fill the gap in my schedule."

He looked back at the machine and then to her, his raised eyebrow mocking her score. As silence took over, Jack watched her fidget.

"So what happened to the pirate novel?" he asked. "All the lace and frippery fun is done?"

"I keep getting interrupted every time I try to read," she said. "Although, it's been interesting company so far."

While she continued to tease him about disturbing her pirate tale, he let his gaze linger over her and in return she unwaveringly met his eyes; he guessed she was trying to be intense and he smiled at her. He wished his hand and not his eyes could be caressing her. His hands actually twitched as he noticed one of her dress straps had fallen, a few inches, off her shoulder. Breathing shallowly through his mouth he could taste the pheromones she gave off and wanted to kiss her. Her prattle got louder and interrupted his perusal of her, which she had not seemed to notice.

"And for your information, I got stood up not once, but twice today. Since my plans were shot, I had nothing to do and I refused to pout the day away in my room; I figured I would come down here for a change of scenery until my appointment this evening."

"I have a hard time believing anyone would ever stand you up," Jack said.

Unfortunately for him, his compliment completely lost on Kama. The more he tried to flirt with her; a few things became obvious to him. Not only did she not have much experience in flirting, she didn't have much experience in being flirted with. Jack watched her struggle to think of something else to say, when Carlos approached him. The man stood stiff and uncomfortable with just a bit of threat in his posture. Jack took offense at his demeanor and the hackles of his wolf rose. Despite Kama not being under his protection he felt responsible for her. He stepped in front of her and met Carlos' eyes. The short man nodded at Jack and directed him towards a small alcove. Excusing himself, he followed Carlos and gave him an expectant look.

"My mate asked me to extend a dinner invitation to you for tomorrow," the man said.

"Tell her I am honored to accept and will see you tomorrow evening," Jack said.

Pleasantly surprised, he gave his attention back to Kama and smiled. He walked back to her side.

*Perhaps the deal hadn't been lost after all. I guess appearing ready to walk away provided the incentive the Garra brothers needed. This woman brings me luck.*

He opened his mouth to invite her to dinner, but she interrupted.

"Boy, rude much? Couldn't he see we were talking?" she asked.

"Guess he isn't big on manners," Jack said, as he had left the original meeting to talk to her.

"That's a big understatement. Besides I sent drinks for everyone. It's not like I monopolized your time or anything," she said, then paused. "Although, I would be happy if you would accompany me to Lucky's. It would be nice to have some pleasant company after a day of being completely alone."

Jack watched her in quiet contemplation, trying his best to again figure her out and failing to do so. All his senses were on high alert; he knew she couldn't stand silence between them so he waited. She flushed with embarrassment, and suddenly found the stool rungs fascinating. He remained quiet even longer, so he could watch her react. He had fun watching her flustered state, not once feeling bad.

"So how about the spa?" she asked. "If you want to come along, we have to leave now, since they don't take late appointments."

Jack nodded and then coughed to cover up a grin as Kama hopped off the stool and almost tripped. She got caught up in the rungs, but righted herself with a sheepish grin. One minute she worked at seducing him; the next tripped over herself and with hardly any shame to acknowledge the clumsy stumble.

"Come on then," she said.

As they neared the front doors, Jack handed the valet a ticket and waited for his car to be brought around. He smiled as Kama gave a low whistle in appreciation.

"Is that the new Hummer?" she asked.

"Yes. Would you like to drive?" he asked.

"Really?"

Jack nodded and smiled, opening the driver side door for her. How much damage could one woman do? Kama winked at Jack and hopped up into the driver's seat, adjusted it, slid on her shades, and turned to give him a wide smile. His heart jumped at the look, but he managed to climb up into the passenger seat, and buckled up before the effect of the sensual smile made itself known. Amazed at the impact this woman had on him, Jack shook his head; his body acted like a long denied school boy and his brain didn't do much better.

"Are you ready?" she asked.

"Sure," he said.

He managed to sit calmly as Kama slammed the Hummer into reverse, almost running over the valet, who shrieked, cursed, and dove out of the way. He worked at sitting still in his seat as she peeled onto Rodeo Drive, towards Lucky's without bothering to look around. Jack leaned back, forcing himself to breathe deep, and raised his eyebrows looking at Kama.

"So, you learned to drive at the Indy 500?" he asked.

"No, New York City," she laughed. "Although there is a lot less traffic here."

"I see," Jack said.

He noticed that she felt speed was the best course of action as she turned a corner, not slowing down at all. He winced as she nearly missed a BMW on her pass and gunned it down the street. To his credit, he managed to maintain a steely but concerned expression as he watched her drive. The thirty miles an hour felt like sixty and he found himself wishing she might spend a bit more time watching the road.

"You do understand the car can go below sixty, yes?" he asked.

"Like there is even enough space to go sixty. I know I'm speeding a bit, but I don't want to lose my appointment," she said.

She didn't look at him as she zoomed through a yellow light. Of all the things Jack had experienced in his life, this had to have been the most scary and intense.

"Yes, but the friction will slow us down if we collide into other cars," he said.

"Don't worry; we'll get there in one piece. I promise," she laughed.

Jack sighed and she continued on, they both swore as she missed the road to Lucky's. Jack wondered just how much insurance he had on the rental. He appreciated a good thrill as much as the next man, but her driving skills were non-existent.

*With all we have been through, this little drive made us terrified. Beautiful or not, she can never ever drive again.*

The wolf shook his head in agreement. Jack unclenched his hands from the tight balls they had formed. He watched Kama unbuckle her seat belt, hop out of the car, fix her hair, and toss the keys to the valet. Thankful to have arrived in one piece, he followed her into the spa, noticing the gentle sway of her hips, and forced himself to think about other things. Kama waved over a female attendant and ordered the whole works for the both of them. He smiled as he let Kama set the tone for the time being. He wondered would happen next.

"Without a doubt, the most intense ride I have ever had," Jack said.

"Well, we certainly couldn't be late. I learned my lesson a few days ago: better to be safe than sorry," she said. "And I certainly didn't want to miss this."

Jack raised an eyebrow, being caught somewhere between laughing and scoffing at her absurd statement that she could use the word "safe" in any sort of reference to their trip there.

*Again, just pure Kamaria. She keeps me guessing and when I think I know what to expect, she changes the rules again.*

They followed the attendant to the dressing rooms. Jack waved goodbye as he prepared to be massaged. He relaxed let his thoughts wander aimlessly as the skilled hands massaged fragrant oils into his skin. An hour later he sat slathered up in mud from head to toe. Jack laughed to and at himself, he would never get used to the sensation. He knew he looked like a huge clay golem, but it came with the process of being pampered. In the dark quiet corner of his mind, he could secretly admit that his favorite part was being able to break out of the mud. It reminded him of various comic book heroes he had admired from his childhood. Not to mention it was just plain fun. His wolf lolled his tongue in agreement.

He stretched as the attendant dusted the last of the mud from his skin. He went to the dressing room, put on silk swim trunks, and made his way to the whirlpool suite.

"Welcome to the good part," Kama said.

She sat on a marble bench near the pool, dipping her toe into the water. She wore a flattering one-piece suit and climbed into the hot tub with a low rumble of pleasure in her throat. Mud gone from her face and the paste and crèmes out of her hair, she radiated contentment from all of the pampering she had received. He soaked in her beauty with appreciation. He stepped into the tub and sank into the water, closing his eyes with a sigh.

"We have a few hours left," she said. "I figure we can hang out for a while and talk."

"Sounds like a reasonable plan," he said.

He let the pressure from the jets further massage his muscles. When he opened his eyes, Kama was watching him with a small smile and in return he gave her a slow look, appreciating her simplistic style that flattered her shape. The cranberry red brought an extra glow of health to her skin. Skin he wanted to kiss and touch, though for now he would be content to watch and talk.

"This is a beautiful spa," Kama said.

"Yes, it is. They would have waited for us," Jack said.

"Really? I lost an appointment yesterday because I happened to be a tiny bit late because of another dress fitting. I wouldn't risk losing this appointment too."

A waiter opened the door and entered the room, causing their conversation to cease.

"We have a full bar and a list of appetizers available for you," he said.

Jack looked up at the man to order and found him entranced with Kama. Out of the corner of his eye, he saw her wrinkle her nose toward him. She then turned to the waiter with a calm look.

"I'd like a bottle of Cristal, and one set of each appetizer," she said.

"Yes, ma'am, right away," he said.

Impressed with the unflappable waiter, who to his credit did not quite blink an eye as she ordered some eight appetizers, Jack sat back. He had been all prepared to order for them, being the gentlemanly thing to do, but Kama had beaten him to the punch. She made him want to laugh a lot, and he found himself looking forward to it.

"Champagne?" Jack asked.

"Why not? We are celebrating and unless something has changed in the past two hours, people tend to have champagne when celebrating," Kama said.

She gave him a lofty look, which the sparkle in her eyes ruined. His wolf berated him for forcing himself to sit still and not kiss her. She winked at him and Jack congratulated himself on his amazing restraint. He watched her switch gears again; she dropped her gaze and seemed very interested in swiping her hands through the bubbles. He couldn't believe she would go shy on him, so with a devilish grin he provoked her.

"I agree it is definitely the drink to have while celebrating," Jack said. "It's just I had expected something with more spice from you, not so sweet and girly."

"Sweet? Girly?" Kama asked.

She looked like she couldn't decide how offended to be and whether or not she might try to choke him. He used her own tactic and switched gears, becoming playfully condescending with her.

"Okay, feminine then," he corrected. "But it's okay, we're here to relax and you're right, it should help."

"I do believe you are making fun of my drink choice," she said.

"Perhaps," he said.

With perfect timing, the waiter entered at that moment. Jack took the flutes off the tray and handed one to her. She tapped her glass against his and took a sip. He got caught up in the caramel brown of her eyes and saw the change of pace once more as she looked him up and down so seductively he choked on the champagne.

"Well, if you can do better…" Kama said. "By all means try."

The challenge of "The War of the Drink" had been issued. The water soothed him with its rhythmic pounding and he sat back, watching her. She tried to continue to look at him in mock severity but failed and laughed as champagne bubbles went up her nose. She moved closer to him, close enough he could smell the subtle scent of lavender rise from her skin. Kama reached across Jack's chest to set her empty glass on a small table nearby, and then sank back under the water. He had almost stopped breathing when the pheromones slammed into his nose. Despite knowing she had made the movement on purpose, he appreciated the close up look he got of her body. Seconds later, Jack's glass joined hers and he watched her intently. He didn't know what game she played, but he knew where he wanted things to end up. When the waiter returned, Jack promptly ordered.

"I would like a 7&7 for myself, and the lady."

"What are those?" Kama asked.

"A real drink," Jack said.

The waiter had left and returned before their conversation had made any real progress. Jack tried his best to listen as she talked, but all he wanted to do was get closer. She gave him a saucy wink and went back into flirt mode. He nodded to her before lifting his glass up. She returned the salute and took a sip. He watched as her face screwed up against the strong taste of gin.

"So this is your idea of a real drink?" Kama asked. "Others might challenge your questionable taste."

Jack tried his best not to give in to laughter at her gall and ended up choking on his drink, again. Kama politely found some interesting scenery outside to look at, while he sputtered and forced the liquid from his lungs. She had set her drink on the small table, and he noticed she didn't touch it again. After a few moments of stifling silence, Jack cleared his throat a few times.

"How are you enjoying the spa?" he asked.

"It's wonderful. There is nothing better than having moments when you have absolutely no obligations," she said.

"So your life in New York isn't all about hanging out with friends and being social?"

Jack knew he baited her and her raised eyebrow confirmed it. He had already learned she had incredible discipline; her musical talent showed years of hard work and training. But his curiosity about her consumed him, and short of grilling her, he wasn't sure how to get all of his questions answered.

"I suppose I'm picky about whom I call friend. Not to mention, practice tends to eat up all my time," she said.

He watched her jab the button and more bubbles erupted in the hot tub. She sounded defensive and with a sigh he watched her try to relax again. For some reason the friend comment had really upset her. He wondered why friends would be such a sore spot with her; he couldn't imagine she wouldn't have a gaggle of friends all around her. She had a kind of sparkling personality that should have drawn people to her. Jack caught himself up in his musings, realizing the depth of his attraction to her.

"Do you have a lot of friends, Jack?"

He almost missed the question, since his thoughts had wrapped him up into knots. He grinned at her thinly veiled attempt to catch him off guard with the same question.

"Very few. It's hard in the business world to keep a lot of friends. Most people want you to believe they are; at least until they get what they need from you," he said. "I have quite a few associates but most people find me down right intimidating."

"Intimidating, really? Here I figured you were pretty good company," Kama said.

"Probably because I am not trying to take over your business," he said.

"I am my business, being a vocal performer," she said. "Not like you could take me over."

His wolf delighted in that challenge and Jack very quickly shifted his questions in another direction before he followed his wolf's lead.

"So, what is your area of expertise?" he asked. "Just don't tell me jazz."

She laughed and even as he joined in, he really hoped she wouldn't say jazz, but very little about her could surprise him at this point.

"Opera primarily, but I also perform classical," she said. "Although from time to time I am asked to perform some contemporary pieces, but I try to take venues that put my training into practice. I have found, however, performing opera at Christmas parties is a big failure."

"I suppose I should count myself lucky Charlie convinced you to go on stage at the club," he said.

"That happened only because you took me to see my favorite jazz duo of all times," she said. "It's not like it was a concert or anything. That was for enjoyment; my professional performances are a completely different experience."

"I'll have to make it a point to come see one of your concerts."

"If you wish," she murmured. "Just don't critique me too hard."

Jack could have sworn she suddenly went shy at the thought of him watching her at a concert. Again he moved to teasing to keep the tone light. She kept him on his toes and slightly off balance, which he found interesting.

"I promise I'll be nice; after all, you don't work for me," Jack said. "If you worked for me, I might have to be critical or something."

"Like I would ever give you anything to be critical about. Are you still thinking of taking me over?" she asked. "I am sure I would be able to handle working for you just fine."

He watched her push a few damp tendrils away from her eyes, and quelled the urge to run his hands through her hair. Soon enough he would have her; he could wait until she was comfortable. The waiter stuck his head back in the room and, noticing the empty glasses on the table, asked if they wanted anything else.

"I believe it is your turn Kama," Jack said.

"Two Appletinis," she ordered.

Jack laughed as the waiter left, and she looked at him triumphantly.

"Well, those sound positively like one of those fancy delicate drinks," he said. "The kind I figured you would stay away from."

He chuckled at the wry look she flashed him with no hint of shame. The waiter scooped up the empty glasses and straightened the appetizer trays. Jack noticed, for all Kama ordered enough to feed a dozen people, she hadn't really touched the food. He popped a stuffed mushroom in his mouth and watched her. He guessed the next round of bantering would start once the waiter left their room; he guessed right.

"It's a good business drink," Kama said. "After all we are sitting here talking about business. Although maybe not so much, because weren't you just trying to convince me you were intimidating and I wasn't buying it?"

"Regular martinis, not the apple," he corrected. "Apple-flavored anything isn't business like."

"The apple ones taste better," she said with a shrug.

"I wouldn't know," he admitted.

"Well why would you? It's not one of your manly drinks," she said. "At least now you get a chance to find out."

He roared in laughter at her proclamation and offered her some food from the trays. He had missed lunch himself, but he didn't want to clear the tray of their contents before she had a chance to get a snack. She took a healthy plateful of the finger foods and ate with gusto. He had to admire a woman who wanted to eat and did so.

"So do you not like fancy drinks Jack?" she asked.

"No, I'm rather a plain sort of guy." he said.

"Plain?" she scoffed "A plain man who just happens to wear Armani? Armani is not plain."

"Carla, my Executive Assistant, insists on my looking professional," he said. "I would prefer jeans and flannel."

"Flannel, hmmm?" she queried. "I would like to see you in flannel."

I would love to see you in my flannel.

His wolf, being more honest, wanted to see her naked.

"Sure, I'll take you on a tour of one of my mills," he said. "I wear flannel when I visit them."

Jack smiled at her, enjoying the thought of future visits. He even looked forward to the little bits of daring she used to taunt him. He leaned in closer and started to make a move to kiss her, when the waiter returned with their drinks. He mentally sighed at the intrusion. He took the glasses off the tray, handed her one, and then raised his glass to hers.

"So are you going to make a manly toast, to counteract the girly in the drink?" she asked.

"Manly? Careful pet, you will prick my temper," he said.

"Should I fear your temper?" Kama asked.

She quirked her eyebrow at him, and then took a healthy sip of her drink. She closed her eyes in satisfaction and sat back. She didn't look the least bit intimidated by him and he wanted to laugh, again. He also wanted to taste Kama again, to feel her lips against his in surrender. He wondered if he were the only one feeling the sensuous vibe that permeated the air as he focused on the beguiling creature next to him. Jack almost shook his head; she had gotten under his skin and then some. The dynamics of her game were so unpredictable that he felt like a novice. He let himself slip back under the bubbles, again not quite sure how to read her body language. Heck, he could barely understand his own; instead he focused on her last question.

"I have found my temper can be very useful," Jack said.

"Oh yea? What do you do with your temper?" she asked.

She looked over the rim of her glass, her tongue darting out to catch an errant drop of liquid. He loved the fact that she tried so hard to flirt but seemed oblivious to innuendo inherent in certain actions. Despite all her apparent efforts at being coy, he relished in her chasing him. He stared at her until she looked away, not to tease her per usual. Jack released a quiet shaky breath and then answered her question.

"Channel it. It's very helpful in business."

"So what is your business?" she asked. "I already told you all about my life, what about yours?"

Jack was confused for a moment; he knew they had already talked about his work. Perhaps the drinks were starting to affect her.

"I work in raw materials; metals and plastics, though mostly steel mills," he said. "I love the mills; they are where I started from. Of course now I'm mostly in the board room, so I used them as my reality base, just in case things get too intense."

"Yea, I can see you getting a bit intense," she agreed.

"Only when necessary," he said.

"Jack?" she asked.

He grinned at her and took a sip of his drink. He vowed to never, ever to reveal to her that he found the drink excellent. It was much better than the original martini, in fact. She gave him a mischievous look and then tilted her head. Jack finally answered her.

"Yes, Kama?"

"I think you are intense most of the time," she said. "Then again, I think it is part of the mystery of you."

"You find me mysterious?" he asked.

"Yes," she said. "You walk around like you are holding something really close to your chest. What deep, dark secrets do you carry?"

"Oh, this isn't the time for deep dark things. We should relax and enjoy the soothing environment," he said.

His wolf urged him to get to the business of enjoyment. The waiter interrupted them again to take the empties and Jack ordered them each a Tequila Sunrise.

"Do you think you are ready for the big bad tequila?" Jack asked.

"I am sure it will be harsh and manly," she said.

"Harsh and manly," he said with a laugh. "Sweetheart, if you even knew…"

He loved that she dissolved into giggles at the look on his face. Very few people made jokes at Jack's expense and this tiny slip of a girl openly laughed at him. The waiter returned again and set the drinks down. Jack nodded in affirmation to take away the plates of appetizers and indicated they were done. He wanted as few interruptions as possible. He watched her turn on the water jets again, enjoying the lines of her body.

"It's pretty," Kama said.

"What is?" Jack asked.

He was afraid she had again lost him in a conversation. A conversation she must finish in head, since most of her truncated sentences didn't make any sort of sense to him. She laughed loudly at the look of disbelief on his face and then explained in exaggerated slowness, like she would talk to a child.

"I said, your oh-so-manly drink, was pretty."

"You dare mock me?" he growled at her.

"I dare a lot," Kama said.

He noticed that she shivered from his intense look, the motion ruined her bold act; leaving him to imagine she felt his growled words all the way into the pit of her stomach. But she said nothing and sank back down into the roiling water until just her chin showed and gave a low, earthy moan of pleasure. Jack sighed and closed his eyes, the sound rippled through him and he wanted to answer in kind. He wanted her to set the pace but, he knew his wolf was past impatient and driving him strongly to act on instinct. After a few seconds of being disgusted with himself for being stupid, he let go and decided to enjoy the time in her delightful company.

'I will let her make the moves in her own time. She has been setting the pace and it has turned out fine. Why ruin a good thing?' he thought, to keep his wolf in check.

His wolf growled in frustration; clearly shoving *the you are an idiot* thought back at Jack. He opened his eyes to find her watching him but saying nothing.

"So, what are you thinking?" he asked.

"I am thinking this is a little slice of heaven. I have not been this relaxed in a long time," she said.

"Indeed..." Jack said. "It is very soothing. The benefits of being the last appointment of the day, we pretty much have the place to ourselves."

"It's like living the fairy tale life," she said.

She gave Jack a wide smile; but all he noticed were her flushed cheeks. Despite having slowly paced out the drinks, the thought passed through his mind that she might not drink a lot.

"Well you know the tales, there's always a big bad wolf waiting in the wings to change things up," he said.

He knew she couldn't interpret the look he gave her. She furrowed her brow, and he knew that she was trying to decide if he were serious or playful. Then she smiled again at him, having apparently decided that he was having fun with her.

"You know the girls in red always win."

"Why the girls in red?" he asked.

*"I sometimes think that never blows so red*
*The Rose as where some buried Caesar bled;*
*That every Hyacinth the Garden wears*
*Dropt in its Lap from some once lovely Head.*

"That's amazing," he said.

"That's Omar Khayyam."

For the first time in a long while, he had the pleasure of knowing a woman wasn't ruthlessly pursuing him. Jack found being the one to do the chasing pure exhilaration. Each time they talked, he found more to be curious about. He wanted to stay mysterious and give her a reason to keep coming around. Not to mention, he found her attempts clumsy but cute.

*I never would have expected her to read a Persian Sufi mystic. I wonder what else is hiding in that head of hers.*

Even as the thought that she might be hiding something passed through his brain, she switched up topics on him again. She looked up at him from under dark fringed eyes. He met her gaze while he sipped from his glass.

"I can't figure you out," she said, acting like she should have been able to.

"Oh?" he asked. "I suppose it's a good thing. If I were an open book, I wouldn't be very good at negotiations."

"I suppose you would have to be in your line of work," she said. "You're funny."

"Am I now?" he asked.

Jack watched her drain the last of the "pretty" tequila drink and then she sat back in silence. He watched her run her hands through the bubbles from the jets. It occurred to him that she might be feeling the effects of her drinks. As he watched her longer, he wasn't sure; she didn't appear tipsy, just contemplative.

"So aren't you going to tell me anything about you?" she asked.

"What do you want to know?" he queried as he placed his glass on the table.

"Well, why are you in L.A.?"

"I'm here on business, negotiating with a small company and trying to convince them to be partners with me."

"Partners for what?" Kama questioned. "Is this for your steel mills?"

He watched her, feeling the beat of her heart as the vibration carried through the water and crested into him. He recognized that she was tipsy but his wolf didn't care. The wolf wanted to possess her and instinct was winning over logic. To his shock, she raised her hand and ran her fingers lightly over his lips. Then she blushed. His lips tingled from the brief contact and he noticed she stared hard at his face in curiosity. He cleared his throat and answered her.

"For a shipping company and yes," he said.

She leaned forward and kissed him. Her feather light touch had an innocence to it as her lips brushed his and then her tongue slowly explored his mouth. Her wet body pressed against his chest, the swimming suit served as a tease to him. So close to naked and yet, not. The kiss lit fiery trails in him; he took control and pulled her onto his lap. He took his time tasting her, touching her, and memorizing her every scent. When he finally released her, he found he needed a calming breath. The wolf was more in control than was comfortable. Confusion fuzzed his brain and he couldn't figure out where the hell when she had gotten this power over him.

"Mmmm, nice," she whispered.

Jack nodded his head in agreement; afraid his voice might crack like a schoolboy if he tried to answer her right then. The wolf offered to take over. Needing to feel her again, he began to massage the back of her neck with one hand, reveling in the dewy softness of her skin. He sat, enjoying the feel of her, when Kama stood up. Her steps wavered as she walked out of the hot tub and grabbed a towel.

"Kama? Are you okay?" Jack asked.

*Right, Twist, because she is the only one unsteady here. You are definitely not drunk, so what is your excuse for acting like some hormonally challenged teenager? Get it together and get this woman back to her room.*

The wolf snorted his disagreement with that plan of action.

"I feel hot," she whispered. "I just need a bit of air."

Crap, definitely too much to drink.

Jack really hoped for a moment that the cool air would help her, and then checked himself. He was amazed at his own spiraling instinctual takeover; he wanted her but knew now would not be the time. He couldn't recall the last time his common sense had been inhibited by strong feelings of lust.

"Let's change and go outside, maybe the fresh air will help," Jack said.

He watched Kama walk in slow steps towards her changing room. Jack rose and made his way to help her. She looked back at Jack over her shoulder, and gave him a sexually heated smile; he promptly tripped over the steps himself as he watched her. Jack, knowing some space a good idea, took a towel and dried off.

*Damn, that woman just doesn't know her own allure.*

He had never had to fight with his wolf this much over a woman. The wolf was constantly pushing, wanting to consummate the relationship and the man had a hard time figuring out why it might be a bad idea. Jack knew she was attracted to him and trying pretty hard to get his attention, but once she had it she turned shy when he pursued her. The experience made Jack react in ways he would have never imagined. So he pushed the tawdry thoughts to the back and gladly decided to ride the wild train to see where it would stop.

Jack had never had an issue with his wolf vying for control. He rationalized his lupine struggles by blaming her teasing behavior, or perhaps he acted a bit rash because of the alcohol and heat combination.

*Just because we haven't bedded her yet doesn't mean it won't happen. I want to be patient, I actually enjoy the fact that she hasn't thrown herself into our bed and set herself up as our arm-piece. Is your stupid ego puffing up because she hasn't spent countless hours fawning and telling you how much she adores you? By the teat of the Great Mother, are we so vain that we need the adoration? Maybe it's part of her charm.*

His wolf just snorted at his stupid human brain and the churning. It had figured out a plan of action hours ago. Jack went to the other changing room and stood under a very cold shower until he had control of his thoughts, as well as other parts of his body.

"Jack?" she called out.

"Yes?"

"I think I am ready to go back to the hotel."

When he came out, he found her sitting in a chair, elbows on knees, with her face in her hands.

"I suppose I should have had more snacks. The heat is really doing a number on me," she said.

"Yes," he agreed.

She looked up at him and made all other conversation leave his head. She wanted him to kiss her, he could feel it all the way...well, he could definitely tell. He leaned in closer to her.

"Hot tubs are good for heat, just not so good for drinks," she said.

"Not quite," he said.

He looked down at her and then pressed his lips to the pulse point of her neck. The taste of her drove him crazy, the texture of her skin was like satin, and he smiled as her breath hitched. Jack firmly shoved the wolf into the back of his mind and regained control. He realized he had been actively seducing a very tipsy woman on a bench in a spa and got a grip on his obviously stupefied hormones.

"Jack?"

"Yes, Kama?"

He savored the way her name rolled over his tongue and around in his mouth like a cool sip of champagne.

"Do you want me to drive?" Kama asked.

His laughter rumbled in his chest; he was going to have to dissuade her from that notion. He tried to think of a way to let her down easily and what to say. To his surprise, she stood up and kissed him on the corner of the mouth slowly working her way across his lips, like a bee attracted to nectar. Jack ran his fingers across the small of her back and slowly returned her kisses. She pulled back and looked up at him expectantly.

"I'm thinking about it," he said.

Jack ran one hand through her damp hair, while his fingers splayed across her back. He drew her for another kiss and felt her shiver against his hard physique. He reveled in the scorching kiss as it consumed him. Learning as he touched her, he changed his tactics until her sharp gasp of pleasure made him aware that they were in public and he was very close to losing control.

*For the love of the Blessed Mother, Jack, get a grip before you make love to her on this spa floor. You are acting like a stupid teenager. You, stand down.*

Jack felt the wolf's disgust at his command as he berated them both for his hormonal regression into emotionally driven actions. He rested his hand on the small of her back as he guided her to the front of the spa. He quickly checked out, and helped her into the car. Jack bent down and kissed her deeply and, as she snuggled against him, he drove with purpose back to the Beverly Wilshire.

During the elevator ride to his suite, he had time to let thoughts mull over in his head. He wanted to possess Kama like no other. It had been years since a woman had made him feel like this – or feel period. He carefully guided her to his room and opened the door. She sank into a lounge chair and gave a deep sigh, one he wanted to echo.

*Well, tonight is a wash. I am not going to take advantage of her being tipsy. I want her to know when we make love.*

"Ummm, Jack?"

"Hmmm?"

"I think I'm going to fall over," she said. "I can't go back like this."

"Don't worry, I've got you. You don't have to go back anywhere,"

He finally admitted that Kama was more than a bit tipsy when she slid off the chair towards the floor. He scooped her up in his arms; she nestled against his chest as he carried her to the bed. Jack placed her on the duvet and tried to make her comfortable. He wanted to groan as Kama wrapped her arms around his neck, pulling him close to her.

*This is not quite how I imagined spending the night with her. Oh well, it's what I get for acting like a stupid kid and having a drink war with a little lightweight who was hell bent on proving her toughness. I bet she had enough after the first glass of champagne.*

"Don't go," she whispered. "I want you…"

"I'll stay by your side so nothing happens."

He said the words out loud to make a point to his wolf.

*We are not going to make love tonight. We are going to watch her fall asleep and then go get some work done.*

"Yes," she said closing her eyes for a moment then opening them to look at him. "I need you here tonight, Jack."

He looked at her and sighed, the deep sigh of a man who had resigned himself to sleeping in a chair, across from the bed where his fantasy would spend the night. Kama had other plans and moved over in the bed and waited for him to climb in beside her. She tilted her face up to his and Jack leaned in to kiss her again, feeling the heat pour out of her and over him. To his surprise, Kama pulled him in closer until he was pressed against her. She nipped and teased his lips in the most blazing kiss he could remember.

*Hell Twist, she is drunk. Get off her and let her sleep. You can give into your stupid carnal desires tomorrow when she is sober.*

He got out of the bed to turn off the lights. By the time he made it back, her soft snores filled his ear. Her breathing, unlike his, was even and deep. He cursed her sensitivity to tequila, then himself for being stupid and for letting her drink so much.

Jack spent most of the night watching her, from the chair. He woke once in the middle of the night as some sense of panic dragged his conscious back up to find her moaning lightly in her sleep. His protective feelings towards her rose, and he moved to comfort her against what had distressed her. He lay next to her, on top of the blankets, and curled an arm around her. The next time he woke, she had thrown off the blankets and had draped a leg over him, claiming him for her personal body pillow for the evening. Jack didn't manage to fall back asleep as his body burned with need of her. He stared at the ceiling and tersely reminded his wolf to behave and then tried to relax.

# CHAPTER Four

Kama woke to a crescendo of thunder; it took a moment for her to realize where the pressure came from. Her head throbbed and pounded as she tried to make sense of her surroundings. She regretted opening her eyes as blinding light greeted her and sent lances of pain through her skull. When the pain subsided, she looked around, not recognizing the room. A rumbling snore startled her, not so much the sound, but because it came from directly underneath her and she did not recognize the chest she lay upon. Thick coarse hair covered the broad expanse and the steady thrum of the heartbeat almost lulled her back into sleep, and then he moved. The full throated scream she had intended, came out as a wispy nothing because her cotton-packed mouth wouldn't allow the sound. She sat up alarmed, immediately regretting the rash action as movement caused black spots to flash before her eyes. Her mind seemed to clear from the panic filled adrenaline rush and she looked down at a sleeping Jack.

*Why am I here with Jack? In fact, where is here?*

The night before began to replay itself and she groaned as she recalled passing out on him. It had all been going so smoothly; great conversation, great drinks, even a kiss, and the clarity went away and she woke up in his room. Granted there were some fuzzy details that she thought she remembered, but Kama didn't think she had done anything terrible. Until she looked down and saw a small drool spot pooling on his chest; embarrassment flooded through her and made it harder for her to think.

"Great going, DeKosse," she muttered.

Her quandary on whether or not to wake him kept her immobile a few minutes more. Then she listened to her pride and opted to sneak out. She eased out of the bed, happy to note her quiet departure had not disturbed him. Her tiptoe past the mirror pulled a gasp from her; her clothes were a wrinkled mess and her hair stood out Medusa style. Kama pulled her hair back into something resembling a neat knot and reached for her purse on the vanity. She felt bad about running from him again, but she couldn't handle feeling stupid in front of him for passing out. She was disgusted at the immature action and the drinking to excess. Waking up after having drooled on one's object of affection classified beyond mortifying.

"Idiot," she chided herself. "Now is not the time to fix your appearance, get back to your own room and do it."

Bolstered into action by her strict talk, Kama stiffened her spine and walked to the door. She busily berated herself in a low whisper as she left his room and never noticed Jack had woken. Had she bothered to look back she would have seen the smile on his face. Instead, she worried he would want nothing else to do with her.

*You drooled like a dog all over him, not exactly what he would find sexy. I am getting worse; ever since I met this man, all I do anymore is talk to myself. How am I ever going to face him again? Where is Gianna when I need her? What is the point of having a best friend if she isn't around to tell you that you weren't a complete dolt? And no, Cynthia doesn't qualify; spa trip or not she still owes us. Damn, the royal we.*

Since she didn't know how to face him, she opted not to, for a whole day and a half. Kama spent the time trying to shop for her last gown and got nothing accomplished. She had lost her fervor and the shopping mission had faded into the background. Nervous that she would run into Jack, she played duck and cover as she walked through the hotel. She sat in her room, moping, when a terrifying thought crossed her mind.

*He doesn't have to wait for me to come to him. It's not brain surgery to call my room or even stop by.*

It distressed her to think that she might return from shopping and find him waiting for her in front of her room. So, she got a grip on her embarrassment and made a point to go down and find him in the hotel restaurant. She would much rather be the one in control of their meeting again.

"Good evening," she said.

She walked right up to him and got a warm rush as she noticed his eyes lit up just a bit when she greeted him. At least she hoped she noticed that reaction. She smiled and sat down next to him, her knee almost touching his under the round table, without waiting for an invitation. Jack put down his paper and signaled the waitress.

"Evening, Kama," he said. "I was afraid you had left for New York without telling me."

"Never," she said, smiling at him. "I just had some appointments. Remember, I already told you about being late and not being forgiven."

"Right," he said. "So you got everything you needed? Because I didn't see you at all yesterday."

She glowed a bit when he mentioned missing her, well at least in his roundabout way. She nodded approval as he ordered a bottle of wine from the waitress and she ordered a light dinner. He seemed relaxed enough from what she could see, so she relaxed too.

"Other than one last gown fitting, then I am all set until I go home," she said.

"What are you plans when you go home?" Jack asked.

"Normal schedule of school, practice, being a diva. You know, the normal," she said. "When are you returning?"

"My business here is done, though I just need to tie up some loose ends," he said. "What are your plans for tomorrow?"

"I suppose wherever you have planned to take me," she said.

Kama congratulated herself for finally getting the flirting thing down, and smiled at him. She noted he didn't seem to be holding a grudge, despite her disappearing acts with him. She could tell he had a lot of questions about her and decided it wouldn't hurt to answer some of them.

"It would be nice if you actually let me ask you out on the date that I had planned for us," he said.

She grinned at him cheekily and leaned to conspire with him.

"Perhaps you need to be less intimidating and more assertive," Kama said with a wink. "Maybe it will help you achieve that goal you had of taking me over."

She stared at him and for once didn't drop her gaze or ramble to fill the silence that she assumed was a ploy on his part to keep her flustered. The stalemate continued until the waitress returned with her dinner. After her wine glass was filled, Kama raised it in mock salute and took a sip. Jack arched his eyebrow and returned the salute.

"I haven't been assertive with you yet. You seemed to enjoy taking charge and I was happy to acquiesce," he said. "However, if you think I should take charge now, I will happily comply. Are you sure you can handle the loss of control."

Kama stroked his arm softly, taking advantage of the fact that he was casually dressed in slacks and polo shirt. She then ran her nails up his arm and was rewarded with a scatter of goose bumps rising up. She took another drink, her eyes never leaving his. Then as she placed the glass on the table, she tucked her chin demurely and then, looked up at him with seductive eyes. She deliberately pulled her bottom lip tight with her teeth and soothed the faux wound with the tip of her tongue.

"I don't think I have to worry about control. You, on the other hand, are showing your cards."

Kama glanced quickly towards his lap. To her surprise Jack leaned back against his chair with a satisfied grin. She reached over him to grab the dressing and made sure that she allowed him enough time to get a decent glimpse of her cleavage. She then made it a point to ignore him as she fixed her salad, even still she could tell when he moved closer to her. Kama was proud that she didn't jump as his warm breath caressed her ear.

"Oh, sweetheart, that was just a preview."

Kama turned to make a saucy retort but lost her chance as Jack's warm hand rested on the nape of her neck and drew her in closer. She thought she was prepared as he leaned in and kissed her but nothing had prepared her for such a carnal and thorough experience. She kissed him back and pressed her hands to his chest as he moved the kiss deeper. She knew the second she lost control, when his tongue swirled in her mouth and she could taste the wine. Her stomach curled and fluttered as desire rose and taunted her.

A clearing of the throat and words spoken in a low deep voice woke her from her reverie and she broke the kiss in haste.

"What are we doing? We are in the middle of the restaurant; I can't believe we were making out in public."

Kama heard Jack chuckle but refused to acknowledge that perhaps he had won their Contest of the Wills. She straightened the napkin in her lap and resumed eating dinner as if nothing of consequence had just happened.

"Don't worry, Kama," he said. "We will have plenty of privacy on our date tomorrow. So you won't have to rely on an excuse when your control slips."

"It never wavered once," she said. "I am not an exhibitionist."

Kama gave him a wry glance as he openly smirked at her. They finished dinner with light banter. She smiled at him and excused herself for the evening. Jack rose as she stood.

"Meet me in the lobby at eight o'clock," he said.

"In the morning?" she questioned.

"Yes, I want you all to myself for the whole day," he said. "I figure if I steal you away on a date, nothing can interrupt us. If we are away from the allure of gown shopping, I just might hold your full attention."

"I will see you at eight," Kama said.

She leaned in and gave him a quick peck on the cheek, turned on her heel, and sashayed her way to the elevator. She stood in the back, for once not minding the press of bodies, and smiled.

*Well that went better than we had anticipated. He doesn't think I'm a total idiot and we have another date tomorrow. And yes, I know I am talking to myself again. But hey, it went well didn't it? I know tomorrow will be great.*

##

Kama arrived five minutes before eight o'clock in the lobby the next morning. The day promised to be clear and warm and she couldn't wait to find out what Jack had planned. She smiled widely as he pulled the car up in front of the hotel mere moments later. She respected a person who kept to a schedule. Jack eased from behind the wheel with grace, opened the passenger door, and assisted her into her seat. He looked great and smelled wonderful, and Kama felt a curl of warmth rush into her belly. She tried to figure out a proper greeting when he leaned over and kissed her. Hot and seductive, the kiss drew her in and made her lose all thought except for Jack. After too short a time he pulled away from her and started to drive off when she realized they actually had not said anything to each other and she figured she should be polite.

"Morning," she said.

"Morning," he said with a smile.

Kama adjusted the radio as he drove; she had to do something with her rising energy. He kept looking over at her like he wanted to devour her, and to quell her nerves she talked as a distraction.

"Where are we off to?"

"You'll see," he said.

"So how did the rest of your evening go? Did you do anything interesting after I left?" She asked.

"I ended up going bowling," he said.

"Bowling, huh?" she asked.

Kama tried her best not to laugh, a giggle escaped anyhow and she turned her head towards the window, but not before she saw his eyebrow rise. She chanced a look from the corner of her eye and saw him watching. Her shoulders shook as she tried to get her laughter under control. Try as she might, she could not picture Jack bowling.

"And what's wrong with bowling?" he asked.

"Nothing at all. I rather like it, but I cannot imagine you bowling," she said. "Quite frankly, I can imagine myself running naked through Central Park before I can imagine you bowling."

She burst into sunny laughter as he stammered in mock protest. His chuckle joined hers and she wondered if he was laughing with her or at the thought that she might run through a park naked. They drove in the rush of highway traffic, having a light conversation about their best and worst bowling scores. Their chatter was interrupted now and again as a favorite song came on the radio and she sang along with it. She appreciated that he didn't mind her musical segues. Los Angeles traffic kept their pace to a minimum, but she enjoyed the time just being together.

"Where are we going?" she asked once again.

"As I said before, you will find out once we get there," he said.

They had been traveling for an hour and she still had no clue of her destination. No amount of prying had given her any sort of hint as to what the plans were. Periodically, she did a sneak attack with the question, hoping to catch him off guard just once. However, Jack made an art of being tight lipped in his responses and gave away nothing about his mysterious plans.

"So, why eight in the morning?" she asked.

"What I have in mind is better done in the early morning," he said.

"Well thanks, I think. Care to elaborate a bit more?" she asked.

"You don't give up, do you?"

"Would you expect me to?" she countered.

"No, based on your dedication to finding the perfect gown, I know you are persistent. But you aren't going to weasel it out of me. I worked hard on these plans."

Something in his voice made Kama pause. A tone of pride had laced his words.

*Maybe he doesn't do this often. Wow, did he make special plans just for me? Damn, I want to know where are going.*

## Enter the Moon

Another half hour of highway and music went by, when suddenly Jack took an exit off the freeway and they drove up to what looked like a gated community. She looked over at Jack confused. They were waved through as Jack showed a pass and wound their way through the lush scenery.

"So, are we almost there?" she asked.

"Yea, it's the newest hot spot amongst celebrities. We are going to have a day at a nudist retreat," he said.

She watched for some sign but he remained deadpanned.

"I hope you are kidding."

Jack cracked a small grin, rolled up to small marina, and got out of the car. He quickly walked around and opened the door for Kama. She let him draw her into a deep kiss and then watched as he walked to the back of the car. She sat with a bemused smile on her face, waiting for his secret to be revealed.

"Well?" she demanded.

"We are spending the day on the lake. After all of my business meetings and your gown gathering, I figured we could both use a day of relaxation and quiet."

Jack motioned to the dock and a lavish pontoon as they walked toward it. Kama nodded in appreciation, the expanse of the day overwhelming her out of a response. However, when she did finally come up with something to say, she made it memorable.

"So, can I drive? There shouldn't be too many old people to push out of the way," Kama said.

She gave him an impish smile, remembering how he had reacted when she drove his Hummer to the spa. She couldn't be faulted if he couldn't handle a bit of excitement. Jack roared with laughter, which kept the smug look on her face. The lake was private and self-contained. Despite never having driven a boat, she figured it should be as easy as driving a car. Kama joined him in laughter, loving the start to her day. As they approached the docks, a man with a deep tan approached them. She waited for Jack to introduce them but the man beat him to it.

"Hi, I am Hunter. How did someone as beautiful as you end with an old scoundrel like Twist?" he said. "Good to see you, Twist."

He addressed Jack as if he were an afterthought and patted him on the back as they gave what Kama considered a "man style" hug. Of course she would have been gasping for breath if he had "patted" her on the back with such vigor.

"Morning, Hunter," Jack said. "This is Kama. Kama this old coot owes me a favor or ten; he thought he could buy me off by offering me the use of his boat for the day."

"And he was anxious enough to fall for it," Hunter said with a laugh. "Glad to meet you."

She smiled, greeted him and while the men laughed and made more references to things that were obviously private jokes, Kama walked out onto the dock. The clear blue green of the manmade lake had not been touched that morning, so it remained glassy smooth and looked cool and inviting. From where she stood, she would have never been able to tell that the chaos and smog of Los Angeles lurked only a short distance away. The houses encircling the lake were huge, gorgeous, and immaculately groomed, a far cry from the style of home in Manhattan. She wondered what it would be like to live in one.

Kama jumped as Jack came up behind her and put his hands on her shoulders; she had gotten lost in her fantasy musings. She smiled up at him and he kissed her, before pointing across the lake to a dark brown and glass house.

"There is Hunter's house. He was smart enough to buy in the area before all the celebrities found it to be their new haven," he said. "If I had planned better, he would have been gone today and it would be all ours."

He nibbled on her ear, sending shivers up her spine as his words sunk home. She leaned back into him and tipped her head to engage him in another kiss.

"I think being on a boat all day with you will be fabulous," she said. "Not to mention, who wants to be cooped up all day when we can be out here?"

Jack nodded in agreement and walked back to confer once more with

Hunter, leaving Kama to look around the area by herself. She looked over at the boat the men were loading and smiled; it was large enough for at least eight people.

*This whole thing is so surreal. We have known each other for what, a week? This is just crazy. It's been a huge whirlwind of dating fun and I can't wait to spend the day alone with him uninterrupted. I wonder if Jack can swim.*

She thought back on their date at the jazz club, one of the best nights of her life, and hoped that their day together would top that experience. Kama lost herself in the remembrance of that special night.

"Now mind you, you will have to really have to maintain your self-control," Jack said.

His soft voice broke into her reverie and for the second time, he sneaked up on her. She tilted her face up to smile at him with a decidedly naughty twinkle in her eye.

"I'll try my best," she said in a husky whisper meant to challenge his mock command. "I promise there will be neither naked sun bathing nor skinny dipping at all."

She grinned and enjoyed the reaction his body couldn't hide.

"Now, now, let's not be hasty," he said.

She saw Hunter walk off the boat and waved to them. As she walked down the dock, Kama had a nervous flutter in her stomach. Alone with Jack again, and this time she didn't plan to drink anything and ruin their plans. Kama started to climb aboard, but Jack stopped her.

"I have a present for you," he said.

She looked at him in wonder; for the first time since she had met him, his eyes were cast towards the ground, apparently nervous she would not like his gift, which she found laughable. The day had been perfect thus far and she doubted he could ruin it.

"Really Jack, you didn't have to; this wonderful day trip is present enough," she said.

"No, really Kama, I had to," he said.

She alternated between confusion and excitement as she took the large bag he proffered. She opened and removed the decorative tissue paper with a flourish. Kama stared in amazement at the contents as she rifled through the items. There was a two piece bathing suit, a sun cover up, a hat, and sunglasses.

Rendered speechless, Kama turned and embraced Jack in a crushing hug as her lips sought his. She let him feel every astounded emotion running through her as she kissed him. She didn't notice the bag had dropped to the dock, or that they had gained an audience of one. An embarrassed cough intruded on their passionate embrace, and they turned to face Hunter.

"I was going to encourage you two to let go and have a good time" he said. "But apparently I'm too late. Anyhow, keys to the house are in the dash in case the weather gets crazy."

Hunter walked away shaking his head and Kama joined Jack in laughing.

"I've never seen the old man shaken by a little display of affection," he said in her ear. "Let's go have a good time."

"Jack, this is the most beautiful gift I have ever gotten," she said.

He kissed her again and then handed her the bag.

"Why don't you go change in the boat house, and I'll meet you back here in a few moments," he said.

A short while later, Kama walked back out, dressed in the lacy cover with hints of the silver and cardinal suit underneath. She thought the sunglasses made her look like a movie star and with Jack's lavish attention she certainly felt like it.

"Wow," Jack said.

"Yea, not too bad," she agreed. "I'm rather surprised at your good taste of color."

"I knew it would look great against that gorgeous skin of yours."

"Oh, you knew?"

"Yes," Jack said. "I had no doubt it would do you justice."

"You don't have to be smug," she said.

"Yes I do."

She stopped in front of him and leaned up to kiss him softly, intending to tease with the promise of more to come. It took every ounce of will power Kama had to pull away from him and to saunter down the boat. She sat in the captain's chair and waited for him with a smile. She took the hand he held out to her with an incredulous nod of his head. Kama settled in the chair across from his as he took the boat out away from the dock. They glided across the lake at a turtle's pace, looking at the lavish houses with well-groomed and flowered yards. When they had done a lap, he found a nice empty alcove and anchored the boat.

Kama walked to the deck of the boat, grabbed towels off the leather seats, and laid them out. She took off the cover up, revealing the very tasteful bikini that fit her like a glove. She pulled off the hat, plaited her hair and stretched out on a towel. She leaned up on her elbow and watched Jack lay out a fabulous spread of delectable bits they could nibble on throughout the day. She smiled as she watched him, something she had gotten used to doing. Kama admitted to herself that she couldn't imagine not seeing him once they got back to New York.

*He really thought of everything. Maybe when we get back home, I can surprise him with a horse ride in the park. I wonder if he likes horses. Either way, I will make it up to him. I hope he doesn't mind me planning on seeing him later. Then again, why would he? We are having a great time.*

The morning progressed better than Kama could have imagined; she and Jack spent most of their time talking. She kept the topics on the Fine Arts and where to find the best performances in Manhattan. She had worried Jack might find it odd she kept the conversation away from herself, but she noticed that he seemed to do the same. Kama changed pace and started talking about the most amazing places she had found good food in the city.

"Really the best tacos are from a truck on 87th West," she said.

"I will have to remember that and try them," he said. "Maybe we can meet there for a lunch break."

Kama smiled at the thought. As the sun rose in the sky, she sat up, deftly unbraided her hair, and shook it into loose waves with a sigh of relief. The hot and clear day made it perfect for lazing around as the boat gently bobbed in the wake from others passing them by. Looking up at Jack from under the shade of her hand she wondered how he could stand to be fully dressed still.

"You don't believe in bathing suits?" she asked.

"Oh I have a suit on, but I will warn you I don't tan well," He said as he shucked off his clothes.

His black and silver suit had a slim tailored fit, which took her breath away. Kama watched him arrange himself on a big soft towel under the shade of the boat's canopy. He lay back and motioned for her to come closer to him. She complied and placed her head on his chest, nestling in until she was comfortable. She giggled when he began to feed her grapes, but accepted them nonetheless, nipping at his fingers.

"Don't make me punish you," he said.

She responded to his playful tone by nipping him harder before answering him.

"I don't think you are capable," she said.

"I am a powerful business man, I'll have you know. I am very capable of punishments. You should be happy I have taken time out of my busy schedule to dally with you."

"Right, as if I didn't know your business has been concluded," she said.

Kama laughed off his severe look and offered up a cherry to him as an apology. She watched intently as he took the fruit between strong white teeth, and flinched despite herself when he playfully snapped at her. She tried to cover her reaction by attempting to force feed him a handful of grapes and then threw them at his chest when he refused to open his mouth.

*You're acting like a besotted idiot. Sheesh! A few kisses and you turn into one of those women who get all gooey and dopey. Who knew that dating could be so much fun? For the love of cheese, will you stop talking to yourself?*

Kama only half paid attention to him while he told her more about the steel mill industry; she paid far more attention to the warmth of his fingers as he touched her. He caressed her arm and she melted even closer to him. Finally, the sun's heat turned from sating to uncomfortable and she stood to stretch. He stood up next to her.

"Care for a swim?" she asked. "I'm a bit warm."

"Aren't you worried about your hair?" he asked.

His mocking tone made her roll her eyes and she leaned in to pinch him, but Jack caught her hand and pressed it to his chest. Kama resisted the urge to run her fingers through the coarse hair for a better feel. Although, with the way he watched her, she could tell Jack would not have minded. She very much wanted to kiss him, but she really didn't trust herself. She brought herself back to his question to get under control.

"Not if you don't plan to take me out to dinner," she said.

"You can actually swim city girl?" he asked.

Kama deftly freed her hand from his and pinched him, and then danced backwards just out of his reach. She scooted over to the side of the boat and taunted him.

"Of course I can. I can even wear a bathing suit without fear of the sun."

"Be nice," he warned.

She gave him a sensual smile and then arched a brow as he moved in close. She knew his look was meant to intimidate her but instead she just laughed. She leaned in and kissed his neck then pinched him again, tiny little plucks against skin of his chest. It was amazingly tantalizing to her and she knew he must have felt something because of his intake of breath.

"And if I don't I suppose you are going to threaten to spank me?" she asked.

Jack pulled Kama close, kissed her hard, smiled softly at her, and promptly jumped off the side of the boat into the chilly water. She came up sputtering.

"You..."

"Yes?"

"Jack!"

"I warned you to be nice," he said. "Maybe you should have listened."

Before she could protest again, he swam next to her and kissed her again. His strong legs treaded the water to keep them afloat as they embraced. Kama broke the kiss with a hazy smile, placed her hands on his shoulder and shoved him down. She had to admit she was shocked when he grabbed her by the waist and took her down with him. Even more so when he kissed her under the water. More sputtering ensued as they surfaced.

"The movies lie," she gasped.

Kama swam back to the side of the boat and looked at him. The water did much to enhance the sleek lines of his muscles. He smiled at her, obviously trying not to laugh.

"They do?" he asked.

"Kissing under water is all well and good, until you try to breathe through your nose. Then it becomes less romantic and more like drowning," she said.

Jack laughed and swam away as she splashed at him.

"That wasn't very nice of you," she said, splashing harder at him.

"I did warn you; I'm ruthless," he reminded her. "Besides you pushed me under the water."

"After you pushed me into the water."

"Well not so much pushing as pulling you in with me," Jack acknowledged.

Kama shook her head and swam out towards him, some vague sort of revenge on her mind. She had to chase Jack around the boat as he played hard to get. He swam stronger than she did and despite her best efforts to catch him off guard, he seemed always prepared; he was even ready when she swam under the boat. Much to Kama's chagrin she couldn't find him and spent a few laps around the boat trying to catch up with him, before a cough from the deck of the boat gave away his position.

"That's cheating."

She pulled herself onto the deck and frowned at him while re-braiding her hair and squeezing out the excess water.

"There were rules? Hmmmm…"

Kama laughed at him; the swim had used up her reserve revenge ambition. She stood and grabbed her cover up.

"Well then…"

She walked over to him and leaned in mere inches from his lips before spinning and walking toward the food. The shade provided a cool comfort and after fixing a couple of plates, she sat and patted the empty space next to her.

"Lunch?"

Jack sat next to her and took a fat juicy strawberry off the plate and held it over her mouth. Kama bit the fruit and closed her eyes in bliss. The berry tasted sweet and after their water games, she needed the sustenance. She let him feed her various foods until she was sated. She changed position so she could lie back against him to watch the other boats on the lake. The even rhythm of his heart and warm sun lured her to sleep mere moments later.

Kama woke to harsh whispers around her, confused as to where she was until she saw Jack. She watched his muscles flex as agitation increased his pacing and wondered how she could have slept while he picked her up and moved her to the cushioned bench. He was clearly agitated and despite the quiet tone she could hear every word.

"Now? I am at least an hour outside of the city. It will take me some time to get back but I will call Carla and set up the transfer immediately. I know you didn't want a merger but this is the only way that I know to keep the company in your hands."

Kama sat up; the sun had traveled quite a bit since she closed her eyes. Embarrassment flooded her as she realized she had slept part of their perfect afternoon away. But it seemed it would be ending soon.

"I'll be there when I can. No, I understand. This is the only way I know how to make this work. Just get everything ready; when I show up I want this taken care of immediately."

He snapped his phone shut and then turned to look at Kama. She noted that he seemed rather unsurprised to find her awake. He walked over and hugged her close. Then moved to the captain's chair and started the boat. She stood behind him, with her hands on his shoulders feeling the tension roll from him.

"Hi," she said.

"I guess I will be the one this time," he said. "I have some urgent business I have to attend to."

"Okay," she said.

She kissed his cheek and started to pack up the boat. He drove towards shore, pushing the upper speed limit of the vessel. They made quick work of docking the boat and getting back to the Hummer.

"I promise to make it up to you," he said.

"You have nothing to make up; you have business to attend to." she said.

They rode in silence back to the city. Jack drove fast and made her wonder how he could have ever been afraid of her driving skills. He wove in and out of traffic, in barely there spaces and never once did the needle dip under eighty. Kama reached over and placed her hand against his thigh, and smiled at him.

*Funny, he seems way more upset than me that our day got cut short. Maybe I'm just starting to grow on him. Anyhow, I had to leave him a couple of times; this at least makes things a bit more equal. Wow, he seems tense. I hope everything is okay. I would hate to see something go wrong with his business.*

Jack returned the smile and caressed her cheek with the back of his hand. He dropped her off at the front of the hotel with a kiss and a promise to call as soon as business was taken care of, then left.

*I'm surprised the tires didn't squeal or smoke. Oh well, I'm sure he'll be back later. Maybe I can convince him to take me bowling.*

# CHAPTER Five

Kama walked through the lobby after another fruitless day of shopping. It had been three days and counting and still no word from Jack; so she had tried to fill her days with shopping. Thrilled with the heady experience that came with dating Jack, she enjoyed their time together. Never once had she imagined that hanging out with someone could be so topsy-turvy on the emotional scale. She tried her best not to call his room repeatedly, but she found herself restless and searching for something she couldn't quite put her finger on. She stopped by the front desk on the way back to her room.

*I hope to hear from him before I go back to New York. I wonder what happened; it all seems so cloak and dagger. Maybe I ought to learn a little bit more about him and not just what he does.*

"Are there any messages for DeKosse?" she asked.

The clerk handed her a small pile of notes which were on top of a black envelope. Kama looked at it with curiosity. Certainly there had been a mistake; she was only in town for four more days. The soft suede envelope caressed her hand as she turned it over; her name was in a delicate silver-embossed script which contrasted with the deep black of the envelope.

*This has to be from Jack. I wonder what this is all about. This is so pretty.*

Kama pulled out a card done in the same rich black color, with the same delicate silver script. She held an invitation to a social gathering hosted by Garra Shipping at the Los Angeles Convention Center, the very next day. She smiled; it would be her first formal business party as Jack's date. She nodded her thanks to the hotel clerk, quickly rummaged through her purse for her phone, and called him on the number from the included business card. Kama was thrilled to have a legitimate excuse and even more excited to finally have his cell phone number.

"Twist here," he answered.

"Hi, Jack," she said. "I take it you are back and all is well?"

"Good morning, Kama," he said. "Yes, I got back late last night."

"Are you at work again? I thought you had it wrapped up."

"I did, but another merger took place and now there is a lot more paperwork to process," he said. "I take it you received the invitation?"

"Yes, I just got it, thanks. Though I have to admit I almost didn't notice. I mean, I have hoards of invitations from my fans. I almost tossed it aside with the others," she teased.

His beautiful, rich chuckle sent a shiver down her spine and filled her with a rush of warmth. She realized how much she had missed his company over the past few days. She got lost in her musings for a few more minutes before she realized he had asked her a question.

"I'm sorry, can you repeat that?" she asked.

"May I formally request your presence at this event with me?" he asked. "I realize it is short notice, but it should be a fun evening out."

"It sounds like a fabulous time. I am thrilled to accept," she said.

"I'll be round to get you at seven," he said.

Kama's mind began to whirl; she would have to get her hair and makeup done for the affair.

*I hope I can find an appointment this late. Oh crap, I don't have time to chat. I need to find out what I brought. I wonder if anything is gala worthy.*

"I'll see you tomorrow at seven then," she said.

"Thank you," he said.

There were so many implications in the tone of his voice that she blushed. His sensual timbre brought to her mind the remembrance of just how perfect his lips felt against hers.

"Good-bye," she said.

Kama hung up before hearing his response, because she was afraid she might fall into the insipid trap of saying "good-bye" over and over like a love sick idiot.

*Right. Kama, get your head in the game. He just gave us thirty-six hours to find a hair salon, pick an outfit, pray we already have shoes to match, and be ready to arrive on his arm.*

Abject panic set in and she rushed up to her room to scrutinize the dresses she had brought with her. Two hours later she stood in front of the hotel closet frowning.

*It's all outdated crap. I cannot possibly wear this with Jack.*

Kama blew out a stream of frustrated air and wanted to scream about the unfairness of it all.

"Great, I have to go shopping and find a new dress, pay for instant alterations."

For about a tenth of a nanosecond she considered calling Jack and telling him it wouldn't work.

*Stupid girl, DeKosse's don't give up so easily. You can beg forgiveness later for the blown budget. Get yourself together, wash your face, get back out there, and find the perfect dress. Now where to shop...*

Her day passed in a panicked flurry going from boutique to boutique. Nothing met with her approval; they were too black, too short, too ruffled or too little fabric. She managed to hunt through an unprecedented twenty of the twenty-two shops on the Drive. Close to weeping by the time she had finished her whirlwind attempt, Kama dejectedly decided to find some food. She had lost count of how many dresses she had tried on, though she did bear the war wounds of sequins scratches and bead imprints on her skin. She sat at the Café and tried to drown her sorrows with cappuccino and biscotti.

"I'll never find anything," she moaned. "Dammit. I have got to find a dress. I am not going to miss a chance to see him in his element because the selection sucks. Okay, we are going to go for 'looks sexy-as-hell' instead of perfect."

She stood up; her determination renewed, and knew that she would walk out with her outfit from one of the last two stores. Kama cringed as she realized that in her dress finding flurry that she had forgotten to make an appointment at a salon and time had simply ran out on her. Oblivious to her crisis, the stores had the nerve to close at their regular time.

*So, this means I get up with the sun tomorrow and find a dress, no matter who I have to kill to do it. Right, and of course I'll have to settle for any hair appointment I can get. Since it will no doubt be early in the morning, I hope I will not mess up my hair the rest of the day.*

Kama went back to her hotel, had a hot shower in a pitiful attempt to soothe her frazzled nerves, and then went to bed at eight o'clock. Despite her stress and disappointment, she fell asleep easily. She slept until the chipper ring of the alarm roused her at six the next morning, and set her back upon her path. Kama got up, showered, and dressed, in a mere thirty minutes. The walk from the elevators to the front door seemed impossibly long as her sleep-fogged brain tried to focus on the activity for the day.

"No one should ever have to get up this early when they are on vacation," she muttered. "Stupid three blocks worth of shopping and I can't even find anything."

She continued her verbal assault against Rodeo Drive as she walked through the lobby.

"Ms. DeKosse?"

Kama turned her head and looked at the concierge. From the look on his face, she guessed that he had called her name a few times before she recognized it. She gave him a bright smile and walked over to the desk.

"I have a message for you."

Kama took the proffered envelope and opened it.

*Dear Kama,*

*I realize I gave you extremely short notice to get ready for our date this evening, so let me rectify my oversight. You have an appointment at La Belle Age at eleven. Please feel free to pick any dress and accoutrements you find necessary. At three a car will be waiting for you at the hotel to take you to Lucky's for some pampering. At five you have an appointment at Raison D'être Salon; be sure to take your dress as they will assist in you getting ready. A car will pick you up promptly at seven and bring you to the gala. I look forward to seeing you tonight.*
*Sincerely,*
*Jack*

She reread the letter three times before everything had sunk in. With tears of joy in her eyes and a sense of awe, she turned back toward the restaurant for a leisurely breakfast before she started her day of luxury.

The day progressed easily and Kama found herself riding in a beautiful white and gold limousine at seven as promised. She had been disappointed to find it lacked Jack's presence, but she quickly made a plan. Kama decided making a grand entrance would leave a stronger impression on him. As she relaxed against the seat, she played with a small box encircled by a silver ribbon. She read the small card attached and shook her head.

*Dear Kama,*
*I noticed you forgot to get jewelry, and took great pleasure in picking out these pieces to accompany your outfit.*
*Jack*

Kama fingered the diamond choker at her neck.

"Damn," she muttered. "I really had envisioned my own jewelry to go with this dress, but I can't very well spit in his eye after he went through all this. Though I will have to ask him how he knew what I bought."

The necklace, nestled on a satin pillow, was also choker-style: three bands of diamonds with an oval cut cabochon of red jasper in the middle. Matching earrings were also included. Kama sighed and took off her own jewelry and put on what Jack had bought for her. She put hers into the small box and slipped it into her clutch. After a complete day of being pampered, Kama thought she was ready to take on the big night. The ride felt very short, and she felt her stomach knot as she got nervous. The car stopped, she took a moment to compose herself, put a smile on her face, and got ready to see Jack.

*Pull it together, Kama. We have been to black tie affairs before. Right, but not as Jack's date. What if I picked the wrong thing? Maybe I should have worn my hair down. Oh God, maybe I shouldn't even be here at all. Okay, breathe. We don't need to be sick. Okay, chin up, smile, and give eye contact. We can do this; it's no different than any other performance we have done.*

The valet at the convention center held the limo door for her, and a doorman opened the heavy glass door. She walked towards the exhibition room, slowing her pace by forcing herself to take tiny steps.

"Don't rush," she said to herself. "And stop talking to yourself, dammit."

She turned a corner and headed down a hallway richly decorated in rosewood and brass accents. Crystal lights twinkled from above, and in front of her stood large oak double doors with brass looping handles that looked like they were made of leaves. She walked through the small foyer and into an empty elevator. The ride was quiet but rapid, and she stepped out onto a small landing. Before her, a wide row of steps curved down and landed in the middle of the gala, which was already in full swing.

Kama wore a strapless, floor-length dress that had a fitted waist and ties that fell into gentle, scalloping waves down the back. The iridescent persimmon color fluxed from red to gold as she moved. It fit her well enough to show off her well-toned body, but it didn't constrict her. To keep her nerves in check, she thought about the jewelry he had bought and tried to piece together how he knew what she had.

*He certainly picked the perfect set. He must have asked the sales lady what I bought. Then again, why wouldn't he know? He has hosted me for the entire evening; I'm sure he knows exactly what I bought. Well, what he bought. I wonder if all men do this. I will have to ask Twin when I get home. Okay, mind the steps; it would suck to trip now.*

Platinum and diamond hairpins secured the loose knot at the top of her head, and cascading curls spilled down the back of her neck to her shoulders. As she walked in precise, graceful steps, she revealed gold shoes that gave her an extra two inches in height. She wore subtle makeup, excepting the faint shimmer on her lips. All in all, she thought she looked pretty good.

Kama walked down the stairs and into the main room, and promptly knew that she owned the attention of everyone there. However, her focus was solely on finding Jack. After spotting him, she carefully navigated her way to him, almost floating from giddiness.

*Wow, that's really all I can say. I thought he was good looking before, but damn.*

Jack wore a finely tailored, black Armani silk suit, with a gold watch and cufflinks accenting his outfit. Standing at six-foot-two, his beautiful olive eyes on her, he made an impressive figure before her. Kama knew he noticed her the moment she walked into the room and his gaze had not once faltered. The room dampened into a deafening quietness, as she stared only at Jack. He seemed a bit dazed and she smiled, knowing her outfit was perfect. She descended the stairs, noting that he watched her every step. He stood so still she couldn't be sure he even breathed. She finally landed in front of him and spoke in soft tones, giving her the true allure of a beautiful woman who is unaware of the sensuality she possessed.

"Good evening, Jack," she said.

"Good evening, Kama," he said. "You look exquisite. I hope I didn't cause too much panic with the last-minute invitation."

"Not at all. Going back to the spa was a lovely treat, thank you," she said.

Kama watched other people mill around, contented her outfit made the cut. Jack held out his arm and she gently placed her fingers in the cook of his elbow and walked gracefully by his side. He escorted her over to the highly polished marble floor; the entire left side of the room boasted a wall-to-wall window revealing the breathtaking view of LA at night from twenty stories up. As they made their way across the room, he introduced her to various important looking people; she smiled politely and greeted each person, but she stayed mostly quiet by Jack's side. A waitress approached holding a tray with several champagne glasses on it, and offered them to the group. Jack plucked two flutes and handed one to her. She tore her gaze away from the party and looked up at him.

"What do you think so far?" he asked.

"I think it's beautiful," she said. "So, who are all these people?"

"These are my new business associates," he said. "Since their last business call kept me here longer than anticipated, they figured I might clean up enough not to embarrass them at their annual gala."

"Like you could embarrass yourself," Kama scoffed.

She continued to look around the party, and was mystified that a lot of the men, and even some of the women, were more than casually perusing her.

*Why are they still looking at me? I already made my grand entrance and yes, I know that we are a gorgeous couple but the staring makes me feel like something is a bit off. I wonder if they expected him to be with someone else. No matter, I will suck it up and smile pretty.*

She had been to formal events and business meetings before, so she tried to project calm, but when Jack left her side for a moment, she found herself surrounded by a pack of young men, too eager and interested in her. She tried her best to dismiss them without causing a scene, but eagerly met Jack as he returned and nodded toward the dance floor. He held her close and his hand caressed hers. Kama tried not to melt against his chest even though she wanted to.

*I feel so comfortable with him holding me. Maybe I've never dated because I was looking for him. I can't imagine anyone else. Oh crap, he's chuckling about something. I can feel the vibrations, but I have no idea what he just said. Okay, ask something quick.*

"What do you do for fun?"

Kama watched as Jack seemed to think about her question. She wondered if part of his hesitation was because he didn't have much fun. She started making a list of things she could show him in New York.

"Well, I do enjoy a good run, a good dinner is always appreciated, and I like art. In fact, I am a good friend with the curator of the Metropolitan Museum of Art. Perhaps I could take you some time," he said. "Other than those activities, I work."

"Okay, and then I will take you to the theater. Some wonderful shows are playing this fall," she agreed.

The music switched to a lively tango and after dancing with much delighted laughter, she begged off the next set. The music's Hispanic flavor was bright and alluring, but she found all she wanted to do was talk to him.

"Okay, I need to sit this one out."

She held his hand as he escorted her off the dance floor and over to the dining area, which was a roped off section with a reserved sign on it. Their table sat towards the front and middle of the spacious room, in a small cluster of tables dressed for only two. Kama figured it had to be a show of status for the top business partners. He pulled out her chair for her and as soon as he sat, she resumed the conversation.

"Do you even enjoy the theater? I would hate to force you to endure something that might cause you pain."

"I have a box seat," he said.

"I bet you didn't use it even once last season," Kama said. "I think you do not know how to have fun. Well, other than being out a boat, but not many of those in New York."

"Other than the big port of call? Maybe you could buy me a book on the art of having fun or something," he said.

"Or perhaps I will just show you what you have forgotten," she said with a laugh. "I think you might actually enjoy it."

"Perhaps. Truth is, most of my time has been spent on business," he said, He shrugged. "I may be a hopeless cause."

"I think you just need someone to show you how to laugh again. Good thing for you, I found you in time," Kama said.

She laid her hand on his arm, and noticed he swallowed a few times. When he spoke, his voice had a tinge of tightness and Kama hoped she hadn't inadvertently stepped into a bad subject with him.

"Well, I look forward to my fun lessons," he said.

The music dimmed and a man stepped towards a podium to their left. Kama thought he looked familiar.

*Oh, he is the man Jack met in the bar the other day. I wonder if his friend is here, too. He didn't seem to like me so well. Not that it should matter, considering Jack is now their partner.*

She realized the man had been speaking all during her thought rambling and tried to pay attention. Her timing couldn't have been more perfect; as she tuned in, he thanked everyone for a job well done, thanked them for coming and with a flourish accented by the band, announced dinner would be served.

The lights dimmed even more and then popped back on, synchronized with loud salsa music playing. Servers stepped on the floor brandishing golden trays laden with food, and began to dance their ways to the tables. An expression passed over Jack's face that she didn't know how to interpret, so she smiled again and continued to look around.

"Well, they certainly know how to make an impression," she said.

"Much better than a long and boring speech, don't you think?" Jack asked.

Kama bowed her head and tried not to give in to laughter. Their conversation wound down as the waiters placed soup and salad before them. She noticed Jack looking at her with intensity and met his eyes.

"There is a bit more business I will have to attend to, since all the members have now arrived. We will go upstairs, but you can continue to enjoy the party."

"I can't come with you?" she asked. "I can sit quietly in the corner."

"Sorry, it really is a closed meeting," he said.

Kama made a moue, and then frowned at Jack. She looked around the room and noticed a group of younger adults who were clustered together; she wondered if they would be staying or going to the meeting. She tried not to be offended at being forced to stay alone, but understood as she sensed that the meeting might encompass things other than the shipping business. Kama's eye caught an interesting detail as she studied the others around the room. Curiously, she noticed quite a few of them had dark tattoos across the back of their necks. The designs were the same, but they varied in size and she wondered if they were in some sort of gang. Jack followed her look to the group, so Kama quit staring and focused her attention back on their meal.

*I can find out more when he goes up for his secret meeting. Interesting to think a street gang has big business ties. Or maybe not. If I nose around too much, they might kill me and hide the body. I'll just eat and then stay out of the way until he gets back.*

They had finally come to the end of their main course. It had been the most perfectly cooked steak she had eaten, which was saying a lot; her mother was a chef with a catering hall and a gourmet restaurant, so she knew perfect steak. Kama had been focused on the succulent food in front of her, but became aware that their conversation had dwindled, and made an effort to revive it with her next question.

"What do you figure is for dessert?"

"I think it's something chocolate," he said.

"Excellent, I love chocolate. As long as they don't do something stupid and make it insipid."

She watched him smother a laugh at her enthusiasm over chocolate. She hoped she hadn't insulted his new partners. She hated when he got silent; she always ended up saying something stupid.

"I'm sure the dessert will be lovely," she said, then paused. "Jack?"

"Yes?" he asked.

"Why did you pick the steel mills as a business?" she asked.

"I bought Cypress Steel Mills after I left the military and it grew from there," he said. "Working at the mills was my first job so I went back to what I knew."

Kama had been ready to respond with more questions, but then the server put her desert before her and she lost her train of thought. Hey eyes grew larger as she surveyed the gorgeous work of chocolate art before her. Her world narrowed in focus to the dish before her. A rich moist cake sat in a pool of deep dark sauce. A small taste brought a nod and smile to her lips.

*Oh, yes, it is a very mellow dark chocolate, how awesome. The tartness is just right and I bet this cake is going to make me shame myself. The filling looks interesting; I can't wait to try the whole thing.*

Kama lifted a forkful of the cake to her mouth and paused just a moment to inhale the scent. The cake melted on her tongue, covering it in a subtle mocha flavor, which the decadent sauce enhanced beautifully. The light pink mousse filling caused her to smile when she tasted the dessert as a whole.

"Wow, a chipotle raspberry mousse. I can't believe it; that took some daring, but wow, it is awesome. The pepper is just reaching the back of my tongue right now and the chocolate and raspberry are nicely intensified by the heat."

She noticed Jack's smile and took another bite. She savored each successive bite as if it were the first time she was tasting it; the cake deserved that much respect. She noticed his eyes watching her movements as she licked a bit of icing from the fork. "They were brilliant with the dessert," she said. "I don't care if they think I am greedy. I intend to enjoy every moment of this cake."

"I'm glad you are enjoying it," he said.

Jack took a back seat to the delectable dessert in front of her and she cherished each rich bite of the cake. She closed her eyes with the last forkful and let satisfaction flow through her. A low clearing of the throat brought her back to her surroundings, and she looked at Jack. He stood and held out his hand.

"Come on. Let's walk off some of this food," he said.

*Okay, did I just embarrass him or something? Crap, did we moan while eating? I know it's a bad habit, but we only do it for really good food. He's looking at me oddly. I bet I just embarrassed him in front of his new associates, damn.*

He led her out onto the balcony, which was decorated in soft white lights that twinkled in the night and no one else could be seen. Kama looked at the Los Angeles skyscape and enjoyed the buzz of traffic below them. She could still hear the strains of the music from the gala inside and looked up at Jack.

"Care to dance?"

"Out here?"

"I want some alone time with you."

She smiled as he pulled her close and danced with her on the balcony. Kama contented herself by placing her cheek against his chest and swaying to the steady thrum of his heart which was in time with the music. Jack said nothing, but she didn't mind. The whole night had been perfect: delicious food, a gorgeous setting, and the most wonderful date she could imagine. Then he lifted her chin and kissed her. Nothing else mattered except his touch and Kama gave in. After a blissful eternity, Jack broke the kiss and they resumed their private dance.

*Wow, this will definitely be one for the memory books. Can you imagine anything more romantic? This is so amazing, just absolutely perfect.*

Kama would have gone on with her musing, but a low tone sounded. The music dampened and with no words Jack led her back inside.

"Gotta go. Have fun," he said.

He escorted her back to their table, and then walked up the stairs and out the doors. No other announcement had been made, but at least forty people, she counted, made their way to the double doors and quietly left the party.

She watched Jack walk away, feeling a bit uneasy at being left in a room full of people she didn't know. She noticed the crowd left in the ballroom was primarily the younger adults and the DJ changed the music to encompass more of the latest popular music. Kama didn't know what to do; she studied classical music and found herself completely at a loss.

*Okay, so do I stay in my seat and look like I don't want to dance? Do I get up and dance with them uninvited? Hell, I'm not even sure that I could dance to this music. This sucks. I didn't know Jack would be leaving me.*

Kama sat in her seat and contemplated the situation until a duo of girls approached her and smiled invitingly. She smiled back tentatively. Other than Cynthia and Gianna, she didn't have female friends back home. Julliard prepared her to be great; however, it left very little time to build relationships other than rivalries.

"They will be up there for a least an hour, there is no reason to sit here by yourself and wait."

The speaker was a tall and curvy Latina woman who gestured to the dance floor, and waited for an answer. Kama looked around and noticed the only other people sitting were quite a bit older than herself and she didn't know if she wanted to be in their category. She must have paused a few seconds too long, because the Latina woman spoke to her again.

"I know it's hard to be the stranger in a group like this, so just come on and have a good time with us. If you stay here, you are fair game to the boys; at least with us you have safety in numbers."

Kama stood. To her knowledge, there were no rules saying she had to wait for Jack at the table. Being a prodigy from a young age, she had not grown up with a lot of acceptance from her peers. So Kama decided since she had been offered an invitation, she would revel in being accepted, dancing and having a grand time in general.

*It's nice to be out and have a good time without people looking at me like I'm some freak or stuck up bitch. I can see the appeal of moving away from what you know. Maybe I'll come out to L.A. for a while after I graduate from Julliard.*

With her new friends, Kama laughed and dared to try some dance moves that she had never seen. She didn't fall and counted it as a win. She did notice that neither of the women had the black tattoo on their neck, but couldn't think of any ways to bring up the topic.

*I still want to know what it means, but I am not going to wreck our fun by asking a stupid question. Maybe Jack will know.*

She felt eyes on her, and turned away from her group of dance buddies to see Jack watching her. Kama gave him a devilish smile and as he approached her, pulled him into a sensual and pulsing dance to some loud beat; to her surprise he stayed on the dance floor and impressed her with some moves of his own.

"So last we talked, you thought this music amounted to cat-gyrating-in-heat drivel?" he asked close to her ear.

"Yea, well, when abandoned in Rome…"

He laughed, but continued to dance with her. The evening was filled with dancing, food, and conversation. Despite the party going on around them, Kama monopolized as much of Jack's time as she could. A benefit of wall-to-wall windows included being able to watch the magnificent sunrise as it crept over the Los Angeles horizon. Things had begun to die down, and after making the social rounds with those who were left, Jack ushered her out of the party. She leaned into him, holding his arm. A giggle escaped; she figured dancing all night had made her a bit giddy. From her best guess it was around six in the morning.

"I had a nice evening, Jack. Thanks for taking me," she said.

"Very much my pleasure, Kamaria."

"We agreed on Kama," she insisted.

"Except for in formal situations, yes?"

"Okay, Mr. Twist."

"Touché," he said.

Despite the gala having broken up, there were still plenty of people waiting out front for their cars and Jack conversed politely with the others while they waited. Kama looked at him as she rubbed her hands up her arms to drive away the morning chill and smiled. Jack took off his jacket and placed it on her shoulders completing the image of the chivalrous hero for her. The valet brought his car, and after a short but silent ride, they were back at the Beverly Wiltshire. He escorted her from the car up to his room.

*This will be a beautiful ending to a great night. It will be nice to erase the embarrassment of coming here drunk and stupid last time. Okay, let's not go there because we don't need to be nervous. Sheesh, look at this place. My suite is nice, but this is incredible. There is a big difference between the seventh floor and the Penthouse. It had a full kitchen and dining room; it's more like my house than a place you rent for a week.*

The large and ornately decorated Penthouse seemed to fit him despite his earlier protest of being a simple man, and she smiled at its opulence. Jack held his hand out to her. The master bedroom had been designed with pure luxury in mind. While Kama gawked a bit more, Jack laid a box on the bed and then excused himself to the living area, which left her the entire bedroom and the master bath to freshen up. She waited until the door clicked shut, and then ripped open the box.

*Well, that was nice of him to give me a bit of privacy. The good news is there are three bathrooms, so I'm not depriving him of …oh my. This is exquisite.*

A silky, crimson negligee caressed her fingers as she picked it up. Kama had never owned anything like it and smiled.

*Although it is awfully presumptuous of him to think that just because I went to this gala with him, I would sleep with him tonight. Then again, here I am. Not to mention, it's early morning and not night at all.*

Her mind tumbled back and forth about what would be happening. Granted, she wasn't given to casual romance, and her relationship with Jack still had new status. She couldn't help but admit the attraction between them.

*Even still, I could have just gone back to my room. Yet I am here. Okay, so then how do I proceed without looking like I am throwing myself at him? Well, probably not throwing myself at him since he bought me lingerie. Should I let him just take the lead? He seems to be the type who would rather have a partner. Okay, let's do this one step at a time. Get comfortable, and maybe I can think straight.*

Kama took off the jewelry and placed it on a highboy, again admiring the beauty of the cut and quality of the stones. Jack certainly knew something about jewelry.

*One more thing we have in common. Maybe not so much in common, because my father is in the industry. I'll just keep that quiet so he doesn't think I am judging his choice of jewelry. I think we're nervous, but why? We really like him. Darn, I cannot get these hooks. So much for comfort before the hard decisions.*

Kama walked over and cracked the door open. She peeked through and saw Jack watching her with an amused smile.

"Help?" she asked "I can't get the hooks."

Jack nodded, walked to the door, and motioned for her to turn around. She turned her back to him and he began to work at the multitude of fasteners on the dress.

"I should have known better; the most stunning outfits are impossible to get into and out of by yourself," she said.

*But I looked damn hot in it and wanted to impress you. His fingers are warm, why am I getting goose bumps? He's pretty competent with these hooks. I wonder who else… Okay, bad train of thought, let's not go there.*

"There you go," Jack said.

He walked back to the couch, picked his drink up, and sat back down. Kama watched him for a second and then closed the door. She shrugged the dress off and tossed it over a chair. After a moment of hesitation, she put on the negligée and pulled on a thick plush robe. She went to the bathroom, brushed her teeth, washed the makeup off her face and took a deep cleansing breath. She had been wondering how long she could actually stall, when she felt him behind her. She looked at his reflection in the mirror and turned to face him with a smile.

"You're stealthy. I'm almost done, I promise. Although, you can most certainly go to bed if you are tired."

"I'm not really tired," he said. "Would you like some breakfast before we retire? It is seven in the morning."

She nodded as she walked over to the vanity, sat on the chaise, and began to work at getting the pins out of her hair. She heard Jack talking, but really didn't pay attention as she tried to find each one of the little devils poking into her scalp. Kama smiled as he came to stand behind her, but almost swallowed her tongue as he started to help her pull the pins from her elaborate updo.

His gentle touch took them out one by one, and peeking, she noticed he let the curls fall over his fingers as he helped. She swore she could hear the loud thumping of his heart, or maybe it was hers. Kama wondered for about a moment, until his fingers brushed the back of her neck as he took out the last few errant hairpins. She couldn't meet his eyes in the mirror; the intimate touching overwhelmed her.

"Thanks for the help; I never would have found them all."

"My pleasure," he said.

Kama knew he meant it as he brushed his fingers over her neck again. He pressed his lips to the back of her neck, kissing down to the collarbone before tilting her head up and giving her a kiss that made her stop thinking. She lost herself to his ministrations, feeling heat coil and tense in her stomach.

She turned on the chaise and stood so she could press closer to him. Kama had no idea what to do besides kiss him, so she moved in as close as she could, running her fingers over the soft material of his shirt. She grumped as Jack paused the kiss a moment, and then sighed as a knock at the door sounded. He went and retrieved the food, setting it aside. Kama had time to take a good breath, and smiled as he came back into the room.

Jack gave her a look and she felt a shiver to run down her spine.

*Damn, that was a possessive look. We want him.*

He moved in close, and Kama stared up at him. She placed her hand on his chest, and then began to unbutton the silk shirt, pausing to kiss the hollow of his throat. Despite being lost in the heady sensation of desire, Kama could have sworn he growled as he tugged her closer.

He caught her in a soul scorching kiss and all attempts at unbuttoning his shirt failed. She moved against him, in small impatient movements, not sure what she wanted; from either him or from herself. But the heat and tension spiraled out of control and Kama couldn't think. She made mewling sounds in her throat that seemed to drive him into a frenzy of touches. Nothing was off limits or untried as they sampled each other. They couldn't and didn't want to keep their hands off of each other. She gave in to the wild abandon and found movements that worked them both into a frenzy. The height of attained passion left them sated; wrapped in each other's arms, the fell in to an exhausted slumber.

# CHAPTER Six

Jack's mind began reaching towards consciousness. The extra warmth and shifting in the bed made him aware he shared it with someone who had just left.

*Kama...*

He lay there with his eyes closed, a smile on his lips, but barely moved other than the gentle rise and fall of his chest. He could hear Kama's movements; she stretched with an earthy moan that directed his interest towards touching her. The night had culminated much as he had anticipated, yet he had been surprised at what had happened: his unsure little vixen had turned full-blown temptress on him.

*I could get addicted to her. This is just weird; I am acting like a stupid teenager, and yet I am enjoying this. I would love to be in Kama's head for just a moment and figure out what makes her go. She put me through paces I didn't know I could endure. She...*

His rambling thoughts stopped quickly as Kama began to kiss his chest and moved upward. He gave in and opened his eyes to look at her.

"Good morning," she said.

Moments later, his brain still buzzed from the lengthy kiss. She snuggled in close and Jack encircled her with his arms.

"Good afternoon," he responded. "How did you sleep?"

"Well, despite the horrible snoring. How about you?"

"Pretty good, even though I only had the edge of the bed to sleep on."

"Jack," she protested vehemently.

"Yes, Kama?"

"I did not take up half the bed," she insisted.

He knew she tried to look irritated, but his eyes were drawn to soft curve of her shoulder, where a lazy curl rested and Jack resisted the urge to pounce on her.

"No, you did not," he said. "More like three-quarters of it."

Jack tried his best not to laugh and failed. Kama pinched his chest, and in retaliation he tickled her. He thought she might have been a bit tender from their love making, but only mere hours later she teased him. Her hands felt soft against his body; just the act of her brushing them through his chest hair made an army of goose bumps rise. He closed his eyes and concentrated on her touch; she alternated between kissing him and caressing him with her hands.

"I think a shower is in order," she said.

Before Jack opened his eyes, Kama slid off the bed and walked to the shower.

*Not that I mind such a gorgeous view, but she is not going to start a fire and leave me to put it out by myself.*

Kama sang a bawdy song. The sound carried through the spacious bathroom and when he joined her a few moments later; she raised an eyebrow at him. He grinned in response, and traced a finger through the bubbles on her stomach, coming to rest on her breast. She stroked his arm from wrist to shoulder, made her way down his chest, and then knelt before him showing him something so powerfully sensual he clamped his hands hard around the shower rail to stay on his feet. It took Jack more than a few moments to catch his breath. With a self-satisfied smile, Kama wound her arms around his neck and kissed him.

"My turn," he said.

Jack lifted her and guided her legs around his waist. He pushed closer, and growled in satisfaction as he felt her cover him. A rush of heat ran up his body as she pressed in to him. Jack looked in her eyes and kissed her. Kama looked every bit the siren. Water rained over their joined bodies and the sensual touch of her hands drove rational thought out of his mind. His focus became possessing her, all of her.

Jack led Kama out of the shower, and took pleasure in running the soft towel over her body. He almost shook his head at his thoughts.

*Here I was worried that she would be too tired. That woman just amazes me; I can't wait to see what surprises she has in store. I have no doubt Kama will keep me on my toes for a long time. Just when I think that I can anticipate the next move, she makes a sharp right turn.*

As Jack let Kama return the favor, he looked in the mirror and had to laugh at the smile on his face. Her amazing passion called to him and infused his soul with her effervescence for life. Her touch was gentle, but she didn't tease him deliberately.

"What are your plans for the rest of the day? Don't you leave tomorrow?"

Kama's voice interrupted his thoughts and he kissed her again.

"No plans, other than finding some food. I have worked up an appetite," he said.

He loved the way her whole body went into her laughter, and he shook his head as he pulled on clean clothes. He hoped that she would like the sun dress he bought for her. To his amazement, shopping for her had been fun. Jack had enjoyed imagining what she would look like in the dress.

*Maybe we can go shopping on 5th Avenue. Although, she is a pro and might wear me out.*

Jack stopped his thoughts short with a furrowed brow. While he wasn't scared his future plans already started to include her, he did have to think about the impact it might have on her life. His life wasn't easy; in fact, his life was complex on a level that most people could never understand. He wasn't so sure that he wanted drag Kama into the fray, but as that thought crossed his mind his wolf snorted.

*Okay, so I've known her a little more than a week and I can imagine dating her a bit longer. I have to consider her safety; that only makes sense. If she is going to be in my life, I need to make sure that she will be all right. Nothing wrong with those thoughts, she's the most amazing person I have met in a long time. I will make this work and screw the naysayers. Shoot, everyone will be surprised how I rushed into dating, anyhow.*

He dropped the towel on the nearest chair and headed to the closet. When he came back out, he noticed Kama staring fixedly at the bed, her face pale. A loud red mark on the sheets all but screamed for his attention. Jack stared at the damning stain, not sure what it meant and he had no idea what to do about it. There was only one reason that he could think that there was blood on the bed they shared, and it made him sick to his stomach.

"Gods, Kama please tell me I didn't hurt you."

Her silence made him nervous; she had been so vivacious that her shutting down made him all the more worried.

*Crap, did I get too rough with her? Well if so, I doubt what we just did in the shower would have happened. Not to mention I'm pretty sure I had no control over what we did last night; she seemed perfectly comfortable setting the pace. Why isn't she saying anything?*

He moved closer to her and put a hand on her arm. Her eyes snapped to his, blazing with worry but before he could say anything to soothe her, she smiled at him sweetly.

"Don't be silly Jack, I am fine," she said. "Can you please zip this up?"

He moved behind her and after finishing his task, kissed the side of her neck. He smiled and admired his choice of garment on her; the dress was white with a splash of scarlet on the petticoat and neckline. The color suited her, but it also made him think of the problem at hand. There was something wrong, he could sense it.

"Good, I would hate to think that I had caused you any harm."

"You didn't, but you are really embarrassing me just let it go."

Jack pulled her close against him and looked over her shoulder at the spot again, more carefully. He stood there trying to figure out what he saw, tried to make some logic of it and came an answer that didn't make any sense to him. He even tried to deny it, tried talk his way around the unlikely scenario, but no other alternatives made sense.

His inner wolf howled in triumph.

*Mine! She is all mine, no one else has touched her and no one ever will. I cannot wait to see her round with my child.*

However, the man side of him froze. Jack shoved his instinct to the back of his mind and tried to think logically.

"Damn, sweetheart, I wish you would have told me."

"It's not a big deal Jack, you were amazing."

*There is no way she could have been a virgin. Virgins do not react with such passion nor such adventure. She did things I didn't even ask for. This just isn't possible. Then again why am I acting like it is such a bad thing. There is nothing wrong with her not having slept with half of New York City. So why does this feel so wrong? I didn't coerce her she came to my bed willingly. There is something else about this, why is she acting like she did something wrong.*

Jack wanted the red damning mark that nagged at his conscious to disappear, yet the proof of her virginity displayed itself loud and proud on the sheets.

Jack sat down hard on the corner of the bed as she smiled sweetly at him and sat on the side of the bed next to him.

"Thank you so much for the dress, it's gorgeous. I'm starving; do you want to go to dinner?" Kama asked.

"That sounds nice, if you are feeling okay," he said.

He couldn't read the look she gave him, but from the look on her face it seemed she had carefully considered her answers before speaking. Almost as if she weren't sure what question he really asked of her. Jack went high alert; the woman could change topics in a microsecond, the long pause wasn't in her character. He waited to hear what she would say. She put on a too perfect smile and gave a light laugh.

"I had a wonderful time last night. That was one of the most exceptional business parties I have ever been to. I rather figured it would be filled with stodgy boring people," she said. "And then afterwards, we came here and spent a lovely evening together. Please don't ruin that by being all upset. You did not hurt me other than making me sit here instead of going for food."

Her performance was brilliant but not real to his nervous and sensitive ears. He knew she had deliberately misunderstood his question and stared at her for a good minute before she raised her head and finally met his eyes. She held his gaze for three seconds before she found something else to take her attention. He didn't like the tingle going up his spine; the type of tingle signifying the shit would hit the fan, soon and hard.

*Breathe Twist; this has to be some simple explanation. Damn it, you be quiet and let us figure this out. Stupid wolf, first blood does not mark a claim.*

Kama said nothing as she smoothed the front of her dress and tried her very best not to get trapped in his eyes again. He focused on her odd behavior and tried not to be thrown off track especially when she wrinkled her nose and winked at him.

"You are awfully tense; do you need some more distraction?"

"Kamaria, we need to talk," he said.

"Kamaria, huh? This sounds serious," she said.

"Your first time is a pretty serious deal. Don't you think we should at least say something? I don't want to embarrass you but seeing the bed was kind of shocking for me."

Jack watched Kama pale but he admired her ability to recover. She said nothing, but he looked at the stain again and back up to her. He watched her still uncomfortably and as he took her hand in reassurance, he felt her pulse racing. Jack made up his mind to get to the factual information, he didn't like her fear.

"Why didn't you tell me?" he asked.

"Seems to me, a long winded conversation might have broken the mood up just a bit," she said.

Kama stood in an abrupt motion, moving away from him. Jack stood as well, watching as she found things to do to take her out of his reach and away from his probing eyes. Her odd behavior damned her more than her silence, the whole time they had been together she had been nigh unflappable but he could almost see her flight instinct take over. Why would she be so afraid? Something just didn't add up, even his wolf's pride awaited the answer. She picked up the dress and jewels from the previous evening, as she held them in her hands a small smile played on her lips. But when she caught him watching her, he caught a look in her eyes and it gave him a cold feeling. A cold sinking feeling.

"Kama?"

"For Gods' sake Jack," she bit out tersely. "All I have are some lovely memories of last night, so you can stop worrying."

She stepped closer to him with a genuine smile, leaned up to kiss the hollow of his throat and wrapped her arms around his waist. He cupped a hand on the small of her back and looked down at her with clear affection in his eyes. Jack felt like he should shake the answers out of her but she fit against him like a warm sexy glove. Her body molded against his and despite their conversation he wanted her again.

"Memorable is good," he said. "I am more concerned you might have regrets."

"Jack, you act like we live in the dark ages. We had some beautiful love making. What could I possibly regret? It's not like we are bound for life because we slept together."

His wolf begged to differ with her.

*Of course we will be mated, it might take some time but I will not allow another to touch her, ever.*

Again Jack found himself having to hold the wolf at bay and focus on Kama. He didn't need to fight off his instinctual nature just then; he had enough to figure out right then. Despite her assurances, something still didn't add up. He watched her pack and noticed she went out of her way not to have to look at him. He stepped up behind her and circled his arms around her.

"I just needed to make sure I didn't hurt you."

Kama stepped away and sat at the vanity. She began to brush her hair but he caught her eyes in the mirror; the guilty look had returned but he couldn't figure out why. One moment she swore there were no regrets and everything was fine. But every time he even alluded to her being a virgin she acted like she had some huge secret attached with it.

*Okay usually women are more ashamed about not being a virgin, why is she acting like this? Hell I'm sure there are plenty of virginal professional women of her age.*

Then the question he had never asked hit him like a splash of ice cold water and he forgot to breathe. It finally occurred to him that he really didn't know her age, and with the way she acted... he stopped breathing for a moment as his brain tried to answer the question.

*I met her in the bar drinking wine. That's proof enough, excepting why wouldn't the hotel cater its wealthy clientele however they want to? She drank at dinner in the restaurant but I was there with her.*

Jack walked over and waited for her to put the brush down. She smiled at him with a sensual innocence, making it hard for him to think of anything besides touching and tasting her. He forced himself to remain focused and smiled at her and resist the urge to shake her.

"Kama?" he asked.

"Yes, Jack?"

"How old are you?"

She looked at him with fear and the ability to breathe went away again.

*Okay let's get an answer before we panic. She might just think she is too young for me; women get funny about age differences. Hell if we mated, does it matter what her age is? Of course it does, in her world this is rape and so very illegal. So how do I get an answer from her?*

"Old enough to drink?"

She pressed her lips together in a thin line and looked out the window. He tried to be calm but he wanted to shake her.

*Ok Jack stay calm there might still be a chance; she doesn't have to be old enough to drink to be legal. Hell, she's not answering and she still looks like she wants to bolt.*

"Old enough to vote?"

Jack felt his world spin, this couldn't be happening.

*Come on, this is not possible. She is not a little girl, she had grace and poise and class. We had drinks in the hotel and at the spa; surely they would have said something. Right because they would ever question her drinking with an older host at her side.*

"Old enough to drive?" he whispered.

"Do I really look like I am too young to drive?" she said. "Of course I am old enough to drive, Jack."

Her voice snapped the words out defensively, and he closed his eyes against sudden dizziness. In one quick response she had answered all of them. He felt bile rise in his throat.

*Holy hell, she's a baby.*

Thoughts raced through his mind top speed, but made absolutely no sense to him as he tried to figure out what to do. Jack paced back and forth; the wolf rose to the surface, but was pushed back down. As he finished getting himself under control, he stood across the room watching her like she were a live bomb were about to go off. Jack felt terrible as a mix of fear and hurt played across her face and he felt the need to protect her.

"Oh shit," he said.

"Jack?" she whispered.

*I can't have her.*

For the first time in years, Jack had to contend with emotions and their paralyzing effects. He felt helpless, confused, and angry, and for the life of him couldn't figure out why he wanted so much to protect her. He should be furious with her for all of the problems she represented, but instead he wanted to feel her curled up against his chest. The wolf howled in rage at him and Jack fought back the urge to toss the couch at the wall.

A shock coursed through him when he realized her age didn't scare him as much as the thought of not being with her. He remembered the way they connected, the way his wolf wanted to claim her, and became heartsick. As he berated himself, he jumped when she touched his arm because he had not heard her call for him.

"Jack please," she pleaded. "Talk to me."

"What can I say? Do you even understand what this means? Kamaria, you are a child; you are a minor. Despite what you may think, I could go to jail for this and if I had known, I would not have let it get this far," he said. "Why didn't you tell me?"

Jack had tried to keep his voice calm and low, despite warring between rage and fear in his own mind. He lost the battle to shout at her and yanked his arm away from her touch, as if it were tainted. Fury covered her face, erasing the fear, and she shouted right back at him. His wolf rumbled in contentment at her strength.

"Why didn't I tell you? I wish you could see yourself: the pacing, the anger, and the fear. I didn't really think it was a big deal; we connected and had a good time. Do you ask every woman you pick up her age?"

He opened his mouth to retort, but closed it again, rendered speechless, not only by her reaction but also her logic. He tried hard to picture her as a child and failed. Every memory he had showed her to be a competent young woman, not some giggly teenager. True, had he known she were seventeen, he would have patted her on the head, sent her on her way, and gone on with his life. It didn't change the fact he had twenty-five years of age and experience on her, nor the reality of this sordid adventure costing him everything he had worked so hard to earn.

"You can think what you want, but I am not some stupid little kid and I never lied to you," she said.

Her indignant stare met his furious one, but neither looked away. Jack just wanted her to acknowledge that the situation was serious. If exposed, things could get nasty, maybe even blow up and hurt both of them. From where he stood, he knew she couldn't fathom what kind of chaos and hell this mess could put them in.

"You let me think you were a college student," he said. "You said you study at Julliard. So, what you started when you were twelve?"

"I have gone to Julliard since I was seven," her tone frosty.

"A youth program no doubt, he snapped back. "Great that makes it all better,"

"It's not like you don't have secrets. I didn't pry into your secret society stuff," she said. "I am seventeen and half; six months is not that big of a deal."

His fury rose at her rebuttal and refusal to accept any blame in the matter. She was the one who conned him; she allowed him to think her older.

*Hell, the only time her acting weird was when she got so distracted in the restaurant...*

His synapses started firing and filling in the pieces that hadn't had context before.

"You're here with your parents, aren't you?"

She blanched and he knew he had guessed correctly.

"It's why you got so jumpy every time we were downstairs. You were afraid they were going to see us and upset your little ruse. Kama, it is illegal for me to even think of you," he said. "Was this some big game to you?"

He felt immediately like an asshole at the look of panic on her face, and he doubted he could have done more damage if he had struck her. For the first time, she actually almost looked young; her eyes welled up with tears and she looked so stricken he wanted to make it all better.

"No, Jack, no games. This is my life. It's who I am. I felt like you were the one person who might actually understand me and like me for me," she shouted.

A stifling silence descended and Jack began to pace again. He knew more needed to be said but he couldn't adequately put his feelings into words. His wolf snarled at him for pushing her away.

*Why are we even having feelings? We've known her for a second and look at the disaster already brought down on us. I don't care what the wolf thinks; this is wrong and will only end badly.*

He found Kama staring at him. He couldn't read the look on her face, her emotions seemed to flux and change as rapidly as his. The wolf kept reminding him just how her flexing fingers felt against his skin. As he stared at her, Kama seemed to gather her composure and calm herself. Again her maturity rang out, and she became the poised young woman he had fallen for, her age non apparent. He cut her off before she could speak.

"We still have a lot to talk about."

"Were you okay with me before you knew my age? We conversed, went out, danced, and enjoyed each other's company, and never once did you complain I acted like a teenager."

"Yes, I enjoyed my time with you," he said. "But…"

"Apparently then, age is not everything," she cut in. "We had a great time, and I was seventeen and a half all the while. Remember that while you are condemning me. You either want to continue to talk to me or not. Not a lot else, is there?"

"I guess not," he said. "Don't you understand that I will not risk going to jail just to date you."

"Well then, let me give you the out," she said. "If you want nothing more to do with me, that is your prerogative. You act like I am about to turn into this clinging and stupid chit who has no life of her own. Quite frankly, Jack, my life is complicated enough without having to worry about your bruised ego and drama."

Jack looked at her, speechless and confused. He had not expected to hear a telling off coming from her. Fury sparked up again at her self-righteous attitude; the deception came from her. He couldn't comprehend why she wouldn't even give him a second to breathe and figure things out. The wolf paced restlessly in his mind, begging for control.

*You think too much. Just feel it for once and act on it. You know what she is, you know who she is, and you are standing on rules and conventions which don't apply.*

He just wanted her to look at the whole thing from his point of view. She would be seen as the victim. The innocent seduced by an older, lascivious man, who had no morals. Her life would be redeemable; his would be examined, and some things just couldn't come to light. Kama stalked up to him and stood so close he could hear the thunderous beat of her heart. Jack found his words again.

"Right, so the next move is to bring me home for dinner with your parents? I see that going over well," he snapped. "Tell me, Kama, do you think your dad will call the cops before or after he punches me in the face for sleeping with his child?"

"So all this is because you are worried about going to jail? You selfish asshole," she said through clenched teeth. "Don't worry, Jack, I don't plan on telling anyone about this whole debacle. You are so certain I will run screaming about how you took advantage of me and you will be locked away. You forget it would mean admitting to ever having slept with you."

He stood in shock as her threat of denial hit him like a ton of bricks.

*You know she would never place you in harm's way. Idiot, go to her, don't stand and watch her watch out of our lives. She will admit to being mine. And again I am more worried about what will happen to her. Dammit this is crazy. Yes I know she is our mate, you stupid wolf. Shut up and let the logical part of us figure out how to make this work. Can it even work? It has to, she can't just walk out.*

While Jack tried to calm back down and figure out just what made him try to keep her around, Kama did the unthinkable. She walked out and closed the door behind with finality. Immobilized and not believing what had just happened, Jack took a breath and tried to calm his erratic thoughts before he lost control to the wolf.

*I could go after her and force her to talk about this. Because a screaming match in the hall is what we need, and right, take the chance to also run into her father who no doubt will want to know why some crazy man is chasing after his daughter? What just happened here? I cannot believe she just walked out.*

Jack needed a moment to catch his breath and not be absolutely furious with her so he might be able to make sense of things. He turned and began to pack his own belongings and caught sight of the dress she had left behind. He couldn't get home soon enough called to have his pilot file a flight plan.

*Perhaps the distractions of work will allow you to get over this moping little boy act. I should call Carla and find out a bit more. Although, Kama seemed pretty offended I would even suggest she would turn me in or try to extort me. Her pride is pretty powerful, not to mention her temper.*

A smile tugged at his lips remembering her threat of denying she had ever been with him.

*What the hell is wrong with me? My life has just been turned upside down, potentially destroyed, and yet I am still enamored and want her. What is it about Ms. Kamaria DeKosse that had me acting like I am a teenager too? This woman… girl…child cannot be in my life. Obviously not only is she a distraction, but makes me question my own good judgment.*

The wolf snorted at his self-assessment and with a sigh, Jack picked the phone back up.

"Carla, can you get me a dossier on the DeKosse family in New York City please? Yea, business is finished and I'll be home in six hours."

Jack moved to finish packing and get ready to meet his jet. At first, the immediate return home seemed a great idea. However, he started to have doubts about such a hasty exit.

*But how can we contact her once we leave here? Yea right, we're going to stay here and hope for a glimpse of her? Get it together, Twist; there are things to be done and deals to finish. Are you really thinking about waiting around "just in case" she decides to come back and let her temper fly at us once more? And the outcome? We would end up back in bed and still be in the same situation. New York and its millions of bodies to press us into anonymity is probably the safest place for us to be. Not to mention our Pack is waiting to hear about this new merger and what is means for future relations.*

Even still, Jack had a hard time leaving his room and putting an end to the fairy tale they had lived. But he did, with his wolf cursing him the entire time.

# CHAPTER Seven

*Sixteen days and counting. Damn Kama, stop counting. It's not making him call us; it's just giving us a headache. Really? Is this the way we are going to start our senior year? What happened to it being the best year of school and? Oh right, we just lost the best thing we have ever found. Of course, now we have the nerve the whine about it.*

Kama walked through the halls of Pembleton Business Preparatory School with dread weighing down on her shoulders and loud sighs that drew stares from those she passed. She didn't care about the prestigious title it carried. She couldn't even muster any enthusiasm that it had held the number one spot of all the private schools in Manhattan for ten years running.

*It is a hellish jail with hordes of people streaming by me, suffocating me with their eager-to-be-back attitudes. What a load of crap! Why do we have to go school to learn about stupid stuff, instead of being able to live our lives? Oh right, we're not adults yet. And that's why Jack doesn't want me. I hate everything.*

Even though she had not really expected that she would ever hear from Jack again, a small part of her had hoped that he would at least reach out to her. In a brave moment eight days prior, she had called and left a voice message apologizing about the whole mess. Then mortified, she turned her phone off for two days. She had called him twice since but hung up as the phone rang. She then spent hours worrying he would see her number and charge her with stalking. The lack of communication allowed her thoughts to spiral into a dark place where he wanted nothing more than to torment her. It all seemed unfair, since she still burned for him and she would swear he still cared for her.

*Of course he should be mad, you did lie to him. Yes, I know it was just not telling him what he didn't bother to ask, but still a lie. Maybe next time you will act like an adult instead of trying to play one. Although I guess I did prove my point, he freaked out about my age. Six months isn't such a big deal.*

She knew only time would help him to get over the bombshell of her age. Time after time, she replayed the whole fight in her head. It kept her up at night; she warred with being mad at him for being upset with her and being madder at herself for letting her temper push them both into a place where things just might not recover. If only she had never walked out of the room.

*But you did, didn't you? You never gave him a chance to think; threw stuff at him and expected him to fall at your feet like a lovesick idiot? Not the way to treat someone you love, DeKosse. How do I fix this mess? Can I even fix it? What if he refuses to talk to me again ever? Do I go throw myself at him in February?*

This new world of emotional distress tore her to pieces; as she started her senior year, she found the expectations crushing her in ways they never had before. Pembleton had a reputation for being academically strict, and they wouldn't cut her slack in her last year just because her heart had been broken.

Julliard didn't play to sympathy either, as she had been told time and time again; the strong survive and the weak wither up and go away. She had never once faltered with her determination and drive since her admittance at the age of seven. She had worked hard, practiced long hours, and sacrificed her childhood in pursuit of her dream. One relationship gone wrong would not be enough to snatch her life's goals away from her. No matter what, she would survive because she didn't know how to do anything but succeed.

*He's acting like I lied to him every time I opened my mouth. I wasn't the only one keeping secrets. Jerk. I'll tell Gianna about him this weekend. If I am going to have to suffer for my mistakes, at least I can have a friendly shoulder to cry on.*

Her best friend had returned from her study abroad in Europe only two days before and, since then, the Fates conspired against them meeting up at every opportunity. Their class schedules had no common classes, and even worse, Kama had to eat lunch alone because Gianna left early each day for an internship. Kama walked through the lunchroom with her thoughts drowning out the cacophony of student voices.

*This schedule sucks. We are going to have to have a skip day or something. Explaining this whole mess with Jack just can't be done over the phone. I mean, how do I tell her I had this great relationship and never even called her once? She's going to be mad.*

With a look of disdain, she ignored the five-star cuisine being served. No matter the quality of the food, it certainly had the atmosphere of any other high school cafeteria: loud, rowdy, and hot. It suffocated her with the childish attitude of it all, and she headed for the door leading out to the terrace. The weather conspired to keep the terrace vacant, despite the allure of privacy and peace. The tiled area came under the continual assault of bright sun, rain, or snow dependent upon the season. And if the weather didn't deter the students, the occasional bird droppings certainly did. She walked over the threshold, ignoring the not-quite-whispers about her as she went outside. The door shut, and the sudden quiet brought relief. Despite a muggy day, Kama felt like she could finally breathe as she made her way to a bench across the yard. She dug through her backpack to find her lunch, and pulled out a container of her favorite soup.

*Of course, it's cold. Now I have to walk back in there and heat it up. I am so not in the mood to deal with all of those stupid children. Dammit, I just want to eat. What else could go wrong with my stupid day?*

She stood up and all but stomped her way toward the door, taking the short route. She tripped over something and was relieved that she managed to not drop her thermos. Then she noticed feet. She sighed heavily and turned to apologize. To her dismay, the motion caused the contents of her thermos to spill into on him.

"I am so sorry," she said.

A young man sat half obscured by the bushes and raised a cocky eyebrow at her. Kama flushed in embarrassment and as she stepped closer to do "something", she fought not to fall on him. She looked down at her lunch splayed across his uniform and couldn't help but be upset.

*I guess I'm not going to be eating the soup. Great, so I get to go through the day starving on top of everything else. This blows. Why is he staring at me like that?*

She scowled at the situation as he looked up at her again with a rakish grin, more intrigued than upset, and she found an answering grin forming on her lips.

"No worries, I haven't eaten yet today anyhow," he said.

"Let me get you a napkin or something. I don't want you to get a demerit for going to class in a dirty uniform," she said.

She dug through her bag and pulled out a crumpled wad of clean tissue.

"No big deal, I didn't plan to go to afternoon classes anyhow."

She offered him the tissue, and grimaced at the thick chunks of vegetables from her soup laying there wasted. Kama noticed how he watched her. She tried to help clean his shirt, but he waved her attempts away.

"Well, can I at least get you a cold drink?" she asked.

"No thanks, I prefer to feed my uniform one dish at a time," he said with a warm laugh. "I'm Cade."

She couldn't fault his logic and laughed with him at his lame joke. He stood and motioned her over to a bench in the corner. It looked clean to her so she nodded. She tried not to appear to be staring at him, but as she met his eyes for the third time, she just looked.

She noted how much taller he appeared as he stood, and smiled with appreciation as he escorted her. His lean physique clearly showed his taut muscles, not the kind of body Kama saw a lot from the boys at Pembleton. He had a grace to him which made her feel clumsy and she noticed his long and agile fingers. While she laughed at herself for noticing odd attributes, well at least odd in her estimation. She couldn't help but to really look him over.

*Sheesh, it's like some hormonal switch has been thrown. If I even come close to thinking a guy is cute, I look him over like a side of beef. Crap, I am beginning to act those silly twits in there. Maybe this is how Jack saw me.*

Cade seemed oblivious to her internal speculation, but met her appraising gaze with a grin. His dark hair had a few errant waves, but the rich coca color reminded Kama of smooth chocolate. He had little facial hair; she found herself wondering what he would look like with a goatee, and then firmly yanked her mind back onto safer paths. Overall, Kama found him attractive and the spark of mischievousness in his eyes made her smile wider.

"Done looking?" he asked.

"If you are," she said.

"I am. So your name is?"

"Kama," she said. "I am not usually this klutzy, but I guess I wasn't expecting anyone to be out here. Sorry, I just didn't pay attention."

"So, what are you doing out here?" he asked "You look like you belong in there with them."

"So, I look like a snobbish, rich bitch?" she asked.

She put her hands on her hips in mock annoyance which he answered with a rich laugh, not at all looking contrite or ashamed. Kama relaxed more; he seemed a decent person and better yet, he had her sense of humor.

"Yea, pretty much. Why are you out in the Loser Zone instead of inside?"

Kama looked towards the cafeteria, where one of the more popular head cheerleader-type junior girls waved around a set of key, shrieking in delight about her new Ferrari and gushing on and on about her fabulous daddy. She invited everyone to a huge birthday party, excepting the freshmen girls because they were too "dramatic". She looked back to Cade with a "Does this explain it?" look on her face and then sighed as squealing and more shrieking sounded from the cafeteria.

"I'm here for the peace and quiet," she said.

"Don't let me disturb you then," he said.

"You aren't. In fact, you're the only person who hasn't bothered me in weeks. You actually made me laugh."

"You did throw killer carrots at me," he said. "Should I go get you some lunch? I don't want to tempt fate by denying you sustenance and having you desperate enough to suck your soup from my shirt."

"No, I couldn't forgive myself for sending you into the den of iniquity for some food. I'll just grab a snack later. And I don't know you well enough to suck anything."

She smiled at him as he cocked his head at her. They finished their lunch period in casual conversation about the locals at Pembleton. Kama found Cade's dry wit and sarcastic sense of humor a balm to her wounds and she enjoyed his company. The bell rang and interrupted her out—of-breath gasping at one of his over the top and deliberately terrible jokes. As Kama picked up her books, he gave her a slow and very indecent wink and she grinned.

*Odd, I always thought high school boys so far beneath me. He's not bad at all.*

She shook her head and turned to walk to class. Kama made a point to slowly look over her shoulder at him and gave him a slow wink back and knowing smile. She wasn't certain if she heard his sharp intake of breath or just imagined it, but his reaction felt good to her.

The next day she looked for Cade on the terrace, and began a new friendship which seemed to ease the ache of loss. With Cade as a distraction and snarky comrade, school pressure and all the craziness seemed to fade. He proved to be great company, even amusing, despite the nickname of "Babe" he insisted on calling her. But he kept her happy and regaled her with outrageous stories of his wild rides in his car through the city.

"Like I don't live in Manhattan and know you cannot possibly drive fifty miles an hour through the streets," she scoffed.

"Babe, someday I will take you for a ride. I think you have sorely neglected the thrill section of life," he said.

Though she smiled at his lofty tone, a tinge of sadness covered her; she had had plenty of thrills while dating Jack. Kama sucked it up and focused on what she had, not what she had lost. Her lunches with Cade were an amusing time of stories, one-upmanship, and bashing on their classmates. Kama felt comfortable with him, bordering on "liking" him, but after the fiasco with Jack she shied away from entertaining the thought of dating anyone again. She stayed content with their friendship; there weren't any assumptions or undertones to her interactions with Cade.

*Not as if I even know if he likes me for anything more than just a pal. I've only known him a few days, so who knows what he thinks. He flirts, but I don't know if it's that kind of flirting because – hey, I still suck at it. Well, I think I do; sometimes it's Someday, I will tell him Mom's catering company is contracted to provide the food here. It's not like he would get anything different just because I bring it from home.*

*Hard to tell if he's serious or not about those looks and winks. He's very different. Anyhow, I'm not trying to date him; I should recover from Jack first. I wonder why he hasn't called.*

In her endeavor to work through her heartache, she kept to herself more than ever; she used any spare time to get her homework done and for once, found her time demands seemed manageable. Kama also found having a relaxing lunch period, in which she laughed and enjoyed herself, made a difference in her outlook.

As she spent more time with him, she found out something astonishing: aside for a penchant for puns, Cade happened to be one of the rare anomalies at their school – he attended Pembleton on scholarship. Pembleton had the "grace" to give ten unfortunate, but super smart children a scholarship to their prestigious school, as long as they weren't troublemakers. Usually, the scholarship-receiving students kept very quiet about their status, as they would be ostracized if the shame of needing scholarship ever became known. Kama gave him all the theatrics she could muster- indignant sneers, shock, anger and disapproval- before she dissolved into a pool of giggles. To which he sighed and tried to look long-suffering before winking at her. Cade didn't seem to care one way or another, much to Kama's shock.

"I'm here because my mom always dreamed about me having a fancy, private school education. I applied and got in. She has never been more proud or joyful about my accomplishments."

"So you're not just a smart ass after all," she said.

"Oh definitely, it's just that I am off-the-charts smart too."

"True enough, however do you manage to suffer through us snobby brats?"

"With much pain, although you are easier to handle than most," he said. "I might be able to handle it better if you would bring me lunch now and again instead of leaving me to suffer with cafeteria fare."

Kama laughed and tossed him a chocolate and peanut butter cookie from her bag.

She enjoyed Cade's company in relative peace and quiet for about another week, until the day his cover got blown wide open in the cruelest way possible. They walked through the cafeteria to get to the terrace, per usual, when a shrill and more than annoying voice rang out.

"You will never guess what I found out. You guys will absolutely die."

Kama turned her head toward the voice; she felt the hairs on the back of her neck stand to attention. The voice belonged to the same Ferrari-owning-junior who had made it point to sneer each time Kama and Cade walked by "her" table. The girls at the table all looked alike, pale skin surrounded by perfectly styled hair with fitted uniforms and were made up like models. The ring leader's voice continued to screech out, and the snickering of her friends reminded Kama of hissing snakes.

"The boy there, you know the one who looks poor? He is one of those charity cases we let in here so the school gets a tax break. Not to mention, he works at some car shop in Long Island. I had to visit my Aunt Suze; you know the poor one who married that guy with no money? So, I was being all charitable and stuff and allowed her to drive me to the store in her junker, piece of crap, car. The stupid thing decided to blow up and we coasted into some garage. And guess what? He was working there. Hey freak, change my oil and wash the windows before you leave today. There's a shiny nickel in it for you."

Kama clenched her fists, straightened her spine, and got ready to have a confrontation as her temper rolled. The petty idiots were attacking her friend and she wouldn't stomach it. Cade put a restraining hand on her arm and gave it a gentle caress as she bristled and led her out to the terrace.

"You're better than them. Don't worry about it; I got this, Babe," he said.

He said the words in a quiet pitch only she could hear as he led her out. Kama watched him, acting as calm as every other day, sit on the bench. She vented and paced to relieve her frustration, even though he tried to lead their conversation into more neutral territory.

"She is such a bitch," Kama snarled.

"Yep, so let's not waste time talking about her," Cade said.

Kama calmed because she wanted to enjoy her lunch with Cade, but didn't forget about the incident. Her day dragged by; not only did she want to snatch the girl bald each time she passed her in the hall, but Kama also had to stay after to meet with her academic counselor.

*Like this woman couldn't possibly be on time, ever? What is she going to ask? I am still on track with my musical career, my grades are still in the top ten and I do volunteer work instead of sleep. Sheesh, what a waste of time. Apparently I will be here until my music lessons.*

The meeting went much as Kama had expected and by the time she left for the day, she had worked herself into a righteous fury about her boring meeting and the raw treatment of the one friend she did see in school. Despite having a driver, she periodically walked from Pembleton to Julliard and after the days' frustration, Kama decided it was needed. She walked through the student parking lot, contemplating keying the Ferrari the "oh so fabulous daddy" had bought. Kama knew the twit would be in a cheer club meeting or some supposed "feed the homeless cats brigade", so she had little worry of being caught. She walked by the car, eyeing it, when she saw a pair of feet that stuck out mere inches from under the car. Kama looked around and then crouched down. She frowned as she saw Cade, on his back looking up at the undercarriage, but noted with some amazement his uniform remained spotless. Disbelief kept her quiet only for a few moments, and then she seethed.

"Don't tell me they actually made you change her oil," she demanded.

"Naw, just making an adjustment," he said.

"You're adjusting her car?" Kama said confused.

"Nope, her attitude," he said. "This car will never leave this parking lot again."

"So you really work at a garage in Long Island?"

"Babe, you shouldn't believe everything you hear," he admonished. "I own the garage, and it's in Queens."

He slid from underneath the car, stood before her, and smiled smugly.

Kama looked at him, ready to launch a million questions, but he stood there with unrepentant arrogance. Cade dropped a small pouch into the backpack he retrieved from the ground, looked around, and then pressed her gently against the hood of the car.

"Don't be mad," he said.

Kama had no other warning before he leaned in and kissed her. She stood in shock for a heartbeat, but didn't resist when Cade moved the kiss from chaste to enveloping. He leaned in closer to her and Kama found she missed the intimate connection.

*But he's not Jack.*

Heavy footsteps passed them, deliberate enough to announce their presence. Their kiss had only lasted a few seconds; even still, a tingle and pulse were on her lips when the kiss stopped. A few moments passed before he moved away and helped her off the hood of the car. Kama looked at him, bemused, waiting for the explanation.

"Security guard. I had the timing down until you came along," he said. "Although this makes a much better excuse; the higher-ups will just think we snuck out to kiss and not to mess up her highness's car."

Kama burst into unrestrained laughter.

"Great, so my parents will get a report their daughter ditched lessons to make out with a boy. What exactly did you do?"

"Heavens forbid they ever think you skipped lessons. I did some car tinkering, nothing to worry your pretty little head about. Aren't you going to be late to your lessons?"

"Not if you start walking with me now," she said.

They walked in silence while Kama tried to figure out what had happened. Street lights blinked on above them in the dusk. She enjoyed walking at night, but didn't do it often; it wasn't safe to walk through the city alone. Cade made for good company, but after a few blocks she noticed him staring at her oddly.

"I have never kissed a girl into being quiet before."

"I'm still waiting for you to offer me a hotdog; we've walked by at least three vendors," she said.

He bought her three with a smirk, but Kama got the last laugh; he looked stunned as she easily ate them all and asked in a very sweet voice for another. They arrived in front of Julliard with ten minutes to spare.

"This is my stop," she said.

Cade began to act funny and for a moment, Kama wondered if he had eaten a spoiled hotdog. He rocked from foot to foot and stuffed his hands in his pockets. She wondered for a moment if he had seizures. She stared at him as his face flushed, but then he made eye contact with her.

"So want to go out?" Cade asked.

"On a date?" Kama asked.

Surprise colored her voice and he smiled at her.

"Well, I had intended to rob a bank, but a date sounds okay too," Cade said.

"Ummm, well, I... I need to think; this is a surprise," she said.

"Surprises are good," Cade said.

"I guess so. Although, the last time you surprised me I ended up making out in front of the school security guard."

"On the hood of a Ferrari," he said with a wink.

"A car is a car," Kama shrugged.

She laughed at his aghast expression and silently congratulated herself for moving him off the topic of dating. She enjoyed spending time with him, but she didn't know if she was ready to take that step.

"I don't know what I am going to do with you," Cade said.

"I imagine blather on and on about cars," Kama said drily.

"We can talk about this tomorrow at lunch. Your treat by the way,

Babe."

He walked down the steps and back towards their school, leaving her confused just a bit.

"You're going to be late."

He called the words over his shoulder and jolted her back to her senses. Kama sighed and walked into her lessons.

*So wow, he really just asked me out on a date. Should I date him? I mean, really, what just happened here?*

"Miss DeKosse, I expected you fifteen minutes ago."

Her vocal coach- tall thin and reedy as ever- towered over her as she walked in the door. Professor Ralston, at the age of fifty-three, looked to be years older and had the disposition to go with the curmudgeonly look. His hair had more salt than pepper, and the comb-over started somewhere around chin level on the left side and swept over to the right. His blue eyes always seemed to water, and his pasty skin probably hadn't seen the sun in at least a decade. Still, his voice kept Kama awestruck and his instruction challenged and progressed her forward in her field. So, she treated him with the utmost respect even though his attitude rankled her.

"Lessons are at 5:30 P.M., Professor."

"Unless you have an audition with Professor Ristori today at 5:45 P.M.," he snapped. "Now you barely have time to warm up."

The Italian curses burned her ears and not for the first time, Kama was sorry that she was fluent. She ignored the tirade from her professor, put on her most serious face, and began to warm up.

*Of all the times to forget! This is the most important audition you have this year. Dammit Kama, is a kiss really worth tanking your career? Get it together, you twit.*

Her many years of practice and performance allowed Kama to pull herself into her professional mode and get down to business in seconds. Irritated with herself for shorting her practice by fifteen minutes to hang out with a boy, she redoubled her efforts and by the time her ten minutes had passed, Kama was ready.

She walked down the cool halls and tried to compose herself after the sudden onslaught of nervousness, which caused her stomach to knot. Professor Ristori held auditions once every three years and this year he had three open spots. Kama had worked hard the entire previous year to even get invited to audition; she had been one of thirteen people, and the youngest.

*I need to pass this first round; if not I can't even try again until I'm a junior in the college program, and that would be waste of time. I feel like I might faint. Well, I would have if I were prone to silly drama. Who faints for attention anyhow? Okay show time.*

She arrived at his office door at exactly 5:30 p.m. and knocked with purpose.

"Come in."

The voice caused shivers run up and down her spine as she opened the door. The office was warm compared to the hall, but even still, Kama felt chilled. The professor sat in a chair in the corner of the room, half hidden by shadows. He looked at the clock as she entered. In contrast to her current professor, this one seemed almost swallowed by the chair he sat in. Despite being slight in stature, he commanded respect with a powerful aura.

"Miss DeKosse, I am glad to see you are prompt."

"Si Signore," she said.

"Your opera selection will be in Italian?"

"Si Signore, I will sing the aria Ah Fuggio Rapido from Orlando Furioso."

Professor Ristori gave a barely perceptible nod in her direction, and Kama took a deep breath and began.

The piece only lasted for five minutes, but showed emotional as well as vocal range. Kama had worked with the aria for months and felt comfortable in her performance.

"Tell me about Orlando Furioso."

"The work was composed by Antonio Vivaldi and first performed at Teatro Sant' Angelo, Autumn 1727. It's about a knight named Orlando who falls in love with the wrong woman set to marry another, and he ends up going crazy. In the end he breaks the spell, regains his mind, blesses the new couple, and extols the virtues of love. Vivaldi set the story to some of his most amazing music, in a score filled with arias and recitatives said to be the most emotionally filled found in any Baroque opera.

"Sing the aria in English."

*What? It's an Italian opera; I've never practiced it in English, oh crap can I even translate it?*

Despite being fluent, in Italian Kama had a hard time pulling the words together in an even tempo. The English rendition came out stilted and amateurish. She couldn't help but wince as she tried her best to make the translation sound like beautiful, fluid music instead of choppy sentences.

"The A minor scale, then a half diminished F chord from the top."

Kama straightened her stance, and after a good breath, began the scales.

"D sharp scale and then G flat minor scale – three octaves each."

Kama went through each scale set, with no mistakes she could hear, but didn't dare smile for fear the wizened man would take it for cocky assurance. He nodded again.

"You may go."

"Grazie, Signore."

Kama curtsied and walked out the door.

*Shouldn't it have been longer? Didn't he want me to show him another piece?*

She walked back to Professor Ralston's room, confused.

*Well heck, I am so messed up I totally forgot about the most important audition of my life. On top of that, Jack won't talk to me and Cade asked me out on a date. Even better I am still talking to myself like a lunatic. Let's just hope lessons go better than the audition.*

She knocked on the door and at the invitation, pushed it open. Professor Ralston stood there looking agitated as she entered the room. He shut the door behind her and began her lessons. Forty minutes later, his torture of her ended, but his odd behavior did not.

"Kamaria, a moment," he said.

Oh hell, he just called me by my first name.

"Professor Ristori would like to extend his recognition of your audition and preparation. He hopes you will audition again for him the next time there is an opening."

*Did he just tell me I didn't get it? Did I really hear him correctly? In the three minutes it took me to walk between offices, Professor Ristori made up his mind? Oh...*

Her thoughts stopped there.

"Thank you for telling me, Professor Ralston."

She thought those were the words she managed to force past dry lips and a throat that felt like it had swollen shut in disappointment. She took her bags and walked towards the front entrance. It loomed and stretched before her like a hall of doom.

*I didn't make it. I should have. Dammit, I was ready for this audition.*

Her car and driver were waiting, per usual, at the entrance and, on autopilot, she went to the car. Her mind shut down on the ride home. She walked in the door to her building and into the elevator in a numb trance.

Kama made it into the house and to her room before she broke down on the bed. The last straw had broken with this newest rejection and, with sobs that burned her chest, she cried into her pillow. She heard her door open and the side of the bed bowed the weight of another. Her mother's soft touch and familiar scent enveloped her and she allowed herself to be cuddled like a baby. Soft Gaelic filled her ears and Kama gave in to exhausted disappointment, wrapped in her mother's comfort.

# CHAPTER Eight

Kama spent the next few days feeling like an emotional zombie. For the first time ever, she contemplated skipping school. Instead, she went and passively sat through each course. Even lunch time with Cade had lost its appeal and she felt drained. She told him all about the failed audition, but his sympathy wasn't the comfort she wanted. After the first day, Cade sat by her side and gave quiet companionship, but Kama felt boxed in and restrained. Everything seemed too loud, too bright, and too over-the-top.

At night, she would go home and sulk in her room. She ate dinner with her parents and Ajani, the brother who still lived at home, but went immediately back to her room, claiming homework to do. Even her home didn't give her the solace she hoped it would. The familiar smells and sights seemed overwhelming. She ignored the looks her parents passed between them; hoping one of them wouldn't decide she needed a talking-to.

*For the love of cheese, I am the youngest. I get to be moody every once in a while. They are acting like I am going to jump out a window. It would be better if they just let me brood. One would think they would be thrilled I am acting like a normal teenager. Tomorrow will be better. I'll get back on track and just handle my business like normal.*

Tomorrow showed up and Kama didn't feel any better. To avoid spending any more time sulking in her room, she stayed at Pembleton and finished all the projects she had let slide. Kama stood in the halls at a loss, wanting to do something to feel better. She sighed loudly, trying hard to pull herself back together, but couldn't figure out how. She had an epiphany: she decided to go for a run, so she tossed her bags into her locker. She came to the edge of Central Park after walking a few blocks, and glanced up at the dusky sky. She had lived in the city her whole life, heard many horror stories about the park after dark but she didn't care.

*If I don't work this feeling out of my system, I'm going to pop. As it is, my skin feels too tight and I feel like everyone is watching me all the time. Look, there goes the loser girl who couldn't make her audition. I can't handle this. Okay, let's just run.*

She pushed all the thoughts to the back of her mind and began to run. Soon enough, everything came forward in a jumble of "what-ifs" and "I could have". It didn't help her work through anything. All her run had accomplished was bringing up all the pain she had felt for the past few weeks. She made it through her favorite running trail and ended on the opposite side of the park. Bent over and panting Kama, realized the folly of her actions.

*I am not running back through there in the dark. Who knows what kind of nasty things are just waiting there to get me? Dammit, it will take me hours to walk all the way around. Like that would be any safer. I guess I will have to take a cab.*

Then, sudden inspiration hit; she could just walk to her brother Dante's and get a ride from him. She had not seen him in a few weeks and figured she could really use some "TLC" from her big brother. She turned right and began walking. She knew it couldn't be too far, "just up the next block" her mind told her, and her spirits lifted at the thought of seeing him. She thought about calling him, but remembered that she had left her cell phone in the locker with the rest of her belongings.

About an hour and a half later, she finally found Dante's apartment building. She had gotten turned around, and had spent time retracing her steps and walking up and down streets that seemed familiar. He didn't answer the door buzzer, his windows were dark, and Kama had to admit he wasn't home. She finally gave in to the very bad day, stood in the small foyer of his building, and wept.

*This day is useless. I am going to take a cab home and go to bed. I might even just stay in bed tomorrow and try to forget about all of this crap. Hell, I am two hours late. I should call, but right all of my stuff is at Julliard. Let's hope I get a cabbie who will let me pay when I get there.*

Kama went outside and quickly hailed a cab. To her surprise she got one on her first try, and a few minutes later it pulled up in front of her building. The driver had been very accommodating and took her at her word. She had had to get money from Nate, the doorman, who cast disapproving looks at her, but at least she had gotten home drama free. She walked into the foyer of her building, her relief at being home being cut as she noticed Nate scribbling as he looked from her to the clock and back. Kama knew she should just go up to her apartment, but she couldn't take any more disapproval.

"What?" she asked.

"Excuse me, Miss DeKosse?" Nate asked.

Kama glared at him; he had stressed the word miss in a tone she knew all too well.

"I know I'm later than usual and like usual it is none of your business," she said.

"Actually it is my business," Nate said. "I note when you come and leave as your parents have requested."

"You're spying on me?" Kama asked.

From the look on his face she must have hissed the words or at least sounded like she would take his head off at the smallest provocation. But he stood his ground and looked her in the eye.

"No, my dear. I am merely doing my job," Nate said.

"Go to hell."

She screamed the words at him and punched the elevator button until the car arrived. The doors opened with a fetid smell, and she stomped her way through the doors to the stairwell. Fifteen flights of steps seemed preferable to being trapped in the tiny car. Kama's angry thoughts carried her easily up the stairs.

*I cannot believe they asked the doorman to spy on me. What gives them the right? I am not my pothead brother who does nothing. I have been responsible since the age of eight. Like I need this. I refuse to let some door man make me feel like I have done something wrong. I think the problem is, for once I am acting like a normal teenager. Well tough, they are just going to have to deal with it.*

She braced herself for her parents' reaction to her late arrival as she opened the door to her house. Just when Kama thought she might be able to get in and sneak away to her room, five foot eight's worth of fiery Irish temper descended upon her as she stepped past the threshold. Her mother seemed to fill every inch of the large space, including the rapidly shrinking gap between them, and Kama cowered under the irate glare. There was no explanation that would justify why she had been so late and why she hadn't called. She could see that the worry on her mother's face; fear and a hot temper made for a terrible mix.

"An' I would be supposin' the reason you have a cell phone, is for decoration?" Brenna DeKosse snapped. "Or perhaps as an accessory to swing around like you have no parents to worry then. Why bother to call the people that might be worried that you were dead?"

She looked at her mother and tried to compose herself enough to give a coherent answer, but her mother closed the distance between them and Kama shrunk back against the wall. Despite having had five children, Brenna had kept a slender figure, but that didn't make her any less terrifying. Red blotches of fury dotted the cheeks of her normally fair skin and her cinnamon colored eyes sparked with rage. Kama swallowed hard at hearing her mother's Irish accent out in full force; in fact, it went past accent and heavily into full brogue. She and her siblings often joked their mother's accent metered just how hot her temper ran, and acted as a warning system that had proved more than accurate over the years. The more pronounced the accent and slang, the larger the temper that all of her children had learned to fear. Kama sighed, knowing this would just the perfect ending to her day.

"I left my bag at school, when I went for a run to get it, and my phone was in it. Then I just came home instead of going back," Kama said. "I'm sorry I didn't think…"

"No, you didn't think. What would possess you to take a run this late? Central Park is full of muggers at night," her mother said. "Ye know damn well New York at night is no place to walk by yourself unless ye be wanting to invite trouble."

"By the time I finished my run, I realized it had gotten too dark to walk back through the park, so I figured it might be better to go to Dante's to get a ride, but he wasn't there. So I got a cab," Kama said. "I didn't try to walk home alone at night, Mom."

She spoke as fast as she could without tripping over her words, needing to get the excuse out before her mother's temper broke. She hoped she might be granted some leeway because at least she hadn't tried to walk through the park. Brenna's spine straightened so quickly, Kama feared it might snap. It wasn't a good sign.

"Dante's?" her mother's voice rose more in volume.

*Oh hell, she's going to start now. Really, all I want is to take a shower and go to bed.*

Kama closed her eyes: her life would certainly get much harder before it got any easier. Her mother's voice broke into her tired thoughts, and filled with her dread.

"Do ye know how bloody far that is? And all those places ye had to be walkin' through by yerself. Dammit Kamaria, ye could have been snatched up and sold. Of all the bloody stupid things to do - Ye would think I raised a damn eejit with how ye be acting lately. I just sent your father and brother out to get you from the school. What is wrong with you? It canna just be this one audition. What is going on?"

In the middle of the maelstrom, the door opened and Kama's father and brother Ajani walked into the house. Her father looked at her with more than irritation, but she knew he wouldn't interfere with her mother's tirade.

*Great, I am being spared a lecture from him, at least for now, which means he's going to let Mom do her bit first. Oh hell, Ajani looks too happy. What does he have planned? He is such an asshole.*

"Hey Kama-lama, how were your late-night antics? Dad and I searched all over for you, only to come home and hear you cussed Nate out. Good show little sister," Ajani said.

"Son, I think we need to let your mother and sister finish their talk," Malik DeKosse said.

Kama narrowed her eyes at Ajani, but he stood watching until Brenna waved them away. When Ajani didn't move fast enough, Kama at least got to enjoy her mother giving him a slap upside the head, and he moved away fast as a blur. Her face had turned a shade of purple Kama had never seen, and she could only hope her death would be swift and painless. She swore if she made it through the night she would make Ajani pay; she didn't know how, but he would.

"Mom," Kama said. "Nothing is wrong with me. I'm tired and upset; I have worked my whole life. Don't I get a break? I bombed my audition with Professor Ristori and won't have another chance again for years. I think my actions are understandable."

"Kamaria, I have never seen you this upset about an audition. You know this is part of the process," Brenna said. "But you canna fall apart just because you didn't make it this one time."

"Why can't I be upset, Mom? I should be able to be, sad and probably even pissed off that I didn't get placed. I worked my tail off for it. I did everything that hideous little man asked me for and in three minutes, he crushed my dreams. I don't understand why you people won't allow me to mope for a day."

With tears glistening on her cheeks, Kama walked past her mother, into her room, and shut the door.

*If she wants to yell at me, she can follow me in here and do it.*

Her mother did follow her into the room and pulled her close. Kama didn't want to want the cuddling, but she couldn't help but fall into the comfort.

"Well, I suppose you can be upset, but it's more Kama. For instance, you forgot tonight is family dinner and your siblings are here. This just isn't like you," Brenna said. "You have been distracted for weeks now, so much that you don't even behave like yourself. However, you will have to be the one to work through it. But Love, know I am here to talk to; trust me, I willna be surprised by anything you tell me. Now, wash your face and let's go have dinner."

*Yea, what happened with Jack would surprise you, so I have to suffer. I wish I could tell you about my first love and first heartbreak. I want to have you tell me that it will all be better and that love hurts but is wonderful. I just want my Mama.*

Kama nodded, put on a happy face, and followed her mother out of her room. Ever since she could remember, her home had been filled with boisterous noises and a flurry of activities that had been a hallmark of her family. They worked hard, played harder, and enjoyed each other's company around the table. Their mother's passion for food and family molded their relationships, and weekly family dinners helped keep their bonds close. She and Ajani were the only two children left in the home, and since they both were out of the house most of the day, things had calmed to a dull roar. Kama shook her head; she couldn't believe she had walked in and not noticed the chatter coming from the dining room. It's not as if her older three siblings were quiet.

"*Arachidi!*"

"Dante."

Kama smiled, and went into his wide open embrace. She knew his care would soothe her hurts. He had always been the elusive older brother due to the eight-year age difference between them, but out of the two brothers she had, he definitely ranked as favorite. He had moved out three years before, and his visits home had dwindled since he had gotten engaged earlier that year. Kama still didn't know how she felt about Jill, his fiancée.

*She's pretty enough, but I think a sponge has more personality. Hell, she's about as exciting as a cup of milk, excepting milk is refreshing. I can't actually believe that he and Jill moved in together instead of just getting married. I would have thought her values a bit more old fashioned. She must have some smarts; he would never deal with an idiot, but she's so... Jill.*

"Hi Jill how are you?"

She tossed the greeting into the air, but didn't wait for an answer, but instead went to hug her twin sisters, Bella and Bridget.

"Hi Twin, how's business?" Kama asked one of them.

She had started calling them "Twin" at the age of two, when she had begun to speak, because she couldn't tell them apart and the nickname had stuck. She still had a hard time telling them apart, but had come to the conclusion that it was okay to treat them like one person because they were changelings. They acted the same; all of the jokes about twins finishing each other's sentences and having a mind-link were fact in Kama's mind when it came to her sisters. They were six years older than she; never once in all her time growing up had she seen them do anything alone.

*Not like they are actually two people; I swear on all that is good and pure, they are one soul put into two bodies. I honestly think the only person who can tell them apart is my mother. Even scarier is that they like being one person. Although I wouldn't say anything to them, my time is better spent staying on their good side and being safe. I wonder what would happen if they ever got separated. Yea, on second thought, it would probably never happen because their radar would activate to find each other. I wonder if they have ever been subject to government testing. Good thing they are pretty.*

To say her sisters were stunning would be like saying a tsunami might be a little wave. Quite literally, they had been the cause of at least six accidents Kama knew of. Men just stopped and stared, regardless of what they had been doing. The only consolation her parents had was Twin refused to date singly. It always had to be the two of them, and their parents figured they would have safety in numbers. However, what Kama knew was that Twin looked at dating as social research. The men they dated were subject to any number and sort of experiments. And yet, the men were willing participants.

*I mean they are beautiful and all, but - sheesh - I wouldn't want to be subjected to their whims.*

Twin might have been elusive and gorgeous, but they also happened to have an odd sense of humor. Kama had been prey to many of their pranks growing up, and she wasn't stupid enough to rile them up deliberately. They were just as prone to be vindictive as fun when playing said pranks. Not to mention, she didn't know if she would survive really making them take a serious interest in what she did.

*And then, there is Ajani.*

She watched as he strutted into the dining room. They were only ten months apart, but to Kama's disgust, he acted like a wild child. Of all the DeKosse children, Ajani defined "black sheep".

*He is a loser and doesn't want to be anything else. Dante helps Dad run the business, Twin has their own jewelry shop, I sing, and he does nothing, besides workout. Even worse, I know he smokes pot and my parents know about it. He is such a stupid jerk. I can't believe he is my brother; he does nothing with himself except hang out with his loser friends. What a waste of the DeKosse genetics.*

If possible, her mood became even darker as she watched him laugh and have fun with the rest of her siblings. In fact, her whole family seemed determined to ignore her grumpy demeanor and have a rollicking, laugh-filled dinner as if everything were normal and fine. She ate and answered questions by rote, but otherwise didn't join in. After dinner, she excused herself and left, and much to her ire, no one called her back to the table.

*They could at least give me some coddling. I am the baby, dammit.*

She walked, head down and the seeming weight of the world on her shoulders, back to her bedroom haven. She felt like karma had repaid her with the harshest punishment six times over, but she wasn't sure what she had done to merit such a thorough ass kicking. As she sat in her room stewing, her chest tightened, and she felt like something would snap, hoping it wouldn't be her psyche. .

*If I have to sit home and listen to the family happiness for one more second, I will scream. This doesn't even seem fair. First, I get yelled at because I went to Dante's and forgot about dinner, then no one cares I'm in here alone. They are all sitting out there laughing and having a great time while I am in here feeling like my head will pop open. Life sucks.*

A few seconds later, she heard her door open. She looked up to see her father in the doorway.

*Wonderful, I start crying and Daddy chooses this moment to come in. Like he wants to deal with my tears instead of being out there with them. The look on his face is almost comical. I think he would rather deal with me shouting and cussing rather than sobbing. Well either way, I'm not going to talk until he does.*

Malik DeKosse, all six foot two of him, shifted from foot to foot in her door way as Kama had a hiccupping sniffle. His dark chocolate skin and rich mocha eyes peered at his youngest child in obvious concern. Kama looked up at her Dad, and refused to hide her misery.

"*Bambina*, what is wrong? Your Mamma told me you are still upset about your audition. What else has you so very upset? You left your family dinner to come in here and cry."

"Daddy, I should have placed. I practiced all summer for it; hell, freshmen never get invited to audition, but I did. I even translated the damn song from Italian to English on the spot. I don't expect to clear every audition, but I should have made that one."

"Kama, *tesora mia*, are you sure there isn't something more bothering you? You aren't acting like your normal self."

"Normal self? Dad, would you be happy if you lost a bid? You and Mom act like I'm supposed to be Miss Sunshine every day. I'm just upset."

To her pride, Kama didn't stamp her feet in the middle of her tirade, but she felt like it. But since she had her wounded pride in hand, she vented all her frustrations.

"Your son hangs out with his friends all day getting high and doing nothing. Yet, you and Mom come down on me because I am upset because I couldn't further my career along?" Kama asked. "Really Daddy, I think you have your priorities messed up."

"*Cara mia*, it's been weeks now. Not just this audition, but ever since we got back from Los Angeles. I doubt it's because you didn't find all of your dresses," he said. "And you are right, you can be upset. But as your parents, we will always worry if you are okay. And because we worry, expect us to pry and ask until we are sure it is true. And bambina, you can talk to us. We aren't so old and out of touch we cannot help you with things that you think we cannot understand. We were young once."

Kama stared at her father for a moment, then went into his outstretched arms and allowed herself to be folded in and comforted. Her tears returned full force and she finally gave in to all the disappointments she had suffered. When her father finally left her room, she crawled into bed, and just ended the day.

Instead of restful sleep, she reentered the world of nightmarish images so dark that she woke in a panic as something feral and vicious chased her. In the dark of her room, she could still hear the cries of pursuit echo in her ears long after she realized it had been just a dream. She sat up and looked around; trying to prove to herself it was not real. She couldn't quite make sense of all the images that crashed down into her mind, trying to push through and give her a message. Kama rushed into the bathroom and spent the next moments being sick repeatedly.

"Come on darlin', let's settle you."

The soft words offered her comfort and she allowed her mother to lead her back to bed. For the first time in many years, Kama put her head in her mother's lap and let her stroke her hair. The dream images faded, wiped away by Gaelic lullabies from her childhood.

Maybe because of her night, or maybe because her father managed to convince her mother she was not the first teenager to do something as incredibly stupid as walk home, the parental tempers were eased by the next morning. Even though she still remained subdued and quiet they left her alone. The horrifying dreams, muted by the light of the sun, still flitted through her memory.

*All I want to do is stay home and sleep. I bet the moment I close my eyes, they will come back and haunt me. It shouldn't affect me; they were just dreams. They weren't real.*

The images of the absolute mayhem haunted her and continually forced their way into the day, which made her nervous. Kama wondered if the stress had finally gotten to her and made her snap. She had plenty of dreams that were odd, but never before had they manifested themselves so vividly or in such gore.

*I need a break, just a little peace and quiet to get over Jack and get over this failure. Maybe I should plan on going to another college instead of Julliard. Just get out of here and start somewhere new.*

For the first time ever, Kama skipped school and practice, pleading ill to her mother. She stayed home, curled up on the couch in her robe. Despite thinking she was taking a mental health day, Kama dozed off at least three times. She gratefully accepted the pampering that her mother lavished on her; a tray for dinner and tucked back into bed. But once she got to sleep again, the nightmarish images resurfaced and plagued her. She woke in a blind panic, until her mother came in and talked with her about things she couldn't even remember until darkness claimed her once more. She woke at false dawn and lay there exhausted.

*It might be manageable, except for on top of all this weirdness, I feel like my stupid emotions have been thrown into a blender and spit back into my face. I feel all jumbled up and crazed inside, and it's hard to hide. What did I ever do to start this downward spiral into hell?*

Kama sighed and pushed herself up into a sitting position.

"Okay DeKosse, enough is enough. Get yourself together and let's move forward. Everyone is right; you are sulking and acting like a spoiled brat in general. It's just an audition; life will go on."

She got up and showered. Despite her determination to stay positive and move forward, part of her mind nagged at her.

*Maybe it's more than just the audition. It might be we haven't gotten over…*

Kama shut down the rest of that thought before it could ruin the good mood she forced upon herself, and went out to start her day.

# CHAPTER Nine

*I want to talk to Jack. I don't know if he cares or will even want to listen to me whine, but I want to hear his voice. Damn, life sucks; stupid audition. I know I am good enough. What is wrong with him? Maybe Ristori wanted me to be eighteen so he could ogle me legally as well. I hate this; I don't want to feel like this. I should just call Jack; even hearing his voicemail message will be okay.*

Kama walked out of school and headed towards the New York public library to get some homework done. Despite having computers at school and home, she found the quiet atmosphere of the library much more conducive to getting her work done in a timely fashion. After three hours of reading the same passages and writing a paper that made no sense, she gave up and dug through her purse to find Jack's business card. Because of her neurotic behavior of calling him and hang-up after one ring during the first week, she erased his numbers from her phone. She found the card after she had dumped her purse onto the table and expelled a nervous breath.

*I'll call his work number; there is less chance of him actually picking up, which I know he will do if I call his cell phone. I mean, why wouldn't he? I only want to hear his voicemail; so of course, he would answer and then yell at me. Yea, business line is safer; besides it's after five, so he might be gone for the day.*

"Twist Enterprises, Carla speaking."

The voice rang out and Kama felt like she had been reprimanded for calling, from the simple, yet firm greeting. She had expected to reach his voicemail; she never once had counted on his assistant answering the phone for him.

"I would like to speak with Jack, I mean, Mr. Twist please."

"One moment please, I will see if he is available."

Kama paced on the ramp behind the library as she listened to the "on hold" music. She actually had a chance of talking to him; after all, if his assistant worked after five, Jack might be there himself. She paced faster, not sure if she wanted to talk to him anymore or not.

"I am sorry, Mr. Twist is not currently available; I'll leave you to his voicemail."

Kama felt her knees buckle in relief. She listened to Jack's rather dry greeting before realization hit her.

*Oh hell, I have to leave a message. Crap it's already beeped. What do I say? I mean, I can't hang up on him again; I'm sure he has caller identification. Okay, talk now because it's already been waiting.*

"Hi Jack, I guess give me a call on my cell when you have a moment," she said. "This is Kama."

She hung up and wondered how much of an ass she had sounded like.

*Well, first we left a twenty minute pause and then we sounded all shaky and a mess. So much for being calm and sounding neutral. Once again, I sounded like the child he thinks I am. Well hearing his voice didn't make me feel any better. I guess I'm going home; maybe food will help. I'm starving.*

She gathered her things and left the library feeling worse. At home, she didn't even pretend to smile. Her mother and father sat in the living room having coffee, and from the low thudding bass, she figured her loser brother sat contemplating how to be an idiot in his room. She grabbed various snacks and retreated to her room before her parents could question her well-being again.

The next day she continued to force herself to keep the grab-the-bull-by-the-balls attitude. Kama made it a point to get her school work taken care of before heading off to lessons. However, her week of moping hadn't done her any favors as she had barely practiced. Professor Ralston took it as a sign that she was still sulking about her audition with Professor Ristori, and had even less patience than usual with her.

"Get out and come back when you can focus. This is a waste of my time, Kamaria."

"I'm sorry, Professor. I'm a bit off today…"

"A bit off? Your music isn't memorized, you are tripping over basic pronunciations, and you are breathing like a steam engine. You haven't done this poorly since you were an untrained child. Do you think you will be successful at every audition? You will fail sometimes. What makes a great performer is getting over it and preparing for the next step. Get out; you are no use to me today."

"Please, Professor Ralston, let me try…"

Her plea met the solid thunk of the wood door she had just been escorted through. Kama stood there dejected, trying to figure out what to do next. She had been waiting on pins and needles all day, but her phone never rang once. Over everything else, she missed talking to Jack.

*Dammit, does love really have to suck so much? I swear, it's like being on a crazy roller coaster and I don't think I want to ride it anymore. All these ups and downs are making a mess of the rest of my life in the process; I'm done. I probably shouldn't have called him. It's not like he has even tried to contact me. How much more time should I give him? I want to see him, but maybe it's best to just put it behind me and get on with this year.*

She walked out of Julliard, ready for the fight to hail a cab home. She had been so put out the last few days; she hadn't wanted to use the very cheerful and talkative family driver. She was forcing herself to smile and be more social, but it was hard to do with family. When she finally dragged her chin up from her chest to begin hailing, she saw Jack standing in front of a car at the curb. Kama stared at him, not one hundred percent sure her mind hadn't produced a hallucination due to stress and fatigue. He waved at her, and encouraged, she forced herself to walk and not run over to him. She tried not to smile too widely, but relief filled her at seeing him and she couldn't help her reaction.

"Good evening," he said.

"Good evening," Kama said.

"Do you have time to go for a walk? I'll get you a hotdog," he offered.

"Sure," Kama said.

*Are you kidding me? Sure? Kama, pull it together and just talk to him. But I don't even know how to start a conversation with him. I mean, I called him earlier and now he's here. Wow, he looks good; I probably shouldn't stare at him though. I am already making a mess of this. Okay, just breathe and walk; we can figure out what to say after the hotdog. Oh crap, did I just use the royal we again?*

From her peripheral vision, she watched Jack walk at her side with his arms behind his back looking ahead. He led her onto the street where a hotdog vender stood; a man with a thick accent smiled and greeted Jack by name. Kama ordered two hotdogs with mustard and relish, and began to eat them to buy herself more time to think about what to say to him. Jack grabbed his order and they walked back towards his car. She looked back and forth between Jack and the pavement in front of her.

"I got your message when I returned from my afternoon meeting," he said. "So, how have you been?"

"I'm not sure," she said. "Things are really different. School is driving me nuts I tanked the audition of my career, and I feel like I am slowly suffocating."

She noticed him watching her with an unwavering stare, waiting for her to finish talking.

"And I hate that I left things how I did," she added.

"I am sorry. I wish I could have handled things differently, but I have never had to deal with a situation like this before," he said.

A long paused followed, and Kama focused on walking.

"You have been on my mind ever since I let you walk out the door."

"I know not telling you my age made things horribly wrong, but I don't think we are. I care for you, and enjoyed our time together. I don't think we should have to let it end based on a stupid number."

Jack stared at her again, and Kama wished for another hotdog to justify the silence. She couldn't read the emotions in his beautiful olive eyes, and fear began to prick at the back of her neck. She watched him tense and prepared to hear the worst.

"I don't think we are wrong either. I am not a stupid man and despite my life experiences, I have never felt like this for anyone before… which is why I am here now," he said, "But there are going to be problems and we are going to have to deal with them."

"So, what do we do now?" she asked.

"You were right when you said I never once guessed you were younger, because you are an intelligent and graceful young woman. There are plenty of relationships with large age differences. The only difference in ours is that we can't be public for six months, so for a minute, we get the intrigue of keeping this a secret," he said.

"So you want…" her voice trailed off in disbelief.

"Yes, I want," he said. "I can't seem to get you out of my head and instead of going crazy trying; I think it's better for us to be together."

Kama felt suddenly shy at his acceptance and smiled at him cautiously. She was still having a hard time believing that they were working things out.

*Okay, so for here on out, I will do my best to give Jack what he wants and not argue with him. I don't ever want him to regret this decision. We made it work in Los Angeles with no problem; I can't see there being many problems here. Six months isn't even a long time to be low key. Okay, he is talking again. Pay attention and start being the dutiful girlfriend.*

"… I know your schedule is as crazy as mine, so we will squeeze in time to see each other, maybe go away for the weekends," he finished saying.

*Balls, a problem already.*

"Weekends might not be possible," she said. "I live at home."

"Okay," he said.

Kama saw he wasn't following her train of thought and said the next sentence with a quiet stress.

"With my parents."

"Right."

She tried not to flinch.

"Of course you do. Okay then, we will have to work with it," he said. "Don't worry. For the next few months we will be discrete, and then once you move out it won't matter. We'll be just some regular couple in New York."

Kama saw some emotion flicker through his eyes and wondered if he already questioned his decision to contact her again. She nodded in agreement and walked with him back to his car. He opened the door for her, and helped her get settled.

"I think it would better for me not to be dropped off close to home," she said.

He pulled her into his arms and nodded.

"Wise precaution."

She gave his driver directions to the coffee shop around the corner from her house, and cuddled into Jack's embrace. A thought flickered through her mind, but became lost as she looked up at him; he leaned in and kissed her hard. Before, their kisses had been full of passion, but this stole her breath. His scent filled her mind and she moved closer to him, not being able to get close enough. Jack finally broke the kiss; she laid her head on his shoulder to keep contact and realized the car had stopped. Kama wondered how long it had been motionless.

"I should go," she said.

"I'll talk to you soon, so we can make some plans," he said. "I missed you."

Kama kissed him again, smiled, and forced herself to get out of the car. She waved to him until his car drove out of sight and then walked home, happier than she could have imagined.

*We can make this work. I need to be calm and collected and not push him. I can see us just holing up at his place, having Chinese food delivered. Well, unless he doesn't like it, then we can get something else. Too bad we have to be so low key; there are some pretty good venues at the theater this fall. Oh well, maybe I'll see him there when I go. Of course, we're going to have to navigate around my stupid curfew. I wonder just how many aspects of my life will remind him of my age. February needs to hurry up and get here.*

## ##

For the next few weeks, Kama floated through school, practice, and dating. She reveled in her time with Jack, but she began to fizzle out. She not only burned the candle at both ends but straight through the middle as she tried to balance it all. On the upside, her parents were thrilled at her turn around.

'Come on, stop whining. Jack is making sacrifices too,' she told herself. 'He still has a job and yet finds plenty of time to spend with you almost every other night. In a few months it won't be a big deal.'

They spent most of the time at his home, much as she had anticipated. She didn't complain, because she enjoyed their time together. Jack had explained the high risk of being seen in public, and she agreed the drama could easily be avoided if they didn't tempt Fate. She couldn't remember the last time she had seen so many different movies, played card games, or talked about herself. Of course, there were the times they spent in wild and passionate lovemaking, leaving her exhausted but sated as she languidly cuddled next to him content in his embrace. Kama felt guilty as she left his bed to return home before her curfew.

"This isn't too weird for you, is it?" she asked.

"No, I just wish you could actually spend the whole night."

"Soon enough. Then you won't be able to get rid of me," she said.

She had asked him the same question on more than one occasion, but still needed some kind of reassurance from him. The demands on her time wore her thin, and she began to fear making a mistake or giving something away. Kama tried her best not to remind him of her age and the drama surrounding it, but instead tried to recapture the excitement and fun they had enjoyed over the summer. Still, she worried what would happen when it became too much of a burden for him.

*I hope I can withstand this pace. I get home, do homework for three hours, get three hours of sleep, and start the routine all over again. Thank God for the weekend, else I would be falling over. Even Mom mentioned I looked like I have lost some weight and Daddy is giving me the "You're tired, slow down" speech. But Jack is worth it. I wouldn't trade my time with him for anything. Just another two months and we get a break for Thanksgiving, and then I can sleep for three days straight. Damn, it also means I can't see Jack because I won't have a good excuse.*

Her grueling schedule finally pushed her to the edge wore her down in ways she never had anticipated. She was jumpy, snappish and in general a miserable person to be around. Kama tried locking herself in her room after returning home from a day at school but the walls seemed to close in on her. She opted to go for a run just so she could get out, and headed out to Central Park. Despite it being dusk she reasoned she had enough time to have a quick run to take the edge off. She had been running for the past few weeks to keep her sanity.

*Run, then a hot shower, eat enough to fall into a food coma and then go to bed blessedly early and get more than a wink of sleep. Thank God Jack didn't want me to come over tonight; I would have just fallen asleep on him and wasted a night together. Well, I do like sleeping on his chest.*

She arrived at Central Park twenty minutes later and hit the trail that encircled the Great Lawn at a brisk pace. Adjusting her headphones, she picked up speed, not paying attention to those around her. Tears blurred her vision as she jogged, and she ran faster until her breath came in ragged pants. Kama pushed herself, and after eight laps, she was frustrated. Even the run hadn't calmed her; she had an agitation she couldn't shake off.

*What is wrong with me? My skin is crawling like millions of spiders laid webs across me and I can't scrub it off. It feels too tight for my body, like it has shrunk against me and will split. And why the hell is everyone looking at me? There are a lot of people running, so why me? Hey, watch it!*

Her inner ramblings blinded her to the traffic coming toward her, and Kama veered off to the left. She found trails and continued to run but at a lighter pace. She wasn't too worried; she knew she was close to the pond near the castle and would reach the road-path soon. Only then did she notice it had gotten darker. She checked her watch and noticed she had been running for 43 minutes. The number of runners had tapered off and it was really too dark for her to be there alone. As she gulped in fresh air, she looked around. She saw the amphitheater to her right as she walked through the paths. They weren't particularly well lit, but they had railings and were well traveled.

*Damn malfunctioning sense of direction. I'm in the middle of the park, crap. Okay, so if I follow these trails, it should take me close to the puppet theater. You know, why do people make puppets look so sinister? For something that is supposedly made for telling stories to children, some of them are plain scary. Maybe that is the whole point, sort of like fairy tales- subtly teaching a lesson in those most disturbing way possible. Anyhow, once I get to the creepy theater, I can just follow the road and eventually get back to a running trail and get home. Yep, because getting lost was exactly what I needed to fix feeling out-of-sorts. At least, I'm not trying to walk to Dante's this time.*

It was almost peaceful walking through the trails; they wound around the gardens and despite night having fallen, a few couples strolled by. For the first time in weeks, she started to relax- just a little bit. Being in nature was calming and when she came to a bench, Kama sat down.

*Now, if I can just figure out how to bottle the calm and take it home. What I don't understand is that I thought all the tension was from my fight with Jack, but apparently not, because we are dating and I'm still stressed. Maybe it's his expectation for me to move out when I am eighteen, but I still have to finish school. I won't be able to move out until I graduate. And then there will be the new breaking-in period, when we start to date publically. I don't know that my parents will allow it, even when I am legally an adult. What a pain. I just want to enjoy dating him.*

With a sigh, she stood up, stretched and realized just how quiet it had gotten around her. The meandering couples had left the trails, and Kama felt alone. She started to walk toward what she thought was the road, but after a few moments, she realized she was walking in circles and was getting lost. The trails around the Shakespeare Gardens should lead back to the puppet cottage, but she wasn't seeing it; and the beautifully sculpted foliage blocked her view. Thus, she was surprised when she walked up on a trio, smoking and having a harshly whispered and heated exchange. Packages exchanged hands, and Kama had the feeling she shouldn't be there. She stopped in surprise, staring at them, and noticed that she had gathered their attention as well.

*Of course, we would have to walk up on some idiots smoking pot. We should be happy it isn't Ajani out here; he would somehow blame me. Okay, just put our head down, and walk back the way we came.*

A rough hand grabbed her just above the elbow and sent a wave of fear through her. She had not heard anyone walk up behind her, so she

## Enter the Moon

flinched at the pinching. The hand pulled her back into the dark recesses of the unlit the path and turned her around. Kama looked up, trying to weigh her options, and forced herself to be calm. She took in her surroundings; now that she was closer, she could see the group better; two men and one woman stood clustered together, passing a joint between them, while the fourth man gripped her arm.

*This is not a good situation at all. Stay calm, Kama, and let's figure this out. All we need to be able to do is run out of this blasted garden and we're okay. Relax and maybe he will drop his guard long enough for us to escape.*

Kama swallowed hard, but then met the eyes of the man who invaded her personal space and blocked her from escaping. He smirked at her, looked her up and down, and then gave a low whistle.

*This is so not good. Crap, his friends are coming over.*

The others seemed a bit more cautious in approaching her, and their body language was guarded. They came over and looked at her, taking in her appearance in a questioning way. The lone female of the group had a scowl on her face; the rest just looked a bit scared. The guy holding her chuckled in her ear.

"What do we have here? Maybe you want to join us, take a hit or two?"

The guttural voice filled the small space and sounded too loud to Kama's ears. She shook her head "no" and tried to look small and non-threatening. Her captor easily stood over six feet and despite a wiry frame, he had a strength that would be her biggest problem. She could feel his fingers pressing into her flesh and knew she would bruise.

"No, just made a wrong turn, thanks," Kama said.

She swallowed hard against a very dry throat and tried to slowly ease out of his grasp and evade his touch. She could see the man as he pulled her closer to him, gripping tighter. His eyes peered out from a surprisingly well formed face, but the fetid breath made her nostrils burn. He could have been handsome, but his red-veined eyes betrayed his drug use.

"Come along, sweetness. I know girls like you. All bluster and denial until stress hits, then you want some," he said.

149

Her eyes darted back and forth, looking for an exit, and she pulled her arm away. An ugly look passed over his face, and he pinched harder. He laughed- a mirthless, bitter sound, breaking against her ears in tinny shards. Kama panicked and tried to move away from him, to get home.

"If you aren't here for goods, why are you here?"

The soft, female voice surprised Kama, and her eyes snapped up to the woman. She was shorter, very skinny, and looked around nervously. Kama dropped her gaze to try to compose herself. She was forced to lift her face as the man yanked her hair back. She didn't make a sound, but began to shake as he trailed an invading hand over her shoulder.

"I just got lost, running. I don't want anything except to go home," Kama said.

"No, that doesn't sound right," the woman said. "No one gets lost running; you run in a big damn circle. You're here as a snitch."

Kama could hear fear underlying the malice in the voice and twisted against the hand gripping her. She began to fight, lashing out until her fists connected on someone with a meaty sound. Desperation set in when she realized no one would come to save her.

*Oh God, no one knows I am here. This can't happen. I won't let it happen. I need to go.*

She began to kick and punch out more, receiving a slap across the head that stunned her for her troubles. Kama noticed the other two men had come closer, but oddly, there was little other noise around them.

"What the hell are we going to do with her? You know what we were told about dealing in this spot again," the female snapped. "Okay, let's just finish the deal and go."

"It was stupid for us to come back here. That bitch scares me," the male snapped back.

"Look, we came here to get some stuff, not get all up in your crazy," a short, paunchy man said.

"Yea, we are out of here. We want nothing to do with this mess."

Kama was surprised as the owner of the last voice and the chubby guy ran quickly away from the scene, but his words chilled her. She understood that there would be very little time left for her, if she didn't find a way out. She jabbed her elbow back at her captor, who grunted, but only gripped her tighter.

"I like it rough, so fight all you want. Maybe we can have some play time."

"I need to go; they will be looking for me."

"Shut that bitch up!" snapped the female. "You want to feed your stupid strangle fetish now? Whatever. Make sure she is dead when you are done."

*They are going to rape me and kill me and no one knows I am here. They talk about it so calmly, like it's no big deal. Oh gods, they have done this before.*

Kama knew that she either had to fight and escape or end up another casualty of Central Park. The duo stood on either side, watching her. Her captor made lewd comments about the experiences he would subject her to. A slimy lock of hair fell over his face as he ran a hand over her breast. Kama slapped his hand away, and then her head rocked as his fist bruised its way across her mouth.

"You might want to get to it," the female said. "If she sent a snitch, she will be around soon enough to check."

"Impatient to watch already? You act like you do this all for me, but we both know you get off watching me screw and strangle girls," the guy laughed. "Did you bring your toy?"

Kama whimpered and tried to figure out how to live. Part of her wanted to float away, pretend such an event would never happen to her and she would wake up from the nightmare, but something kept her very firmly grounded. Her emotions were turbulent, fear and rage intermixing and coursing through her.

"Don't worry, you will like it."

He spoke low and close into her ear and pressed his groin against her. Kama could feel his erection and knew it was going to happen. She could see the girl standing to the side, watching them intently. Her faced was flushed, and Kama could hear her breathing harder.

"Trust us, Princess, we can show you a good time," he said. "You might even learn to like the pain."

Time seemed to slow down for Kama as total dread blinded her senses. Her eyes went wide as the man ground against her, forcing his slimy tongue into her mouth. She closed her eyes, trying to quell the urge to vomit, but her mind spun in circles, refusing to stay focused. The thick taste of fear choked the screams forming in her throat. The female was moving closer, her breath faster and more erratic. Kama saw her pull a knife. She bit down on her captors' tongue as hard as she could. He pushed her away with a roar of pain. Before she had the chance to run, the female stood before her.

"Wrong answer, Princess."

Kama felt the knife slide in to her stomach, and her eyes widened at the sudden explosion of pain that flashed through her body. The woman thrust the knife again and again into her body; a sudden sense of calm took over as she fell to her knees.

*No, this will not happen to us. We will not let it happen; we have more control than they know. Being touched by these two miscreants is offensive. They need to hurt like they tried to hurt us. My turn.*

Her fight response kicked in and her conscious mind fled. Somewhere in the miasma, an anguished howl filled the air around her. She screamed in terror as her bones cracked and popped, elongating. Coarse fur sprouted from her pores, and she could feel the wind weave through it with a curious sensation. Her fear turned to cold fury, and she looked at her enemies. She found them backing away from her terrified, and part of her brain noted the assailants who had overwhelmed her, seemed smaller somehow. She opened her mouth and a snarling growl came out. She reached out for them slashing, drawing blood. Incoherent cries of pain and fear sounded in short, static bursts.

*You said you liked pain. Let's see how much pain you like. No one attacks me! You will regret touching me in such a filthy way. Disgusting creatures. You need to be punished. You have done this before to others; I can smell stale fear and sordid sex on your bodies. This ends here.*

She moved even closer to them, claws slick with glistening blood, and the screams of terror sounded like a roaring ovation in her ears. With her vengeance spent, she saw there would be little left of them for anyone to find.

*Done. Now they will never harm another.*

The stillness of the area, which was so unusual for New York City, brought her out of her rage. Fear overtook her, and she felt the overwhelming need to return to where she was safest: home. Kama bent over to catch her breath and clear her head. She fought back tears and the urge to vomit, but as a warm salty flavor made it presence known in her mouth, she lost her fight. Her memory gave her shadowy images of dead bodies being flung about and bestial sounds. She could do nothing but shake, and promptly passed out from shock.

With a jolt, she woke up and looked around. The lights seemed too bright, and the bed she lay in was hard with rough sheets. She sat up, and her head immediately felt like it would explode. Dazed and disoriented, Kama looked around to get her bearings.

*How the hell did I get to a hospital? Where are my parents? What just happened? I thought I was at the park.*

She gasped when she found a thin Cuban woman about five feet ten, with dark hair pulled back from her face and the darkest eyes Kama had ever seen, looking her over.

"Hello."

"Where am I?" asked Kama.

"Are you okay?"

The woman was joined by another, who wore a doctor's coat.

"I don't know, I can't remember what happened or how I got here," Kama said.

"You were being attacked and fought back," the woman said. "We brought you here to make sure that you were okay."

"Who are you? Why are you helping me? Are you the police?" Kama asked.

The doctor said nothing, but took her pulse and listened to her lungs. She felt the lymph nodes in Kama's neck, and then pressed on her stomach. She nodded and scribbled.

"Everything seems normal."

That statement was punctuated with a shot from a syringe that Kama had not even seen.

"This will stave off any potential infection. She's good to go."

"Holy shit! She just stuck me. Where am I? Where are my parents? Who are you people?"

Kama looked around in agitation and noticed that the room was not quite right. The harsh lights were suspended from pipes that were set in a raw ceiling. To her right, there was a sink and a bin full of bloodied towels, no hazard containers to be seen. There was no machinery, no anything else that would have been found in a hospital or clinic.

"Why don't we get you some clean clothes and then we can have a little chat," the woman said. "My name is Lorna. What is yours?"

"I'm Kama. Nice to meet you," she said.

Kama wanted to giggle as her manners took over in the very weird situation. She took the clothes that Lorna handed to her. As she did, she felt something pass between them, a familiar comfort, but it passed before Kama could put a name to the feeling.

*Okay, just hold it together. She must be taking me to the police or something so I can get help. But what do I tell them? I barely remember anything, and what I do remember isn't real. I mean, I know I am not in a hospital, but how did I get here and where is here? That so-called doctor just shot me up with who-knows-what. Shouldn't I remember something?*

Lorna pulled a curtain for privacy, and Kama began to get dressed. The clothes were just a black sweat outfit, which was almost her size. She sat back on the bed and waited for someone to come and explain things to her. The ticking of the clock was unbearably loud. Images kept pressing into her mind, disjointed and harsh. She began to laugh as hysteria overtook her.

*Wow, going commando style, in some borrowed clothes. Why am I here? What do they want from me? They wouldn't have saved me from those druggies if they wanted to hurt me. At least, I don't think they would. Shit, that girl was going to kill me. I don't even know what is going on here.*

Reality crashed down on her.

*Oh God, he was going to rape me, and she was going to watch. They were going to…*

Sobs racked her and she curled up into the fetal position on the narrow bed as she succumbed to the stress. Lorna walked to her side and held her hand, giving it a gentle squeeze. Kama held onto her hand as if it were a lifeline.

"I'm supposed to be home after my run," Kama said. "What is going to happen to me here?"

Her throat felt tight and her voice came out small. She felt confused and the urge to scream welled up and spilled out as tears. Numbness set in, and Kama's mind went blank.

"Okay, let's stand up and go get a nice hot cup of coffee. Walking around will help you clear your head, and then we can talk," Lorna said.

She felt her knees buckle once; she took a deep breath, and then stood on her feet.

*Okay, I can do this. When I get home I can call Jack and he will make everything right again. He will protect me and keep me safe. I just need Jack.*

She took another deep breath to steady herself; she pushed back the white curtain and walked into the small room. As she held on to Lorna's arm, she heard the door opened. A wave of dizziness washed over her and she closed her eyes to compose herself.

When she opened them again, she looked at the person who had entered the room. She stared up into Jack's olive-green eyes, and then promptly fainted.

## CHAPTER Ten

Jack rubbed his eyes, which watered from the grit scrubbing across the sensitive tissue. Ever since he had walked into the makeshift medical room and found Kama, having experienced her First Change, he hadn't been able to do anything but pace. Worry twisted through all of his thoughts. How would he be able to talk to her and help her make sense of everything that was happening? He mused that fate had a twisted sense of humor. His wolf hadn't stopped dancing for joy.

*Okay Twist, go and get some food or coffee or something. She will wake up soon, and it's not going to be easy. The least we can do is be prepared to deal with her freak-outs and tears.*

Jack summoned someone to watch her and walked toward to The Lounge. After the war that had ravaged the park, a few of the pack members had designated a section of abandoned subway station as the central meeting place for their pack. Popular belief was that Central Park sat on acres of solid bedrock. While being true, what most did not know was that the city had dug subway tunnels through the bedrock when creating the rail system. Funding had been cut short because of the extreme cost of cutting through the stone. So the tunnels ran completely through the park from north to south, but they were unfinished. The platforms were dry, relatively clean, and large spaces that had made them not only desirable, but also a comfortable place to congregate. Various people had brought down some of the comforts of home, including remnants of carpet, some old furniture, and at least a dozen coffee machines. It had evolved over the years and really had become the hub of their den; at any given point, there were people hanging out and chatting, playing cards, and sometimes even napping. Jack surveyed the tunnels as he walked through them. He wondered how hard it would be to rework the wiring and make the lights stable.

*The damn flickering gives me a headache. I know we have to stay off the grid, but there is no reason to live in squalor. Hopefully someone knows something about electrical work, and we can make this place more secure.*

Then again, the headache could be in the form of one Ms. Kamaria DeKosse who lay asleep in his office. He just had not been, nor ever could have been, prepared to find out the reality of her being Loup.

*What the hell am I going to tell her? The truth is not going to be welcome. In fact, I'm pretty sure she will think I have lost my mind or she has lost hers. Bad enough she got attacked; now I have to explain all of this to her. No doubt, Kama will hate me for the rest of her life. It almost seems Fate doesn't want us to have our happily ever after.*

When he had walked into the examination room hours before, to greet the newest cub, it had taken all of his training as a military special ops soldier not to flinch or react in surprise. Too many eyes and ears would have made for uncomfortable questions, so he had steeled himself for Kama to acknowledge him. Thankfully, she had passed out in shock instead. The tricky part then became how to talk to her before anyone else did. His role as Alpha didn't include taking care of new cubs; but in this case, he didn't really have a choice. He knew he needed to be the one to explain things to her.

Once he had gotten himself calmed and composed, he took Lorna, his Southern Point Beta, aside and made sure Kama's care would be directed by him.

"I'll take this one," he said.

"Not like to you chase a pretty skirt, Boss," Lorna said. "She's a little high-strung, but nothing I can't handle."

"Not like you to be so far off your game. Don't you recognize her?" Jack asked. "She's high profile."

His tone had lacked the teasing quality of hers; and despite her raised eyebrow, he bit his tongue to stop himself from offering more excuses. He had hoped Lorna would just accept his word, being Alpha and all, but like any good Beta she tried to take some of the burden from his shoulders.

"Yea, I have dealt with the princess type before. It will be okay. She didn't come in a drooling mess of hysteria," Lorna said. "Really Boss, I can handle one little girl."

Jack sighed and tried to figure out a proper excuse. It wouldn't be the first time he had chosen to talk to a new cub and explain the situation. In this case, he had to; he just hoped he didn't come off as desperate.

"I recognize her; her family is in the diamond industry. She's most likely one of those high-strung 'won't believe anything' types. It might take a bit of finessing, both with her and possibly with her family. I've got this one."

"Sure, Boss," she said. Despite her attempt to hide it, Lorna's smirk shone through. "Here I thought you might have given in to the lure of a young tail. Nothing else seems to interest you."

Jack rolled his eyes and snorted. Lorna often made snide jokes, not quite under her breath, about her beliefs. She often said he would be a happier person if he got laid more often.

*If she only knew the whole sordid affair and the mess I'm in, she might have not look so smug. Then again she'd probably be laughing her ass off on the floor,'* he thought.

He had carried the sleeping Kama to his underground office and deposited her on his couch. He hoped waking to a familiar face might east some of the shock, because the rest of the night would inevitably be hard. Especially since the news would be dropped on her, and she would have to leave to meet curfew.

Jack rummaged through the memories of their uncomplicated time spent together as he poured himself a fresh cup of coffee. Just as things had started to take on a nice routine, she had surprised him again. The Lounge had a lot of traffic, so the coffee was always hot, strong, and fresh. He was grateful because he needed the caffeine. He paused to look around; a few eyes met his as he scanned the room, but for the most part, people were there chatting and relaxing. Delighted in how his pack had settled in over the past few years, Jack allowed himself the luxury of being proud.

The war that had ravaged the park a decade earlier had left a group of fearful, angry Loup. Jack had stepped in, grabbed the reigns, and reorganized the structure. The first years of pack cohesion were a constant battle of wills; trying to convince them to act like a Pack and work together took more work than he had thought. With Jack's military training, he brought order and through rigorous discipline, he created a strong pack that was a force to be reckoned with. He had two long, satisfying sips of the dark, bitter brew before a fairly new member came loping in, interrupting his calm moment. Jack smiled as Karl managed to navigate the space with a gangly gait that most people would have tripped over.

*That young man is going to be the death of me. I know most people think he's stupid because they can't see past the goofy attitude, but there is more to that boy. I wonder why he is running like a fire is lit up under his ass. She's awake. Right, here I go to ruin her life. We have about two minutes to figure out how to make this easy for her.*

He gulped down the last of his coffee and walked back to his office. Of course, Kama would wake up during the few moments he left her side. Nerves made the walk back down the corridors incredibly short, and he found himself agitated. He had left the Omega to watch her; he didn't want Kama to wake up alone and scared. Jack wondered if he should have just stayed. He didn't know what the girl would tell Kama, and he sure didn't want her spilling the beans.

What is the Omega's name? Billie, Belle, Barb? Something. Anyhow, she should be able to keep Kama calm enough until I get down there. At least, I hope she's able to.

Jack walked down the rapidly shrinking tunnels trying to act normal. He slowed his pace the closer he got; he realized that he really didn't know what he would say to her. For the first time in a very long time, Jack, the master strategist, was stumped at how to proceed. He paused outside the door as he heard talking.

"Why am I here? Are you keeping me here?"

*The voice would be coming from a very irritated Kama. That is not a good sign. Although, I suppose it's better than the door hanging on its hinges.*

"No, I'm just waiting here until the Alpha gets back. He didn't want you left alone."

"Who is this Alpha person? And who the hell are you?"

"I'm Beth. Would you like some tea while we are waiting?"

He gave a mental nod to the Omega for having a calming voice. A long pause hung in the air and Jack could picture Kama giving the Omega a scrutinizing look.

"Okay, I guess tea would help. I am thirsty."

"What's your name?"

"Kamaria, Kama."

"Okay Kama, give me just a moment, and I'll bring back some tea and something to eat. You must be starved."

Beth's offer of tea made a perfect transition. It was the only reason he wouldn't punish for her leaving a cub alone, especially when he said to watch her until he got back. He waited for Beth to walk out and close the door, and then he pulled her aside.

"Knock before you bring the tea in. Go."

He walked into his office, shut the door, and willed himself to be calm and collected.

"Hi, Kama," he said.

He hated the look of relief that flooded her eyes. He knew she expected him to make sense of the questions and bring her some peace of mind. He could see the confusion swirl around and she tried her best to keep calm.

"Oh god, Jack. I am so glad you are here. Hopefully you can make them tell me what is going on."

Her voice never wavered, but he could hear the stress coloring it.

"It's okay, baby. I am going to try to help you make some sense of this," he said and then paused, not sure what to say next. "Do you know what is happening here?"

"I'm not sure. No one really wants to tell me what is going on. I mean, I woke up here, waiting for some Alpha person. But why am I even here? Last I knew, I passed out at some clinic."

Her voice began to rise in pitch and she began to shake. Jack went to her, sat close, and held her in his arms. She shook for a moment, but didn't cry. Jack almost wished she would, just to get it out of her system. So many changes were happening in her body and in her life that he wanted to her release the buildup of energy in a positive way, if possible.

"It's okay, Kama," he said. "Do you remember what happened tonight? Do you remember seeing the doctor?"

She sat up stiff in his arms. He smiled in her hair; even distressed, nothing got by her.

"Make sense of this? Just what do you know about all of this? I mean, why are you even here? Jack, what is going on?"

"Because of the attack and your fighting off those hoodlums, a change was triggered in you," he said.

Jack wished there were some easy way to break the news to her but it wasn't going to happen so easily she wouldn't let it. Kama was far too smart for her own good sometimes. She pulled away from him and turned to stare at him.

"What change?"

He opted for the no -bullshit way and hoped Kama would at least accept it from him. From the way she bored holes into him with her beautiful but awfully pissed off eyes, he didn't think the news would be welcome, no matter how he delivered it.

"You are Loup, Kama," he said. "Werewolf, for lack of a better term. Last night, you were attacked and because of the danger you had your First Change into your warrior form. By instinct, you came here for safety."

Jack watched a plethora of emotions play over her face. Disbelief gave way to shock as she relived parts of her memory from earlier in the night. She started to settle on upset, but instead gave way to rage with a swiftness he had not expected. His ears burned for a moment with the very colorful curses that she spewed like an acid fountain. She took a breath and focused on him again.

"What kind of crap is this, Jack? It's not a joke."

"No, honey, it is not."

A knock sounded at the door and paused their conversation. At his terse command, Beth came in, bringing a tray of tea and snacks for two. She set the tray on his desk and walked out as fast as possible. Jack noticed she never once looked up from the floor and shook in pure terror. He aimed his frustration and disgust at the Omega's fear, and snarled at her to lock the door behind her. He reached out and gave Kama a mug of steaming tea and waited for her to take a sip. He hoped that she would not dump it on him. Healing ability or not, it would hurt.

"I know this sounds unbelievable, but it's true. If you stop even for a moment, you will know it's true."

"Right, werewolves just happen to be real, and I just happen to be one."

"Yes."

He didn't know any other way to tell her. He knew it was hard to imagine the reality of supernatural creatures, even after having been in that form. Jack had accepted the fact that he was Loup, only because he had believed that he was hallucinating at the time of his own First Change. He hoped that having someone familiar explain things would make it easier, but Jack knew that having a moment of questioning reality, and even one's own sanity, was maddening.

"Kamaria, please listen to me. I know you aren't going to want to hear this or even accept the truth, but, baby, give me a chance to explain. This is a major change in your life; it is going to impact the way you live from now on. So just try, for one moment, to listen with an open mind."

She stood up and slammed the mug on his desk. Jack watched the amber liquid crest up the porcelain side and slosh over in gentle waves. He sighed in relief that it wasn't dumped on him. Kama had almost reached the door to his office before he realized her intentions.

*Shit, she is walking out on me again?*

He put one hand on the door to block her from opening it and braced himself for her fury. She turned on him, her lips pulled back into a snarl. His wolf saw his mate and pranced.

*Let her change and experience the truth again.*

He crowded her up against the door and put his face close to hers. Her pupils dilated in fear, his actions hit too close to being attacked for her and she bristled.

"Get the hell off me," she snapped.

"Make me," he growled.

He let his wolf come out just enough to lend a bass gravel tone to his voice and pinned her down with his stare. Her pupils widened even further and she went rigid. While she was staring at him, he allowed his eyes to shift. The whites darkened to black and his normal olive green bled into a lupine yellow. His eyes had a slight glow that betrayed his supernatural status and he saw her, for the first time, as his wolf. Through his changed eyes he saw her heart beat furiously in her chest; not just the physical movement but the sound waves that rippled away from her in a fast pulse. Her body gave off spikes of red-orange heat as she flushed in anger. However, most prevalent to him- and his wolf- was her lupine aura that surrounded and embraced her. It wavered as it wound around her, not settled.

*It would be so much easier to identify Loup if their aura was present before they changed. Of course we might as well paint a target on their heads. Her heat just spiked again. Damn, please don't let her change now. I don't need a fully enraged new Loup on my hands.*

Kama made a choked off squeaking noise, and he watched her throat convulse over and over. A rumbling growl issued from his throat before he knew it. His wolf sensed its mate, and it wanted her to change as well. Kama tried to back up further into the door, but upon meeting the barrier, her fight response kicked in. She struck at him then, pushing him as hard as she could. Jack tried not to smile as he slid back a few inches before bracing to a halt.

"Let me go."

He stared at her and closed in again, forcefully. The sudden movement caused her temperature to spike, and Jack watched her gorgeous brown eyes bleed into the lupine yellow he knew so well. He smiled. He grabbed her before she could make another protest and moved her two inches to the left, where he had a mirror on the wall.

"Look."

He used his Alpha voice for the command, and she complied. Jack doubted that she even realized what she was reacting to. She went shock still in his arms. She pressed back against his body, trying to escape what she saw in the mirror. Her head lay against his shoulder and two sets of Loup eyes stared back at her. The moment she tensed against him, he realized that it would be harder than he expected.

"Oh God, what did you do to me?"

The wailed statement was the last thing Jack expected to hear. He blinked and shifted his eyes back to normal.

"I didn't do anything to you. Kama, you are Loup."

"You did this, the night we were together. Oh my God, you bit me. You passed on this disease to me."

"No, I can't pass on anything. You are Loup because you were born Loup."

He looked down at her, amazed that she blamed him. He wasn't prepared to meet the despair in her eyes. In all the years Jack had been Loup, he had seen many cubs after their First Change, and they always blamed something at first; they blamed their ancestors, they blamed society, they blamed Fate, they blamed God... but no one had ever pointed the finger at him. Kama's accusation rendered him speechless.

"You cursed me, Jack. All the time at the hotel, you stood there and acted all superior and hurt because I didn't tell you my age? Your big speech about my telling lies and how betrayed you were? Well, isn't this great! You lied to me and cursed me into being a monster."

"This isn't a movie Kamaria. You aren't cursed."

"Then what happened to me?" she implored. "Tell me what the hell is happening to me."

"Well, last night you underwent what we call the First Change. To the point, you shifted into your werewolf warrior form," he said. "Our kind is called the Loup. Somewhere in your bloodline there was another who carried the gene. Many times it is so far removed that people end up surprised to be Loup since there hasn't been one in their family for generations. We are a different race all together, but are considered a hybrid between wolf and human. We look and act human in every other way, except we carry the genetic code enabling us to shift to wolf and warrior form. Our wolf personality is rather like a more active, instinctual sub-conscious. We don't know how many Loup are out there, especially in the city; they are often killed or locked away and medicated for being insane. Or in the worst case, they destroy themselves because their mind snaps."

He watched her digest all the information, and she gave a heaving sigh.

"What do you want from me?" she asked.

"From you, nothing. I only offer to help you," he said.

Kama slid to the floor and broke into hysterical laughter. Her eyes shifted back to brown and she shook with her emotional release. Jack knelt near her, trying to offer comfort without crowding her. She laughed until she wheezed, and then looked up at Jack.

"So what you are telling me is I am some wolf beast?" she asked. "Not to mention, it is a family trait, so someone else in my family line passed it on to me."

"You are not a beast. Loup aren't humans that turn into wolves; this is our natural state of being. Yes, somewhere in your family line there is another member with Loup blood. No, I am not joking. This is serious," he said. "You are Loup, as am I, as are the other people you have met here. They are part of my Pack."

"Packs?" she asked. "So we go around like wolves and run in groups?"

She broke back into giggles, and he watched her trying to make sense of all the information and then watched her throw it into the realms of unbelievable. She scoffed at him, moving away from him again. He tried to continue to give her evidence so she would have things to think over later when her mind calmed down and allowed her to think clearly.

"Yes, but we are more like a blend; the best traits that human and wolf have to offer," he said. "You are actually quite superior to regular humans."

"I don't need to be a wolf to be superior," she said. "I don't need this complication in my life. I have goals, and being a wolf is not one of them."

"Well sweetheart, you don't really have a choice. You are Loup, and thankfully you were found by this Den, and now we can help to take care of you until you get settled."

He pushed her hard to accept the truth and start to deal with it. She stood and paced, throwing glares his way, but didn't attempt to run for the door.

"I can take care of myself," Kama snapped. "I don't need you or any of your kind to take care of me. This is my life, and I'm not about to give it up because I have some rogue genetic that supposedly makes me a wolf."

"Being angry and resentful of this is as pointless as being angry at the color of your skin. It's not something you can change or should change; it's who you are. This is not a curse; it is your birthright, and soon I think you will find it to be a wonderful gift. " he said firmly. He had slipped into businessman mode, knowing no other way to deal with the situation.

"Well I refuse," she said. "I just won't change anymore and I'll just go on with my life as before."

"You can't," Jack said.

"Why can't I?" she asked. "You and your Pack have some rules about having a normal life?"

"Baby, your aura is screaming out to every Loup and every other kind of supernatural being out there, announcing your First Change," he said. "Every Loup will instinctively know what you are just by watching your aura spike. You are in such a flux; they can see your inner wolf warring with your human form. Until you accept what you are, and begin to make peace with yourself, your aura will stay split and be loud and noisy to anyone who knows how to look for it. Not every Loup is going to try to help you. If you don't come to grips with what you are, they will find a way to use it to their advantage."

He thought maybe she had started to come to grips with her situation. Just when he let his guard down, she leapt to her feet, tried to run to the door, and looked back for one second to see if he was going to follow her. Jack sighed, and then gave his huge marble-topped desk a hard shove in her direction. Instinctively, Kama stopped the desk with the palm of outstretched her hand.

"Do you know many people that can stop a desk with their hand?" he asked.

"It's not that heavy," she said.

"So, the grooves were made from what?" he asked.

Jack pointed out the thick gouges in the floor. Mentally, he cursed at the colossal bill forthcoming from his little show.

"Look at your hand; you instinctively shifted."

Kama looked at her left arm; it had lengthened, the muscles were more defined, and her nails looked darker and sharper. He watched her eyes widen in shock at the light coating of fur. She raised her right arm to compare, her mouth dropping open when her left arm shifted back as she watched it. She looked back up at him in horror.

"I know it's a scary thing you have been going through. My only goal is to keep you safe while you learn about who you really are," he said.

She nodded, still looking at each of her arms from time to time. It had started to sink in, and Jack hoped she had started to accept it. She walked back to his couch and sat down. Silence drew around them and for ten minutes he allowed her to run through everything he had told her in peace. He watched her shake her head in silent argument with herself and look up at him with venom in her eyes. She finally bent her head down on her knees and sighed.

"How does this Loup thing work? I mean, do I tazz out under a full moon or is this a full time thing?"

"Tazz out? I guess you mean shift," he said. "You are always Loup, just like you are always a woman. We are more instinctual and closer to our wolf nature when the moon is full. On the opposite end, when there is a new moon, we are more intellectual and closer to our human nature. We can always shift, no matter the phase of the moon, but we are at our peak during the three days of the full moon."

"Great, I guess I don't have to worry about walking by myself anymore," she said sarcastically.

"Kama, we have rules in place to ensure our survival," Jack said. "If the human world found out we existed, they would hunt us down based on all of the stupid stories out there. Not to mention other supernaturals don't always play well with each other. I am trying to give you the heads up as much as possible, because until you are fully trained you are vulnerable."

"Well, now what?"

"Now I will take you to meet a few members of my Den," he said.

"So where is this Den?" she asked.

From her tone of voice, he knew she had imagined some run-down looking crack house in the Bronx.

"You're standing in it," he said.

"Your office?" she scoffed.

"No, you're actually in the sub-tunnels underneath Central Park. Which is where this Pack of Loup runs," he said.

"Right, because I've seen so many werewolves running around Central Park. I mean, 800 acres of nothing but wolfy goodness," she said snidely.

Jack wanted to smile at her glib words, but he knew it would incite her. The last thing he wanted to do was topple the moment of calm and conversation they were having.

"We have an underground network that spans the Park," Jack said. "As time progressed and our kind was more feared than accepted, we made changes to allow us to live in relative peace. We have our place here, under the Park and to keep our privacy, we help people buy into the rumors of muggers and the like."

She nodded a few times, figuring it out. Jack stiffened when her lip curled in distaste; he had a feeling he wasn't going to like the next few moments. The look on her face alternated between hostility and rage.

"This is your Den?" she asked.

# Enter the Moon

"Yes, I am Alpha here," Jack said.

"So, you're the big boss?"

"Yes."

"Well, now what happens?" she asked.

"Honey, you belong to another life now. There is a lot for you to get used to, some new rules you will have to learn to deal with," he said.

"First, I am some hybrid wolf creature. Second, my boyfriend is the Alpha leader, and now, there are a bunch of new rules that I have to learn in order live amongst the world of the creepy," she said. "Sure, I'll just learn to deal with it."

"Most of the rules contribute to our group's safety. As Alpha, I am the one to keep things running efficiently," he said.

"And if I don't choose to follow these rules? What if I don't want you to be my Alpha? Hell, you could barely handle being my boyfriend and now you want me to look up to you like some big, great leader?"

Jack wanted to shake some sense into her. Scared or not, the diva routine was starting to push against his Alpha nature.

"Then, you can run alone. But it's dangerous, Kama, very dangerous."

"I want to go home, because my parents don't know that I am a werewolf, and I'm sure I'm late for curfew," she said. "I'm sure they won't accept my being Loup as a good excuse."

"The Park is your home now, too. We want you here; I want you here, and things will get better."

"Well, I don't know if I want to be here. In fact, I'm not sure I want you to be my Alpha."

The sneered title hurt more than he wanted it to.

He watched her head toward the door; she paused a moment and took a deep breath, then opened the door with a slam and left without looking back at him. Jack fought the urge to follow, but instead he stood and closed the door to his office. He knew she had a lot to think about, and until she came to grips with being Loup, he would give her the limited protection he could.

*Yea, because she will last long with her attitude. My Betas will demand either I bring her in or she runs alone and never comes back. I can't believe she blames me for this. I can't believe she walked out again.*

He walked to the mini bar and took out the scotch. He poured a jigger and sat down in his chair, staring at the desk that lay two feet away. His wolf still paced; he very much wanted to go after his mate. After a few more shots of scotch, they both quieted.

*I should have given her some scotch. I will give her one week, and then I will go after her and make her understand. I'll make her come home with me and be safe. I am the Alpha, dammit; I'm not about to be told no.*

He had allowed his mind to go pleasantly numb when one last thought ruined the tranquil state the scotch had begun to knit.

*And when she does come to grips with being Loup, how are we going to break it to her we can't date anymore because it could cost her life? And here I thought her age was the biggest hurdle.*

His wolf howled in frustration, and for the second time in an hour, his ears burned from the cursing.

## CHAPTER Eleven

Kama lifted her head from the report she had been working on for three hours. Her stomach rumbled reminding her a whole two hours had passed since she put any food in it. Her eyes were bleary and she wanted to go home, graze on whatever dinner leftovers she could find, and then pass out. Her phone blinked a reminder that she had a message.

*Yea, it's probably Jack again, trying to tell me to come back and be part of his pack. Like I want to be a werewolf. For the love of cheese, who in their right mind wants to be a werewolf? He makes it sound so simple: come and join the crew. Maybe something he might have mentioned when we were dating. Somehow, being a freak of nature and being an opera diva do not go hand in hand. It's been a week and three days, Jack. Let it go.*

She stuffed her laptop into her carry pack and headed out of the library's side door. It groaned slightly, but for the first time that she could remember, she did not have to put any "oomph" into opening it. The small ramp and walkway that ran alongside the garden were empty per usual, but she noticed the street seemed oddly quiet. Ever since her "experience", her senses had become super sensitive. Her hearing was amplified, which had only annoyed her as she strove to find quiet to study in; even the library was full of ambient noises that were unnaturally loud. Her vision had never been bad, but she noticed details she hadn't observed before; like textures of clothing fabrics and colors that were more vibrant and crisp. And her sense of smell… sometimes having a hyperactive nose led to a nauseated stomach and headache from the odor of millions of people roaming the city. Every scent was pungent and collided with olfactory senses. Looking around the sparse garden, she noticed only a few individuals, and the emptiness seemed a bit odd for a city like New York. Everything felt out of place and put her on edge, even if she wasn't sure she should be.

*Okay, so now I'm jumping at every freaking shadow? I have lived here for seventeen and a half years and nothing exciting has ever happened. Well, the unfortunate incident, but still, after knowing what I am, you would think I would jump less and not more.*

She looked around a bit, and started to walk home. After changing, she had found she needed the physical exercise. Being Loup felt like constantly having a live wire in her hand- extra energy which turned into the jitters and a sense of irritation if she didn't deal with it. And of course, it led to ravenous hunger; meaning her stomach was an ever empty void, which the obscenities it rumbled out called attention to. Kama walked off the ramp and stopped as voices rang out.

"Yes, you do know. You are going to tell me, or I will see to it you stay alive...long after you wish you weren't."

The female voice was laced with a malice Kama felt ride up her spine and make her hairs stand on end. Underneath her initial reaction, something else stirred.

"I swear! I don't have what you are looking for; I don't have any access to important things. I am just a low-level teller."

"No, you are just a liar. I know you are more than that because I killed all of the little lackey's to find out their manager's name. Guess what. Before they died screaming, they named you."

The loud arguing was coming from somewhere on her left and rounding the corner, Kama watched a small, dark-haired man being thrown to his knees, crying out in pain. She moved closer to take a good look. He looked like a businessman in a nice crisp suit. Holding him immobile in the kneeling position was a dark-skinned man in an oilskin duster; he looked like someone Kama would hate to make mad. A young woman, about Kama's age, stood in front of them both and was clearly in control. She wore her pale, blonde hair up in a ponytail and a black trench coat despite the warm evening. She looked so gaunt Kama figured a good wind would knock her over. As she watched, the blonde walked over to the small man and lifted him off the ground by the throat. Holding her breath, Kama stood transfixed.

"I swear I don't know anything about the transfer of funds," the man said. "Why are you doing this to me? I have no idea what you are talking about. If you would just let me call my manager, I'm sure we can get this figured out."

His voice came out in a squeaky wheeze. Kama bristled and felt her ire rise.

*This is how New York gets such a bad reputation. Why are you shaking down some guy behind the library? It's supposed to be a place of learning. I can't believe he is being attacked in my spot. This is my place. She ought to...*

Kama stopped her thoughts, startled by the sheer ferocity of her possessiveness. It didn't make sense to her, but she felt compelled to watch to make sure everything turned out okay.

"Okay, let's start this over. I am Stone, and I will be the one finding out where the missing funds have gone. You are Mr. Mercaw, the very stupid little man who thought that my Boss wouldn't notice the missing funds. He very much wants His money."

"I don't know what you are talking about; I don't remember making any important transactions."

"Help him remember," the blonde said.

Her thug took out a gun and screwed on a silencer. Stone released Mr. Mercaw, and he fell to the ground in a heap. He stayed there, and Kama wondered if he would ever get up again. Her shoulder muscles knotted as she eyed Stone. Part of her wanted to force the blonde out of her territory. The rational side of her wanted to run away screaming.

She watched the scene intently; she moved closer to investigate and didn't quite clear the wall. As her jacket brushed the wall, it made the barest whisper of a sound. To Kama's surprise, Stone turned and looked at her. She met the woman's gaze, noticing the drawn look of sheer irritation at being interrupted.

*Oh hell, she sees me and looks mighty pissed off. Bitch. Crap Kama, pull it together. You are going to get yourself shot. Okay, maybe I can act like I just walked into this little scene instead of looking like I am being nosey.*

Stone walked over to her, and Kama noticed how the thug grabbed the little man and dragged him along. She tried to figure out how to knock the woman down and run away before she became New York's newest casualty.

"Well hello there pretty one," Stone said. "You just couldn't help yourself, could you? Saw a bit of action and maybe wanted to use the drama for a scene in the pithy, creative novel you are writing?"

Kama looked at the woman, but said nothing; her voice just didn't want to work. Stone scared her. She stood shock still as the woman approached and caressed her shoulder in seeming affection. The look in her eyes made Kama want to shudder, so she tried her best to look small and innocent. A smell she couldn't quite name curled up into her nose and made her nauseated, like the trench coat needed a treatment or two at the dry cleaners. The feeling of something wrong hit her in the pit of her stomach, and Kama shifted her stance, just a bit waiting until she could safely escape.

*Wrong is such a weak word. I feel like I am going to be sick. There is something just not right here. Mostly my still being here.*

"Interested in our little business, hmmm?"

"No, I'm just on my way home," Kama said. "No one ever uses the back door; I'm surprised to see anyone out here."

She kept her voice high pitched, sounding young and scared. The cold look in the woman's eyes didn't waver, and an even cooler smile slid onto her face.

"A late night of studying for the ever diligent student. Aren't you just too sweet for words? And you just happened to come upon our little meeting and couldn't help yourself. You just had to see what we were doing."

"No, I actually didn't notice until you came over. I am on my way home; my mom just called me for dinner."

"What do you suppose is happening here?"

"I don't know," Kama said. "It's not my business, so I didn't pay attention."

"You are a very poor liar, my dear," Stone said.

She waved the thug close so Kama could see the gun in his hand.

"I think you know what is about to happen here."

"You're mugging somebody," Kama said.

"Well, I prefer the term torturing, but sure, mugging works," Stone said.

Despite the scary woman's chipper voice, the urge to throw up grew stronger in Kama. The smell coming off the woman turned her stomach over. She couldn't quite describe it because she had never smelled something so completely foul. Rotten food mixed with stale urine and the carcass of a dead thing might be close, but not quite bad enough.

"Well then, I have a deal for you. You help us out, and I will let you go, no questions asked. Does it sound like a good deal to you?" she asked.

"I don't know how to do anything," Kama said.

Stone gave her a look that sent a shiver of pure terror up Kama's spine. She took the gun from her thug and held it out by the handle. The small man on the ground seemed to shrivel up. Kama looked around, trying to find an exit point, but something kept her there.

*We need to leave. She is going to shoot us. Wait until she is done talking and then run. Why are we still here? This is our library; she's intruding. No, fight. We need to go, she scares me.*

Her ego wouldn't let her leave her territory undefended but the realistic side of her brain kept yelling at her.

"Oh, it's quite simple. you just help us take care of our friend here and then you can go. See, darling girl, this silly little man took some money from my boss. He was supposed to buy some goodness for us in L.A., but he failed that venture. So imagine our surprise, when my boss needed his money for an acquisition in Pennsylvania, and it wasn't there. You can see how wrong that was, can't you?"

Kama flinched as Stone pressed the gun into her hand. The weight dragged her hand down, and the cold metal chilled her on a level far from physical. Kama looked at the gun with absolute revulsion. She threw it behind her and tried to bolt, but the blonde stood in her way.

"Well, that was just plain stupid. How do you expect to help us now?" she asked. "Do you plan to kill him with your bare hands? Maybe choke the life out of him?"

*She could try being a bit less mocking while she expects me to kill someone. Stupid bitch, we should kill her and be done with it.*

"How about letting him go?"

Kama knew the tone was snarky and condescending, but the comment slipped out anyhow. Stone raised her hand, and pain exploded across Kama's cheek before she could detect any other motion. She could feel the blood drip from the cut across her cheekbone and down her chin. Her head snapped back, and anger fired through her veins at the insult. Stone pulled her up by her shirt, flicked her nose, and in fury, Kama struck back. Her fingers curled into a fist and punched the woman in the side of the head. Blonde hair rippled as her head rocked, but Stone stood there with a bemused look on her face.

"You know, you have spunk, kid. I could almost like you," Stone said. "That's the second time in ten years someone has hit me."

Before Kama could wrench out of the strong grip, Stone lashed out and this time, when her fist made contact with Kama's face, it propelled her backwards. She found herself lifted off her feet and flew through the air. Stone advanced on her, and for the first time, Kama listened to the fear coursing through her body.

*We need to leave now. We are outmatched, and she will kill us. Oh God, where is Jack?*

Another realization hit Kama.

*She must be Loup, too. Who else could hit me so hard that I would be knocked off my feet? It's just not possible for a human so tiny. Oh hell, she is mad.*

From the look on Stone's face, she was intent on doing some serious damage in retribution; it further outlined just how much she would enjoy doing harm to Kama. She quickly scrambled to her feet and moved as fast as her human form could. She deftly ran through the city, thankful that the streets were mostly empty at 11:00 P.M. and she didn't have to weave in and out of bodies.

*I hope she isn't following me. Only a few more blocks; I have to be close to the park. Please don't let her follow me. Just a few more steps and I'll be safe.*

Relief came at the end of the next block when she could see the entrance to the park, and hope began to rise. At last Kama looked over her shoulder, to make sure no one followed. Thankfully, Stone was nowhere in her sight. When she turned around she ran fully into a petite, blonde barricade. The woman did not so much as flinch as Kama's one hundred and thirty pound frame crashed into her full tilt. Fear iced her veins as she was lifted up off the ground and held before a coldly menacing face.

"You thought you could get away? You made me run. Do you know how much I hate to run?"

Kama tried to twist out of her grip, panic giving her some strength, and she almost got away. Stone's face stretched into a malicious grin, and wicked-looking fangs descended as her fingers tightened around Kama's arm. She felt the bones pop and shatter.

*Oh God, she has fangs. Do Loup have fangs? Do I have fangs? She broke my arm. We have to leave; we need safety.*

The pain hit her full force; the panicked screaming in her mind reached deafening levels, and survival became her first priority. Her instinct took over, and she shifted into wolf form, snarling at the astonished blonde who dropped her due to the shifting mass. Kama hit the ground and after ripping the tangle of clothes off her legs. All fours she ran the few remaining feet into the dark of the park.

"Get the fuck outta here," Kama heard Stone say.

More curses followed as she tried hard to outrun the terror suffocating her. She ran as fast as she could toward the interior of the park, trying to figure out how to get below. The scent of the park surrounded her, and Kama almost calmed when she was tackled to the ground, and then through it. The world spun and pulled with a sickening wrench. When it stopped spinning, she found herself in a bright circle of light; on either side of her were shadowy voids. She seemed to be surrounded by a shimmering wall of light; then she was given a nudge and stumbled into a small room. She looked around in a panic, ready to bite and claw her way to freedom if she had to, but on the ground next to her sat Lorna. Relieved, Kama shifted back to her normal form. She looked over, ready to thank Lorna, but stopped, taken aback by the angry expression on the woman's' face.

"What the hell is wrong with you? Do you have any idea how many people just saw you?" Lorna snapped. "You may have just given away the location of our Den."

"I came out of the library to see her mugging the little guy and then the blonde woman broke my arm and then she had fangs and I panicked," Kama said. "I didn't know what else to do and Jack said I could come back. I need help."

She had gasped out her words; fear making them a tangled jumble that she hoped made sense. Lorna placed a hand on her broken arm and pain coursed through Kama. Heat and the snapping of bones broke through the panic with an explosion of agony. Shock crashed over her like a wave, and she had to concentrate on keeping conscious.

"What woman? Calm down, and talk to me," Lorna command.

"Stone, near the library, this blonde girl had this little guy at gun point and I walked up on them. She wanted me to shoot him, but I threw the gun and then these fangs came out," Kama said. "And she smelled horrible."

She broke into horrified, quiet tears, trying to get out the details. Lorna stood and snarled with an odd look on her face.

*I just want to go home and have my Mom hug me and tell me it will be okay. Instead, I am here, in a dark little room, being questioned for trying to save my own life.*

"What did she look like?" Lorna asked.

"She's about my height, petite, blondish hair, with cold, dead eyes," Kama said.

"And she had fangs too?"

"Yes, I said that. I ran most of the way here as a girl, except the last block. She broke my arm, and I knew if I didn't get away she would kill me, so I changed into a wolf. Oh gods, I changed into a wolf. All of my stuff is back there."

Kama brushed the tears off her cheeks with the backs of her hands. Lorna threw her head back and howled. The sound echoed down the tunnel halls and resonated much louder than Kama expected a human voice to.

"I'm sorry. I didn't mean to give us away; I just didn't want to die."

Lorna growled, not aimed at Kama, but rather the information she gave. She shrugged out of her clothes, shifted into a compact, black wolf, and let out a short series of yips. Upon getting an answer she looked at Kama.

"Stay here. Others will be around to get you," the words were a bizarre mix of growls and words.

*So I have to stay here, alone? Wow, she just got naked in front me. Do they all get naked? Oh god, I am naked. I am just sitting here naked. Why didn't I notice this earlier? Well, probably the dying part. Oh shit, she said something about others. Others are going to see me naked.*

Kama sat in the room, curled in on herself like a small child. The acrid smell of cigar smoke alerted her to the presence of someone else. She didn't know how much time had passed, but it felt like hours. A bundle was tossed at her.

"Come on, gal. No use for you to sit in the dark by yourself. Get dressed and come on out."

"Who are you? Can I speak to Jack- I mean -the Alpha?"

The bundle turned out to be sweatpants and a sweatshirt, and she quickly dressed. A calloused hand gently took her arm and helped her over the ledge of the door that she would have definitely tripped over. The smoke wafted into her eyes and nose. Kama coughed and fanned her face.

"They call me The Judge, and we'll go to his office once we get a few things straightened out. So, what happened?"

Kama reiterated the story, giving as many details as she could. When she started to shake and falter in her steps, he placed a hand under her elbow and continued to lead her down the hall.

"Sounds like you have your first run in with a vampire. First we've had around here in a bit."

"Vampires are real?" she asked.

"Yes, they are, and pretty much just as nasty as the movies would have you believe."

"I didn't realize they would be so strong," Kama said with a shudder. "She broke my shoulder with one hand."

"Yep, they are damned strong. Nasty undead freaks," he said. "But now, we need to talk about you messing up."

Kama felt cold to the core and her brain started to shut down. She took a deep breath trying to get herself calm; she had a feeling it would be a very long evening.

"So what happens next?" she asked.

"Lorna is out there searching for the vamp and will kill it. Now let's get back on to figuring out what to do with you."

She watched him calmly smoke his cigar, and he watched her back.

"You had your Change last week and then decided to go off. But then at first sign of trouble, come running back here-as a wolf, no less- and exposed you and us. It is going to take some working out to make this go away," The Judge said. "Seems to me you aren't so good at being your own; but you can't come and go as you please just because life gets a little harder than you expected. Happens when you are Loup. Time to figure out your life, little one."

Kama stood stunned at the dressing down she had just received until her anger took over. The shock from the evening's terror dissipated and rage coursed through her.

"Did you want me to die?" Kama asked. "Fuck you. What the hell else was I supposed to do? He said I could come back, but if it's such a hardship then I'll leave. Then if I die, you won't have to worry about me breaking protocol anymore, asshole."

She turned to walk out, but his commanding voice demanded her attention.

"Stop."

The voice rang out, and terrifying was too a mild a word for the emotion that curled through her body and forced her to stand still. Kama refused to cower; instead she squared her shoulders and got ready to argue. She turned to face him, seething in cold fury.

"Yes?" she asked.

"First off, you will stay here where you are safe. Don't act any more an idiot than you already have tonight," The Judge said. "Secondly, New York is crawling with vampires and other supernatural beings. The reality is you were bound to have a run in with something sooner or later. Lucky for you, you got to take your head out of your own ass instead of having it handed to you."

"Are you for real?"

Kama watched the old man inhale on his cigar, but nothing could have prepared her for when he blew the stream into her face. She coughed as he spoke in a slow drawl.

"As real as your broken arm, which should be healing. Did Lorna set it? Good. Now let's get back to helping you understand a few things. You can't come here because you are scared if you aren't one of us. So make up your mind to either be with us or not."

"It's not like it was a calculated move. She broke my arm and I freaked out," she said.

He continued as if she hadn't spoken.

"Your choice is to stay here and be a part of our Pack with all the protection and learning. Or go back out there on your own and deal with vampires by yourself."

Kama still mulled over his words as they stopped in front of a door. The Judge knocked, opened it, and pushed her in ahead of himself. She looked into Jack's green eyes and for the first time that evening, relief washed over her. A cloud of smoke enveloping her reminded Kama that the Judge still stood behind her.

"Seems the best choice is to stay here," she said.

"Well, the gal isn't near stupid as I thought. She's all yours for tonight, seeing as she wanted to talk to you. But come six tomorrow night, if she's still going to be one of ours, she needs to meet me at the fountain."

Kama watched The Judge walk out of Jack's office in a slow saunter. She still wasn't sure what to make of the man.

"Hi," she said.

"Guess we need to talk."

"Is he for real?" she asked.

Jack's smile caught Kama off guard. She watched him push the door shut and smiled in relief at the concern in his warm eyes.

*I have missed him. Why is this whole thing so darn complicated? Okay, so how I do apologize and get a kiss? I wonder if Jack will want to kiss me after he realizes what I just did. Probably not. I just endangered his group. If I join his group, do I work for him...? Hell, he's asking me something.*

"What happened? I heard Lorna's howl of pursuit."

Kama started to cry, burying her hands in her face. Mortified she had just broken down; she stood tightly compressed and didn't even look up Jack. She felt his arms encircle her, and hold her. She talked through her sobbing, not sure if she made any sense but she needed to get it out. For the first time in a long time, Kama felt vulnerable and she hated it.

"A vampire attacked me tonight and after a chase, she hurt me. Then in a panic, I ran here, only to get yelled at because I was in wolf form. But I didn't know what else to do."

"Are you okay?" he asked.

"I don't know," she said. "I don't know about anything anymore, Jack. I thought I could just not be Loup. You warned me, and I still thought it wouldn't matter and could never affect me. So now, I don't know what to do."

Kama relaxed in his arms, and leaned her head against his chest as he pulled her closer. He rubbed her back and rocked her in a soothing manner. She wrapped her arms around him and held on, as if for dear life. She sobbed into his chest until she ran out of tears.

"You are safe, and that's what matters," he said.

"When I tried to fight back, she shrugged it off like what I did to her didn't even faze her. I hit her as hard as I could, and she laughed," Kama said. "I don't want to think of what I will have to do to survive."

"Don't worry about it just now. When you accept what you are, it becomes a part of you. You will learn to harness it and use it when you want to, not in reaction to fear or anger only."

"I guess. Is it really going to make a difference, if what I am fighting is so powerful? And if I can win, then why am I so scared?"

Kama's voice had taken on a flat quality, and she tried to compose herself. She didn't like not getting over the shock of the evening and displaying such weakness to him. Her mind still struggled with vampires being real and, there were even more supernaturals she had yet to encounter.

"Because this is a frightening thing, Kama. Just because you are Loup doesn't mean you don't have emotions. Quite the opposite. You are more in touch with them because of your nature," Jack explained. "Most Loup are terrified, and some don't survive their first encounter. Vampires look like regular people, but you can smell the evil and power-sickness on them because they are a mockery of Luna's cycle; they are dead things still existing, so they are pushing against the fabric of what should be."

"How do I kill it?" Kama said.

"Their powers differ, but most seem vulnerable to claws and teeth, taking their heads off, fire, and sunlight, of course. Shooting them will slow them down, but it is always better to go for the kill. In your case, you did the right thing by running."

"I knew I would be dead after she got done with the little guy. It got worse when she wanted me to kill him. I hate all this, new creepy werewolf, vampire, and who-knows-what-else stuff," Kama said.

"It's only natural you would be in shock," Jack said. "Most of us never knew werewolves were real until we became them, so don't feel alone in this. It's what I tried to tell you before; we are here for you."

"But to have a safety net, I have to be a part of your Pack. How does it work, Jack? I don't know I can do it."

"You are always welcome at the Park, if you join our group; then any of the Loup here will take care of you. They will be closer than family to you," he said. "They all will be marked with our Pack Claw so you will be able to recognize them."

Kama watched him roll up his sleeve, until she saw the tattoo she had noticed in Los Angeles. The black marks were fashioned in to two mirrored crescents connected by a line, and each cupped a full moon. She tried to keep her mind on what he told her about how it marked each person in his pack. She learned that it was only given once a person had decided to join as a full member of the pack. Her mind thought back to the party in L.A. and wondered if the tattoos she had seen had been a Pack Claw for werewolves there.

"So The Judge mentioned some sort of training and stuff?"

"Yes, ever since I became Alpha, I made sure that we, as a pack, would be able to defend ourselves. So we practice defense and other training to make sure if we do have a run-in, we aren't easily over powered."

Kama looked at him, trying to let everything sink in.

So, doesn't it seem weird to him to have this werewolf army in the heart of Central Park? I mean, isn't this the stuff the movies are made about? Defense class- wow, he makes it sound like we are at war. I wonder if I will have to get a tattoo on my arm.

"When do I start all of this stuff? When do I get my tattoo?"

"Training will start tomorrow if you are choosing to join our pack," Jack said. "And you will get your Pack Claw when you officially are an adult in the pack."

"Great, more drama to add to my schedule," Kama said. "Like I don't have a busy enough life to contend with."

"It will take some getting used to, but I have no doubt you will be fine. Lucky for you, you were at full strength tonight. Despite what common lore would have you believe, our big secret lies in the phase of the moon; we are more like humans during the new moon, running on intellect, and more warrior-like during the full moon, running on instinct. In the half-phases we flux between wolf and human, depending on our lineage."

"So, this means exactly what?"

"It means during a new moon, you have higher logic and reasoning, but you are more easily hurt. During a full moon, you are nigh indestructible, but you are driven by instinct and high passion. For instance, have you noticed your arm doesn't hurt anymore?"

Kama looked down at her arm in amazement and flexed it. She hadn't thought about it in a while. She knew it had been broken, the blazing pain had attested to the break, but now, she could move it easily.

"Okay, so I need to stay home during the new moon and play it safe. No wonder the full moon has such a bad reputation. I can only imagine the kind of silliness and dares people try."

"I don't know if I am comforted by the gleam of mischief in your eyes," Jack said.

"Well, it's not like I am planning to sky-dive from a building or anything, but so far, invulnerability is the best part of being Loup I have heard about."

"Maybe, but even still, we don't go crazy with it."

"Oh come on, can't we even have a bit of fun?"

"Kama, we have rules in place to ensure our survival," Jack said. "Werewolves and vampires are not the only supernaturals; there are ghouls, benders, and I'm sure things I have yet to discover. Then we have the human world, and if the human world found out we existed, they would hunt us down based on all of the stupid stories out there."

She sat down on a chair and looked at him. His very serious tone and posture made her a bit nervous. Whatever he would say next would be hefty, she was sure of it.

"So, what are these rules?" she asked.

"A very simple set of three: Do not let others know the location of our pack Den, don't reveal our shifted form and do not engage any other supernatural in public, if you can help it," he said.

"Okay, so I have broken all three in one shot. Damn. At least the rules are reasonable," Kama said. "They make sense, since I doubt humans would let us live. So, I have to keep a low profile."

She rolled the word "humans" around her tongue- for the first time excluding herself from the grouping. It felt weird, but Kama figured she had best learn to accept it.

"In a nutshell, yes. So, are you going to join us?" Jack asked.

"Yes, I will," Kama said. "But I know this is going to take time to get used to, so be patient okay?"

Kama allowed him to escort her out of his office, trying hard not to fall over and give in to hysteria. They exited a door and when she looked back she noticed they had just come from the Children's Cottage. She even allowed Jack to call his car but she rode home alone. Once in her bed, she tried to decompress.

*I hope it gets easier.*

The thought replayed over and over until she fell asleep.

# CHAPTER Twelve

Kama walked with agony, but nothing could stop her movement towards her ultimate prize. Only four days had passed since her run-in with the vampire, and the last three had been spent in the torturous situation known as Combat Class. Jack had explained some of her new responsibilities would involve learning how to fight, so, in case she had another altercation she would be prepared. After her encounter with Stone, Kama thought it sounded like a great idea. Their Pack had a regime set in place, and she had been given her schedule.

*Yea, it all sounded easy enough, like a life-saver even, except Jack neglected to tell me he ran this place like his own private militia. Is it even possible that I can want to puke my brains out and eat French fries at the same time? That Aturus dude must get his kicks from seeing how many people have to crawl away from his class. Okay, we're almost there, just a few more feet. I didn't know it was possible to hurt like this. Hell, I didn't know I had so many muscles in my body. Who would have ever thought I would learn to fight like a thug?*

Because her thoughts consumer her, Kama didn't pay attention and she tripped over a small rise in the pavement and stumbled in to Beth.

"Sorry," she said. "I think the sidewalks know how much pain I am in and move just to make it more difficult for me."

Her walking partner smiled and shrugged, but said nothing. In fact, Beth moved to the side to give Kama the majority of the space. From the slow gait, she knew Beth felt the after-effects of the workout also. Knife fighting was much harder than in looked. She looked over at her new friend and tried once again to figure her out; something about her thus far didn't add up.

They had met three days ago when Kama arrived at her training session early, as per her habit, and found Beth standing against a wall. The young woman stood about five foot four, blondish hair pulled back into a tight braid against her head, and hazel eyes in a round face. She had small and delicate features Kama might have associated with a pixie, excepting she knew Beth was a werewolf.

"Hi," she had said. "I'm Kama."

Beth's eyes had widened, but she had smiled in a friendly manner.

"I'm Beth," the young woman said. "We actually met the night you first came in. Welcome to Aturus's class. It will make you hurt; you might even bleed."

Kama had some vague recollection of the night of her Change and shrugged.

"I don't really remember too much about what happened that first night," she said. "Chaos doesn't really explain it. So. Let's go back to the part where you said this class will make me hurt?"

Beth nodded and then clamped her lips shut as more people entered the room. Kama looked at her curiously for about a second. Then she felt like she had become a piece of prime beef on display to some hungry predators. Every eye found its way to her as each person walked into the room. No one said anything to her, but she could feel their curiosity like small electric shocks.

Kama reacted like she did when the people she went to school with, at Pembleton, acted snobby. She straightened her spine and prepared herself to meet a challenge. Before she could say anything, a tall, bald man walked into the room. Kama had never met him before, but the way the class snapped itself to attention, she knew someone important had arrived.

"I hope you are warmed up. Let's begin."

That had been all the warning Kama had before weapons were rolled out in the middle of the floor, and everyone started grabbing them and pairing up. Kama was left without a partner.

*Well, this sucks. New to class and I don't even get a partner. It's like being picked last for a team. Maybe I can just watch this time, to get the hang of things. Oh shit, why is he walking over to me?*

Kama watched Aturus approach. As he drew closer, she swallowed hard. He was at least six foot three with dark chocolate skin, surprisingly light caramel eyes, and a body that seemed to be made of chiseled perfection. He moved toward her, and she didn't spy an extra roll anywhere.

*Damn, he is a beautiful man. He is sculpted like a model; I almost want to touch him. Except, he is here to make me fight with a knife, and I would imagine that he is not going to go soft on me just because I am a newbie.*

Where Jack had a sleek, taught figure, this guy was ripped like a body builder with tight, corded muscles. Aturus could have been on the cover of any fitness magazine.

*Okay so why hasn't he handed me on to an upper classman or something? Doesn't he have a class to run? Are you serious? Oh hell, I am so in trouble. I really don't think I want his personal attention, ever.*

Kama stopped her internal rambling then, because he stood in front of her.

"You're the new cub. You get to work with me."

*So much for a greeting or welcome. New cub, pfft. Why does everyone call me that like it's a bad thing? Why is he tossing a sword at me?*

"Ever held a knife, Diva? Ever hit anything in your life?"

"I hit an E above high C on a quarter note," Kama quipped back.

"I hope you are a fast learner," Aturus said, his eyebrow raised at her sass. "This is how you hold it properly."

The class ended an hour and twenty minutes later, and only Kama's pride kept her on her feet. In reality, she wanted to fall into a heap on the floor, curl into a little ball, cry copiously, and lay there until her hair stopped hurting. Instead, she walked to the stack of towels, took one, and blotted her face and neck dry. She felt someone behind her, and turned to find

Aturus.

"Nice work. I can appreciate someone who comes in giving their all. See you tomorrow."

*I am surprised he had a sort of compliment for me. After the beat down and the do-it-right-or-get-poked mentality, that was the last thing I expected. I think Jack has a lot of explaining to do; he said combat-to-be -safe class, not kill them on the first day. I think I will go find some food and a pain pill, because this workout... Crap did he say tomorrow?*

Kama threw her towel into the corner with the others and noticed she and Beth were the only two left in the room. She smiled at the girl and got one in return. Beth appeared to be just as tired as Kama. She decided to leave before another class started.

"Did he say tomorrow, or did I hallucinate?"

"He definitely said tomorrow," Beth said. "We do combat every day."

Kama groaned. Beth gave a weak chuckle, and their friendship started. After three days of being integrated into the Park and all its routines, Kama felt more acclimated, but the sense of unease still plagued her, like she didn't quite fit in despite being Loup. She had imagined it would be easy, seeing as they all had a huge secret in common, but the others were still aloof. Beth helped things a bit; having at least one friendly face in the crowd made the outsider feeling fade some, but everyone else- they were quite a different story.

*Come on, we can do this. One foot after the other, there we go. Just remember what waits for us up there. Our prize for making it through one more day.*

Kama looked at Beth again as they walked up a slight incline. She didn't shriek like she wanted to as her legs protested the climb. She focused on her friend so she wouldn't have to think about the agony in her very bruised and sore back and buttocks.

*Beth is so unlike the other Loup around here. She is just so quiet and unassuming most of the time. I would have figured she would be as loud and rowdy as the rest of them. It's almost like she shrinks into the wall when anyone comes in the room. Then again, maybe she is just trying to get mentally prepared for our "Torture by Aturus" class. I don't quite get these other people. They act like they want to talk to me, but don't because they aren't sure about me. I wonder if they think I am stuck up. Heck, I know stuck up- I've gone to Pembleton my whole life. This is a different vibe. Almost like they are sizing me up or something.*

Her thoughts broke off as they crested the hill and their goal came into sight. She turned and gave the big thumbs up to Beth who returned it; neither wanted to waste precious breath on unnecessary talk. Their friendship had been building over the last few days and really helped Kama in getting used to all the new craziness she had been facing. She looked forward to chatting with Beth, once their treats were in hand.

*You know, Beth is the one person who doesn't seem to have any reservations about me. Everyone else is just impossible to read; it's like they want to get to know me but they are holding back for some reason. I mean, I can see the curiosity in their eyes, but no one else talks to me.*

Kama's stomach rumbled, breaking her train of thought with an all-consuming hunger. Her appetite had gone from "teen age boy" to "Olympic athlete" status in just a few days. Even her mother had noticed how much she had been putting away. Not like Kama had anything to complain about. The driving hunger gave her the perfect excuse to indulge in her guilty pleasure: hotdogs.

*If Mom even had a clue I was eating anything less than her five-star cuisine, she would melt the flesh from my bones with her glare, which would just be the start. How does she do it? She must have some kind of motherly "you're eating hunk food crap" power. Who knows - heck who cares! There is the hotdog cart now. I finally get rewarded for my hour and a half of hellish torture. Besides, this is all Beth's idea, so I am completely exonerated of any decisions to eat simulated meat products. I just went with my friend to get a snack. Who am I to tell her she can't have a hotdog?*

Kama watched the hotdog vendor's smile get larger as she and Beth approached. She got the impression Beth frequented the cart and hoped for a good hook up. She pushed the pain aside and sped up just a bit as the aroma filled her nose and made her mouth water.

"Hey, Vinnie," Beth said.

"Hi, Miss Beth. How are you today?"

"Just call me Beth, and I'm great. Can I please have three with extra mustard?"

The smile fell off Kama's face and was replaced with a look of abject shock and horror as she watched Vinnie extract three pale, limp tubes of something and place them in hotdog buns. He slathered them with mustard and gave them to Beth with a small flourish. Kama stood there silently trying to make sense of the calamity that had just happened when Vinnie flashed her a bright smile.

"You would like some food too?" he asked.

She nodded in mute confusion watching Beth start to eat. Her attention snapped back when Vinnie held out a tofu-dog to her. The smell of old, moldy feet assaulted her nose. Her disappointment and anger at being offered tofu nonsense instead of her hard-earned hotdog made her want to slap him for his stupidity. She resisted shaking Beth out of her crazy place and tried to make sense of the rude intrusion on her reality. She settled for glaring at Vinnie; she would talk to Beth later.

"I want seven hotdogs. The real ones, you know? The kind made with the unnamable meat product, with mustard please," she said. "And can we get a few waters?"

Vinnie paled at her tone, and Kama internally nodded her approval at the speed with which he put together her food. She paid and noticed Beth had made it through one of the rubber dogs, but had been giving hungry glances to the bounty in Kama's hands. They began to walk back into the park and as they approached a garbage bin, she unburdened her friend of the two travesties in her hands.

"Oh, my lunch," Beth said.

"Those couldn't be considered lunch. They weren't even real," Kama said.

She smiled at her own statement; like hotdogs were real food. Beth objected half-heartedly as Kama handed over three of her own hotdogs. She stared so hard at the dogs; Kama expected a line of drool to escape her friend's mouth at any time.

"Oh no, Kama, this is your food; I can't take it."

"Of course you can. I can't eat seven hotdogs, yet."

Beth's look of anticipation spoke much louder than her words, as did the look of bliss that covered her face when she bit into her first hotdog.

Kama grinned, took a bite, and too was transported to the little piece of nitrate-filled heaven. They walked through the Park toward the Chess house. It would be nice to sit after all the walking, even if it meant going up some stairs.

Kama savored each bite, knowing it would be some time before she could indulge again. The daily workouts would take care of the high fat content of the treat, but her body seemed to demand higher quality of food. She hadn't craved much junk food over the past few weeks. She knew her mother would be thrilled to hear that confession.

*It's not like I don't enjoy her culinary creations. Heck, the woman has a thriving business here in Manhattan. But it would not kill her children to have a hotdog or two once in a while. Although, I wonder why Beth avoids them; she's Loup. Shouldn't she crave real meat? Tofu is awesome in stir fry and soups, but as a meal by itself, ugh.*

Kama enjoyed Beth's reaction as she bit into her second hotdog and for once, saw a true smile cover her friend's face. She had seen Beth smile at her over the past few days, but it had always stopped short of being real. They climbed up the stairs with no apparent hurry, but Kama sighed in pleasure when she finally got to sit down and rest her legs.

"I think Aturus is really impressed with you," Beth said.

"Yea? What gives you that idea? He does nothing but yell, smack me in the head, or try to stab me. Even better, he likes to prove how spoiled I am by making me fall on my butt anytime he can. The only impressive thing I've done so far is not puke my brains up after every workout."

"He gave you a compliment on the first day," Beth said.

Kama snorted and took a too big mouthful of her hotdog. She ignored Beth's expression of amusement as she tried not to choke on her excess.

"He gave me a compliment so I would come back," Kama said. "After bruising me up, he saw the look in my eye and knew I would need some encouragement."

"Oh wait, you will get to know Aturus. He doesn't give compliments just to give them. He would rather beat you into submission than entice you."

Kama chewed another bite and thought about it, shrugged at Beth and picked up her third hotdog. Her look of despair must have comical because Beth broke out into deep laughter. The rich sound was so melodic and infectious, Kama joined in. Again she wondered why Beth held back so much.

"Maybe I am his new pet or something," Kama said.

"Somehow I doubt it," Beth said. "He will just work you harder, so you keep the 'wanting to puke' feeling. Think about it, Kama; he teaches at least six classes a day, and ours is the easiest."

"Oh hell. I bet it's too late to look like a slacker now, huh?"

Kama expected Beth to laugh at her joke, but no sound came. She looked at her friend and was surprised her clouded expression. Their jovial mood had vanished much like a tide would wash away a sandcastle. Beth sat still, hunched over in a protective position.

*Crap, I bet Aturus is behind us. Now what have I said in the past few minutes he might have heard? Heck, how good is a werewolf's hearing anyhow? I mean, if he could hear us talking, wouldn't I have heard him walking up the steps or something? Or maybe Beth can hear better than me, so she heard him coming before me.*

To confirm her suspicions, Kama heard purposeful footsteps behind them and tried to think of an appropriate apology to keep her from having a true class from hell. She realized that there were more than one set of feet making the sound.

"Well girls, what do we have here? I believe it's our darling Beth. Hello, Beth."

Kama straightened up at the tone of voice. The sneer came through loud and clear, as did the intent of harassment. She turned to find four young women, about her age, closing in on her and Beth. The slender blonde clearly was in charge as the other three walked behind her and followed her lead.

"Hello, Sophie," Beth whispered.

Kama watched her friend shrink even more; Beth's eyes were locked on the middle of the checkerboard table in front of her. Kama could feel the misery roll off her, so she turned to look at the women causing such distress.

Sophie, had pale complexion, free of any blemishes, but her nose had a bump and stood away from her face. Her eyes were way too small, and her ears were downright tiny. Despite being thin, she moved in a gangly fashion, and her yellow hair dangled limply from a ponytail on the back of her head. All of the pieces of Sophie seemed to be mismatched. Had they been on separate faces, they might have been pretty; but combined how they were, they looked awkward and did not fit any conventional description of beauty.

Her friends were apparently created from a cookie-cutter pattern as they all were petite and dark. It did make a striking contrast to Sophie, and Kama wondered how contrived it had been.

*I guess she didn't want any competition on the blonde front. This should be interesting. Though, I am really beginning to dislike blondes - well, other than Beth.*

The backup trio stood about five foot each, and their hair trailed down their backs, making them appear younger. One had dark brown eyes peering out from a very round face with full lips and cheeks. Another had wide set eyes fringed in long lashes and a sharp nose; she kept her hands on her hips in tight fists. The last gave Kama pause; she had stunning sharp cheekbones, a lush mouth, and bright hazel eyes forming a very pretty picture, until she noticed the absolute malice shining from them.

*Well, it seems like not everyone in our little pack likes each other. I wonder what Beth could have possibly done to get on their bad side; she's so easy to get along with. Okay, I won't jump to conclusions. Let this play out how it will.*

Even as Kama sifted through her internal thoughts, her spine stiffened, and something deep inside told her to get ready for some harsh words, since they would be needed. Sophie stalked her way around the table and stood between Kama and Beth. She didn't bother to look at Beth, but instead spent a good amount of time looking Kama over and gave her a sniff of disdain. Sophie took another, deeper inhalation and turned to face Beth.

"If I didn't know any better, I would say I could smell food. But that can't be right, because darling Beth doesn't eat real food. Does she, girls?" Sophie sneered.

Beth said nothing and continued to stare at the table. Kama tried to remain calm, but she didn't know just how long she could stomach the abuse. Being the youngest in her family, she had learned to stand up for herself, so she wasn't as intimidated by the group, as Beth appeared to be. Sophie leaned close to take a sniff and then stepped back, with an animated expression of surprise on her face.

"I don't believe it; she actually has something edible. Well, that's not okay. Real food might upset poor Beth's little tummy. Mindy, help Beth. We don't want her to get sick."

Kama's every instinct screamed about the incoming trouble, but she kept still in her seat. With a smirk, Mindy stepped past Sophie, snatched Beth's hotdog off the table, and took a large bite out of it. She made an exaggerated moan of delight as she swallowed. Beth kept her eyes on the table and said nothing as Sophie and her gaggle of girls laughed.

Kama boiled as she watched. She had witnessed the others snubbing Beth the last few days, and it was made clear that the shy girl didn't seem to be anyone's favorite; but this was too much. She had never witnessed such rude and inexcusable behavior, even at Pembleton. She began to bite her tongue, but found she just couldn't. Mind-numbing anger made her tremble, and before she thought about what she would do, she rose from her seat. Kama had opened her mouth, about to give the group a very loud piece of her mind, when Sophie met her eyes. The condescending smile given to her would have been enough for Kama to add cussing, but then, the blonde wench went and crossed the line.

Sophie's hand shot out, her intention clearly outlined on her face; as she snatched Kama's hotdog from the table, shooting her a triumphant grin.

*Did she really just take my food?*

Kama only half registered her own movements as she caught the girl's wrist. She stood smoothly and pulled Sophie off balance. The blonde stumbled, but Kama used the momentum to finish defending her food. The rest of the fight looked like moves practiced from a bar scene. Kama yanked hard down on the invading wrist with one hand, and guided the blonde head downward with the other. A wet crunch, audible crack, and horrified muffled scream followed as Sophie's face met the granite table.

*That will teach the stupid bitch not to mess with me. Who does she think she is? These are mine. Wait, are her girls looking at me? How dare they pick on my friend?*

*Back off.*

Kama looked at the group and a low, rumbling growl issued from her curled lips. The girls began to retreat in slow motion, so as if not to provoke her. Kama's head snapped around to find Sophie sitting on her behind with her hand clamped over her mouth trying with no success to hold back the gush of bright red that seeped through her fingers. Kama walked forward, claiming her territory and Sophie scooted back until she hit a wall. She got to her feet and backed toward the stairs. Once she seemed certain Kama would not be chasing her, she turned and ran to catch up with her friends.

*Good. Mess with me again and I'll rip your head off. Next time I will do more than rearrange her ugly face. I should hunt her down and show her what a DeKosse is made of.*

It took another few moments of pacing for Kama to use up the excess energy she had gathered. She looked around for Beth, and much to her astonishment, found her friend picking up the scattered remains of the food off the floor and depositing them into the waste basket. Beth then opened up a bottle of water and began to rinse off the table.

As she watched her friend wash rivulets of blood away, the full reality of what had happened came crashing down on Kama sending her into a complete panic.

*Oh crap, I just pushed someone's head into a granite table. I don't fight - I mean, besides Ajani. Who doesn't fight with their brother? What am I going to do? I broke her mouth, and I liked it. I wanted to fight them all because they stole our food. I'm going to get kicked out of the pack for some hotdogs. I have never put my hands on someone in anger. What will Jack think about this? He's going to be pissed off I hurt one of his members.*

Kama stopped pacing as all the ramifications came rushing to her mind and overwhelmed her. She sat down and tried to make sense what had just occurred.

*Maybe this Sophie chick will get yelled at for taking our food. Hell, no one grabs another person's food. Crap, Aturus will punish me for hurting someone so badly. I mean a bruise or two in class is expected, but I attacked her. I doubt she even has any teeth left, although she pressed the issue, we didn't start this fight. What will happen now? Beth. Beth will have some answers, she has to.*

"Excuse me," Beth said.

Kama couldn't understand the lack of reaction from her friend. She moved away from the table so Beth could finish cleaning up the blood that dripped down the side. Part of her took immense pride as the bright red puddle on the floor captured Kama's attention. She smiled in satisfaction until she remembered that she had caused the marks, and her stomach began to twist.

*Why isn't Beth reacting? I just beat up Sophie, I broke her teeth. Is she slow? Maybe it's why the others don't want anything to do with her? Maybe she doesn't speak a lot to hide her slowness. Or maybe she's high, I've seen Ajani act the same way. He has the same blasé attitude towards everything when he's smoked a joint. Crap, is she a stoner? I need some answers; I think I'm going to be sick.*

Beth moved in unhurried motions, but sensed Kama standing over her and looked up.

"What's wrong?" Beth asked.

"What's wrong?" Kama shouted. "What's wrong? Didn't you just see what happened? I just slammed Sophie's face into the table, broke all of the teeth out of her mouth, and made her bleed. I really hurt her. They are going to ban me, or hang me from my ankles or something."

"Relax," Beth said, putting a hand on Kama's arm to calm her. "No one will say anything, certainly not Sophie. She got what she had coming. She challenged you. She shouldn't have; but she did, and you answered her. She just didn't expect you to stand up to her, and ever worse you won. Her pride will prevent her or any of her friends from telling anyone what happened. Should we get some more lunch? I think now we can eat in peace."

Kama stood and looked at her friend.

"I think you need to explain what just happened, because I'm missing something here."

Beth gave her a questioning look, but under Kama's hard glare walked over to her.

"Okay, well in our Pack, you can rise in rank by challenging others. It's kind of like our pecking order, or ladder, if you will. It really doesn't mean a whole bunch, unless you are trying to climb your way up to the top."

"So, Sophie challenged you because you rank higher than her?"

"Not quite. She's higher in rank," Beth said. "I'm the Omega, bottom of the ladder. When she feels bad about being herself, she picks on me to feel better."

"It sounds like some high school crap. I thought we had a whole bunch of rules and stuff."

"We have rules about challenges, because the Alpha likes order," Beth said. "For instance, when you first come into the Pack, you are considered to be a cub, a child."

Kama snorted at being called a child, but said nothing else so Beth would continue.

"Until you take your Rite of Passage, you have a child's rank and all adults are supposed to protect and guide you. No one who has adult status would find it worth their time to pick on a cub. Partially because you can't gain any rank, but more importantly, if the Alpha found out, he would punish them severely for child abuse."

"So, Sophie has passed her Rite?" Kama asked.

Beth nodded, and clarity struck Kama full force.

"Oh, so essentially she crossed the line by challenging me?"

"Well, she was messing with me not you, but her problem came when you interpreted her taking your food as a challenge. Sophie thought since you were sitting with me, you would just cower. She never expected you would get aggressive, and never give her a chance to fight back," Beth said with a grin. "She basically got her butt beat by a baby. Who is she going to tell? She's way too embarrassed and even if she weren't she would be taken to task, by one of the Betas' for picking on a cub."

"So, then why don't people just stay cubs?"

"Because you have no rights," Beth said. "You can't vote, or make decisions, and you don't have any rank. You really are treated like a child of about ten years old. Most people would rather take on the Rite and be done."

Kama nodded in agreement; she would have to ask Jack about this Rite and how soon she could take it. The last thing she wanted is for another group of people to think her too young to make her own decisions.

"Come on, let's enjoy the few hours we have before security rotations. I heard The Judge is in a bad mood."

Kama sighed and began to walk with Beth.

*Once again, this whole Loup thing is becoming more complicated. Really? Challenges for rank, Rites of Passage... What's next? Body piercings and dog tags. Just what am I in for?*

# CHAPTER Thirteen

Kama climbed the fifteen flights of steps up to her home. It had been a long day, and she just wanted to be done. Only six days had passed since her run-in with the vampire and talk with Jack, and she could feel every single one of them. She still didn't know how to take the rapid pace changes, but she tried. For once, she really didn't know where her life would go, except at the current moment, she knew she needed to go up.

*Ow, ow, and ow. Stupid combat class, stupid combat class. I cannot do one more day of this. Hotdogs or no, this is torture. A hot shower, that's what I want. Have a hot shower for three hours.*

More than once, she had been ready to quit all the Loup nonsense. Kama wanted to go back to her real life of singing and focusing on her future, until she remembered the broken shoulder resulting from her inability to fight. She knew, intellectually, that Aturus and his painful combat class would help her in the long run. Her physical body, however, had a few choice words to spit at her as she walked up the stairwell. None of the words were ladylike, and none of them were helping her already foul mood.

*The least Jack could do is make it a point to check in and see how my days are going. Well, at least on the days I don't get to see him. Has it only been a couple of weeks? Some days I wonder what my life would be like if I had never met Jack. Although, I can't imagine never having fallen in love with him, so I'll just have to suck it up and get through this.*

She pushed the door open, and to her credit, didn't groan as her muscles protested the familiar motion. Kama walked with determination toward the shower; she locked the door, turned the spray on as hot as it would go, and climbed in. She shut off her mind as the hot water kneaded the knots out of her body. A loud banging interrupted her serenity.

"Kama, Mom's putting dinner on."

"Okay, I will be there in a minute."

She sighed and turned off the water.

*I don't want to go out there and join them for dinner. I just want to stand here until I feel normal again. Except my stomach might suffocate me while trying to crawl out to the food. Damn, is that a bruise? Right, I'm healing slower now, which sucks since I was getting used to the faster getting better part.*

Stomach rumblings aside, Kama would not have missed dinner anyhow. One did not live in the DeKosse home and miss family meals. Her parents expected any children living with them to be present when dinner was served. Even evening classes weren't a good excuse; most times, they were told to adjust their schedule. Kama towel dried her still sore but somewhat relaxed body, threw on clean clothes and went out to join her family. Once at the table, with a plate piled full of food, Kama forgave her parents for requiring her to be at there.

*Oh my, has food always tasted this good? I don't know if it's being Loup or the fact I worked off two million pounds in class, but these potatoes are awesome. Maybe I just haven't appreciated her cooking enough.*

"This is great, Mom," she said. "Can I have some more greens, please?"

"No need to suck up, Dear. I made enough for seconds tonight while you study."

"Can't I give you a compliment without you assuming I am sucking up?"

"I can't recall when you have before."

Kama rolled her eyes and continued to eat, as her mother and father laughed. She wanted to escape into her room and try to get more work done, but having some nice, normal family time was more soothing than she remembered it being.

Like Brenna DeKosse knows how to cook for only four people. She made enough for a study session and leftovers for tomorrow. Oh well, I'm not about to argue with the woman feeding me. I wonder what she made for dessert.

"Your father and I will be going out later to attend a fund-raising event," her mother said.

"So, why are you eating now?" Ajani asked.

Kama ducked her head to hide her grin. Her mother's glare tried to eat the flesh from her brother's bones.

"Because I enjoy real food."

"So, they didn't have you cater and still invited you? Wow, they had some gall, Mom."

Kama watched her mother bristle. She knew her brother trod a fine line with his banter. Brenna only ate the food of the local chefs with whom she was friends, and apparently the dinner would be catered by someone who served something deemed as swill. In reality, the food served would be delicious; but the caterer at some point had crossed Brenna, and she made holding a grudge against professional rivals an art form. A very scary art form.

"Son, use some common sense."

Kama smiled as her father interrupted Ajani's fun. Her mother didn't really enjoy attending all of the fund-raisers, but did so because of the professional expectations. Whoever had won the catering bid must be someone she really didn't like.

"You don't have to stay long," Kama said. "You can just get your applause for giving out vast quantities of your money and leave."

"Don't be embarrassed that you will be eating two dinners," Ajani snickered. "Snacking is okay."

"Not everyone gets the munchies, Ajani," Kama said defending her mother. "Then again, with all of your extra activities, munchies are a part of your life."

Kama ignored the hostile look her brother shot her across the table and smiled.

"Will you please pass the roast?"

Her mother passed her the dish and then faced her son.

"I suppose you would rather have me tired and weak from the poor excuse for food? You know they don't give enough to feed a toddler."

"Yea right, Mom. I guess you had better eat up so you have enough strength to withstand all of the praise and adoration," Ajani snickered.

Brenna's face lit into a sudden smile, and Kama knew she would be hearing something she didn't want to. Her mother, no doubt, planned to torment them by alluding to some sexual escapade.

"Aye, strength would be a good plan, Son. So when your father and I get home, we can have so much needed relaxation."

Kama tried to swallow fast, so she could warn Ajani.

*No, no, don't fall for it. Chew faster, Kama, so we can warn him. Damn, he's falling for it.*

"Why would you need strength to relax?" Ajani asked.

"I'll be needing the strength for all the loving before the relaxing."

Kama and Ajani both flinched. She shot her brother an irritated look. He had broken the cardinal rule and allowed their parents to speak about their sex life. Her brother looked properly appalled, but her mother continued on.

"In fact, Dear, would you like another serving of roast, so we can have an extra go?"

"I have homework to finish," Kama said the words as she grabbed her plate, refilled it, fled the dining room, and barricaded herself in her room for the night.

*I hate when she does that. No one needs to know their parents have sex. What a horrible way to scar your children.*

After finishing most of her plate and getting settled in, she called Jack. She listened to the phone ring and was startled when gentle knock sounded on her door. She smiled as she recognized her father's scent. It was a comforting smell.

"Yes, Daddy?" she asked as she hung up the phone.

"May I come in?" Malik asked.

"It depends," she said.

Kama had learned to be cautious when her parents were in a good mood.

"On what, Bambina?"

"Your topic of discussion."

She heard the rich chuckle she loved from her father.

"I only want to make sure my daughter is okay."

"I am fine," she said. "Why do you ask?"

Kama placed the phone down, walked over, opened her door, and stared at her father.

"Well, the last few weeks were very rough on you, and lately you seem exhausted," he said. "So I am checking because I have to know that you are okay."

"Yes, Daddy, I am fine," she said. "Like I said before, it was just a teen thing. You just aren't used to me acting normal."

She sat at her desk and looked up at him. She wondered about his formal use of English. If Kama's mother's brogue could be used as an indicator of mood, so could her father's grammar. He had emigrated from Italy over thirty years ago and had adopted most American idiosyncrasies. In general, Malik only used formal English when the situation was severe; if he reverted to Italian, things were near unredeemable. He looked her over a moment and then launched into conversation.

"I know the past few days have been tense between us. I want you to know that I did hear what you said, and it is true. Your mother and I have always respected you as an adult because you act so maturely," he said with a light touch on her shoulder. "But you were right that you should be able to get upset about not placing after an audition."

"Well, that was weeks ago, and I have managed to get over the disappointment," she said. "Life throws some pretty amazing changes and challenges at us. I am fine."

Kama smiled as her father nodded, and she stood up and gave him a tight hug. She started out stiff, but melted into the comfortable embrace. For the first time in weeks, she felt secure and steady. His familiar scent curled through her nose, and she relished being held by her father.

"I am glad to hear that you are feeling better. You work hard at your craft, and you deserve the recognition," he said.

"Thanks, Daddy. Maybe you can judge me next time. It might stave off a few fits."

The chuckle returned and vibrated through her.

"Being disappointed is not the world's biggest sin. In fact, your mother acted much worse after learning she lost tonight's bid," he said with a wink. "I am going to finish getting ready."

After a tight squeeze, Kama smiled up at her father.

"Enjoy the fund-raiser."

She had learned long ago to stop using the words "fun" and "tonight" in the same sentence. Her sanity demanded it; although her father teased much less mercilessly than her mother, he had said things that scarred her. Neither of her parents considered talk about sex taboo. In fact, they delighted in using it to punish their children.

*Actually, he is worse. I never see his comments coming. He always waits until just the right moment to throw one in there. Sometimes I get it and sometimes it takes a moment before it catches me. Men are just sneaky.*

He nodded and left her room. Kama picked up the phone and dialed Jack again. Another knocking at her door sounded. She opened it, expecting to see her mother, and to her surprise, found her brother filling the door frame, looking none too happy. She sighed and hung up the phone again.

"Yes?" she asked.

"We need to talk," Ajani said.

His tone of voice low and quiet; even still, Kama felt her hackles rise. Ajani had moved from being annoying to rude, and tonight she didn't want to deal with his attitude. Especially since he seemed out of sorts, and she really was not in the mood to deal with his drama.

"Well, dear brother, I have homework I need to do," she said.

"Yea, and we need to talk now," he said. His tone remained flat but her wolf bristled as he walked into her room, making her move back to avoid being stepped on, and right up into her face. Her teeth pulled on her bottom lip as she tried not to snap at him. She wanted to remain calm and get back to her homework.

"And I suppose it can't wait until tomorrow? Does it interfere with your schedule of getting high?" she said.

Kama looked at him as he looked down at her in irritation.

*Who does he think he is? This is my room. He needs to back up.*

"You know, Kama, just because your little princess dreams got smashed doesn't mean you need to be such a bitch," he said.

"What the hell do you want?" she asked.

"What the hell is your damage?" Ajani snapped back.

*You're in MY space. Watch your tone, little boy, or I'll take your throat to teach you respect. Little piece of nothing.*

"What the fuck is yours?" she retorted.

"Do you have any idea the shit I got because of you? And then you said that 'getting high' crap again tonight?" he accused.

Kama's eyes narrowed in irritation, and she quelled the urge to push him out of her face. She found herself paying more attention to keeping her wolf in check, rather than what he said to her.

"Get out," she said. "I have things to do."

"Your little trick of telling Mom and Dad I smoke pot to get out of trouble a few weeks ago was shit. Dad has been dragging me to work with him all this month."

His words were all but hissed at her as he tried to take another step toward her.

*Watch yourself.*

The wolf growled the warning low in her ear, and Kama's shoulders squared as she braced herself for an eventual fight. Ajani didn't seem to care about her defensive posture and stood toe to toe with her, trying to dominate her with his larger size. She looked up at her brother, and for the first time, really saw him.

He stood at least five inches over her height and had the same kind of muscular build as a basketball player. His arms were tight cords of muscle and his shoulders wide and strong. His torso narrowed in at the waist, but his legs had sinewy, narrow lines of strength.

*I wonder when he started to work out. He would put up a good fight, but it's still my room and I will make him leave.*

She hushed the wolf as she took another good look at her older brother.

*Older, ha. He is only ten months older than me. Hell, we even are the same age for a good month. He certainly doesn't act older; he acts like a jerk.*

Kama's vision narrowed to an irritated haze as her brother pushed into her, but she didn't move.

"Back out of my space, 'Jani. I don't have anything to say to you."

"We're not done," her brother said. "Just when Dad was starting to relax and trust me again, you went and threw out that little taunt at dinner?

I should beat your ass for that."

The low tone of voice and larger physical size made the wolf push forward. Kama took one step toward him and then another, all the while forcing her brother to move back.

"You have some nerve," she said. "I am not to blame because you smoked pot."

Her voice registered to her as more snarl than talk. She could tell her brother's level of agitation from his flushed face and dilated pupils. She glared at him and then turned away, waiting for him to leave.

"I quit smoking after you sold me out. Dad threatened to send me to work with Uncle Giuseppe in Africa," he snapped. "But because of your little joke, Mom is in tossing my room right now."

Fortunately for him, being in no mood to deal with his petty, human bullshit meant she had to calm herself. When she reached calm, Kama turned to tell him to leave, and was surprised when he grabbed her by the hair.

*He just attacked us, in our territory.*

The incensed wolf took control and promptly slapped his hands away. When he raised his hands to deflect her blows, she grabbed his arm and shoved him towards the door.

"I don't think you understand how much I don't care. Get out."

*You should respect us boy.*

She could smell the fear rise off him in waves, and it appeased her anger just a bit. Kama wanted to slap him, just once to prove her point, but instead she backed up a pace and gave him enough space to leave.

"You tell on me again, and I will make sure Mom and Dad find out some things about you," he said. "You aren't as careful as you think."

"Don't threaten me, little boy."

She countered his dark threat with snarling words of her own as she began to pace around him like a predator scenting prey. Kama knew she couldn't take his throat out, but she wanted to. The wolf had more presence than the girl, and she had a hard time not giving in to what felt natural. As Kama fought to get control of herself, Ajani pushed by her forcefully to leave her room. He shoulder-checked her, and she bumped into her door.

*He struck us in our room.*

Kama opened her mouth and actually growled at her brother; hairs rose on the back of her neck, and she could feel the wolf pushing at the constraints of her human skin.

*I'm going to kill him.*

The thought tore through her rage and as fear gripped her, Kama did the one thing she knew that would stop the fight and keep her brother safe - from her. She took a ceramic bank and threw it to the floor at his feet. Kama pushed against him, trying to push him to the door and as anticipated, Ajani grabbed her by the arm. She took a deep breath and began screaming, in apparent panic, and let the tears flow.

"What is going on in there?" Malik asked.

She could hear his heavy steps as he came down the hall. The sound helped her clear the red haze from her vision, and she no longer felt the urge to rip her brother apart.

"Daddy, help me. He's crazy!" Kama cried.

She put more effort into her crying as her father opened the door and stared at them incredulously. She noted his eyes narrowed dangerously, when he registered Ajani gripping her by the arm.

"What in the name..." Malik shouted.

"He said he was going to beat my ass," Kama said.

She felt Ajani release her arm. She was thankful that she was in slow healing mode, as his finger left dark red impressions against her skin. Kama watched the look of shock and disbelief flicker over her father's face as he looked between her and her brother.

"I didn't mean it. You know that, Kama!" Ajani yelled as Malik grabbed him, ushered him out of the room, and told her to go to her mother. Kama started to feel guilty. She had used her father as a diversionary tactic so she wouldn't shift on her brother, but now she had calmed and didn't feel enraged, she felt bad for all the trouble she had just brought down on him.

Kama walked towards her parent's room, still not believing what had just happened. She had fought with Ajani before, but nothing had ever spiraled so far out of control.

*Oh God, I could have killed him. And for what? He came into my room and acted like a jerk. Nothing new for him, but damn new for me. I cannot believe I acted like a snarling beast with him. No wonder Hollywood hates us; we lose control over stupid things.*

She walked into the room and smiled. It smelled like her mother's perfume and nostalgia flooded her mind; she had spent many hours watching her mother get ready for one event or another, and it relaxed her to be doing so once again. She walked over and sat next to her mother on the vanity bench and smiled at her mother's reflection in the mirror.

*I can't believe that we don't really see each other anymore. I used to love sitting here, watching her, and talking about everything. So much has changed, and now I don't tell her anything. How the heck am I going to explain this silly fight to her?*

"Are ye sure you are okay, my dear? I don't know about Ajani sometimes," Brenna said. "You two used to get along just fine, and nowadays you do nothing but bicker. Maybe I should stay home."

*Like she would be able to do anything if we wanted to rip his throat out. Hell, she doesn't even know we exist, let alone how to calm us down.*

"I'll be fine, Mama. Daddy is having a conversation with him now. I'll be surprised if you still have five children after his talk. He's pretty mad at Ajani," Kama said. "Now, finish up before you are late and you miss the dinner. Daddy will just gloat and smile about being right."

She tilted her head as her mother caressed the side of her face with a smile.

*I swear, if I start to purr I'm going to sock Jack in the mouth. Wait, dogs don't purr, only cats. I wonder what dogs do when they're happy. Right, they thump their leg. I don't think I am in any danger.*

"You're a good lass," Brenna said. "We can't be giving your father having anything else to be smiling about."

"What has Daddy been smiling about lately?" Kama asked.

After the words left her mouth, Kama wanted to smack herself for falling into her mother's trap. She braced for the worst. Her mother pulled open her jewelry cabinet and peered through her vast collection of necklaces.

"Well, the other night, after we got back from our board meeting, I helped him relieve some frustration," Brenna said. "He's been smiling ever since."

"Mooother! You know I don't need to hear you talk about those things," Kama wailed.

At least her mother had been predictable, and their easy banter helped Kama shove the wolf back down.

"Where are you and Daddy going tonight after the fund-raiser is over? I know darn well you aren't staying there the whole time."

Brenna laughed, and Kama gave her a dubious look; she really hoped she had not set herself up again for hearing more damaging things.

*Learn to stop asking, you idiot. Just let them do their thing and stay ignorant of it. Please be something like having coffee or playing cards with another couple. Do they even play cards? She's smiling. Why is she smiling so widely?*

"Your father is taking me to a poetry reading; they are doing a recitation of some of T.S Elliot's pieces," Brenna said.

"You are going to hear poetry?" Kama asked. "What does Daddy know about poetry?"

Brenna laughed even harder. Kama could hear her father's low rumbling bass voice and then the slamming of the front door.

*Great, Dad just left. I hope he took Ajani with him. Why is she still laughing? Crap, she's gearing up to scar me. Can I play the hurt card?*

"You, my dear, will have to ask him about it sometime," Brenna said. "Just make sure you have a camera to catch the look on his face. That was an interesting time in our relationship."

*My parents are crazy. At least she didn't talk about anything nasty. Although, I am always amazed they have so many stories I haven't heard yet. I wish I could tell her about my crazy stories.*

"Okay," Kama said. "It's another one of those crazy college references from the Dark Ages, huh?"

"Yes, way back then we only had poetry readings by candlelight for entertainment," Brenna said. "Now, be a good lass and help me put this on."

She took a stunning rope of pearls interlaced with emeralds and diamonds from her mother's hand.

Why did she even bother to look through her jewelry? This is her favorite piece. She must really not like the caterer tonight, because she is jeweled up to the nines. I suppose it's easy because Daddy has given her so many pieces, but she doesn't usually go out so decked out.

"Promise me that there will be no gushy displays of affection tomorrow morning. You know I like to have breakfast in peace," Kama said. "I know how you two get after a date."

"I promise nothing, my darling daughter. If not for our 'gushy displays', you and your siblings would not be here," Brenna said.

Kama scowled as her mother winked at her in the mirror.

*Dang it, I got caught twice tonight.*

"Mom, in case you weren't aware, this is where you head into the realms of T.M.I.," Kama said. "It's talks like this that distract me while I help put on your jewelry and your hair gets yanked."

"I'm sure it would be accidental," Brenna said as she pulled her hair away from her neck with exaggerated care. "Hurry, though. It's getting late and your father is not a patient man when it comes to his poetry."

Her mother chuckled again, and Kama rolled her eyes and held up the pearl choker.

*This is one of my favorites, too; I don't know why she even bothers to keep the others. I can't remember the last time I saw her wear the snowflake piece. The green in the emeralds highlights the red in her hair. I wonder if she dyes her hair. I've never seen any gray.*

Her thoughts were wandering as she began to place the necklace against her mother's skin when a mark pulled her attention into sharp focus and she stared. Kama felt a mixture of fascination and horror rise in her.

She had seen the tattoo since her childhood and never had paid it any attention; it was as much a part of her mother as her red hair or vanilla scent. All of a sudden, the back of her neck began to prickle as the conversation with Jack echoed in her ears, and she knew just what it was that she was looking at.

'All Loup who belong to our pack have a tattoo, called a Claw, Kama. Not every pack has one. In fact, it is a Purist tradition, and we only have them because Lorna had some of the Purist knowledge shoved in her head. She made a pretty compelling case for our group to be marked. It is their way of identification but it works well for us here. It is a mystical bond, and so we try to incorporate the moon into the symbol. Once you start to notice them, you will realize how big our pack is and just how safe you are with us.' Jack had said.

Her mother's tattoo was a beautiful piece of crafted art across the nape of her neck; there were four slash marks forming a hand, which cradled a perfect circle. Dark and glossy, it stood out like a shining beacon against Brenna's peachy skin, and as Kama looked at it, she felt herself growing cold.

Her hands began to shake so hard she dropped the necklace; the meaning of where and why the mark had been made hit her full force.

*It is a Pack Claw, not just a tattoo. She is marked with a Claw. Oh God, she is Loup.*

Kama stood stunned as her world began to crash in on her. All of the stresses of the past weeks swelled up and began to choke her. The key to what she had become sat in front of her and never once given her the precious gift of knowledge that could have spared her some of the agony she had gone through, up to and including the fight with her brother.

"Oh my god, you knew. All this time and you let me ... Mother, how could you?" she asked.

"Dear, what on earth are you talking about?" Brenna asked.

She met her mother's eyes in the mirror and watched as confusion turned into a flicker of surprised recognition. Kama looked down at the Claw and back into her mother's eyes.

"You let me think I was some freak in our perfect family. You knew all along about the Loup and never prepared us. What is wrong with you? Didn't you think we should know? didn't we deserve to know?" Kama asked.

Her mother flinched at the words as they were flung at her like daggers. Kama laughed mirthlessly as her mother turned pale white and leaned away from her.

"Oh my god," Brenna asked "How…"

"How?" Kama asked. "Really, do I need to explain it to you? You are marked with a Claw."

"Blessed Mother. No, no, no," Brenna whispered. "This canna be happening. Not to you."

"Yes, to me," Kama said. "You made me what I am and left me unprepared to deal with it. I was afraid to tell you because I thought you would think something was wrong with me, that I was crazy. Stupid me for thinking you might fear me. I never once thought you would have been the one to condemn me. Do you hate me so much?"

"Kama, please it's not what you think," Brenna said.

"What I think is you knew all along about the Loup and said nothing."

"I wanted to spare you," Brenna said.

"Spare me? Funny, because from where I stand, it looks like you were trying to hide this."

The words were growled from the back of her throat, and tears dropped from her mother's eyes. Kama steeled herself, not wanting to feel anything, let alone compassion for her mother.

"Don't you dare. You are not the victim here, Mother. I am," Kama said.

"I never thought… I mean I thought it would skip … I…" Brenna said. "You were all so normal…"

"Normal? You have been on my butt the last few weeks for my behavior, and even then you didn't think to check?" Kama shouted. "My life is ruined. Everything I have strived for is gone. Years of hard work and sacrifice down the drain because you didn't want to tell us about our history."

"I just wanted you safe," Brenna said. "This was never supposed to happen. This is a nightmare."

"Oh really? Nightmare. Nice way to put it, yes, it has been for me."

Kama rounded on her mother and stood in front of her. Fury emanated from every pore and was directed at her mother. However, before she could get another word out, her mother's cell phone rang. Kama recognized her father's ringtone and looked at her mother.

"It's your father," Brenna said. "I need to go."

"Oh sure, run away and let me deal with your betrayal," Kama said. "You are a horrible, selfish person."

For the first time in her memory, Kama watched her mother's proud figure droop in sadness and defeat. It didn't appease her or the highly irate wolf; instead they were even more incensed.

*She could have helped us. She knew all along what we were. I didn't have to face this alone. She let me suffer.*

Her mother looked back at her with a great sigh and for a moment, Kama saw some regret, but it was too late.

"We will talk later," Brenna said. "When you are calm and can understand, you will see I tried to save you from this horror. I didn't want you to get hurt."

She watched her mother walk out of the room, and the front door closed soon after.

*Dammit, at least she could have apologized.*

The wolf sat close to the surface, wanting to fight. Kama paced in the silent house for a few moments to get herself under control. With all of the drama and heartache Kama had dealt with in the past weeks, she wanted some clear answers. She headed down the stairs to finish talking with her mom. She waited by the elevator door, and felt her irritation rise as her mother refused to look in her direction and resolutely headed toward the front door.

"Mother."

"I said we will talk about this later. I canna handle this now," Brenna said.

"You handled the mark on the back of your neck for your entire life just fine," Kama said. "You owe me answers."

She watched her mother straighten her spine, and knew that any more confrontation would result in a fight. Loup or not, Kama didn't want to push that boundary just yet. She watched Brenna wave away her husband's questions and get into the car. As her brother walked through the lobby, Kama glared, before she turned and stalked back up the stairs, locking herself in her room for everyone else's benefit and fumed.

##

Down in the lobby, Nate the doorman nodded to Ajani as he shuffled past into the elevator and waited for the doors to close. Nate had watched the exchange between father and son and then between mother and daughter. He had stood unobserved by the DeXosse family as their turmoil raged, but he had heard enough. He picked up the phone and made the call that had been almost twenty years in coming.

"Yes, this is Nate. I need to be speaking to the Alpha. It's a Family matter and canna be waiting," He said. "Get him out o' the meeting, and tell him 'tis about his granddaughter."

# CHAPTER Fourteen

Kama and Beth walked back to Kama's building in quiet. They had just finished with a particularly grueling combat session with Aturus. While she didn't mind the workout, sometimes the verbal assaults wore her nerves down. At least her life at the park kept a consistent schedule; it made it almost easier to deal with all the chaos trying to topple the rest of her life. Learning about her mother being Loup still carried a shock, even though she had been thinking about it for the last 24 hours. Instead of working herself up again about the betrayal from her mother, Kama groused about Aturus.

*The man will be the death of me. He acts like once we go all fuzzy, we are all imbued with kung fu fighting skills. Sheesh, does he think this is a vampire movie? I have never fought hand to hand with a knife. Where does he think I grew up? I would like to see him come to a formal dinner and survive, jerk.*

Kama nodded to Nate as he held the door open for them. She would have said 'hello', but breathing had become a chore as they walked and she looked at the stairwell with disdain.

"I am pretty sure that my ribs are bruised. If elevators didn't make me feel so boxed in…"

Beth nodded and Kama took a good look at her friend. Beth looked more pale than usual and seemed to be taking shallow breaths as well.

"How are you?"

"Sore but healing. Some days I hate to practice when it's this close to a new moon. Aturus uses it to remind us that no matter what the time of the month, we still need to be able to fight."

The girls started to climb the stairs and Kama grunted. Her legs felt like lead, and her chest felt like it would split. Her pride wouldn't allow her to cry, not to mention crying would take far more energy than she had to spare.

*For the love of cheese, you are Loup. Suck it up and get up those stairs. This is only week six. Did you expect it to be easy? Let's move, DeKosse; we're not getting home by standing here and whining.*

Her internal scolding kept Kama moving. She made a mental note to try the elevator again, but since her First Change, she found tight and confined spaces unbearable. The small box of the elevator had closed in on her and made her pace like a caged animal the last time she had taken it.

*I bet no one else at the park has to walk up fifteen flights of steps every day. Shouldn't it count as conditioning? Who knew becoming a werewolf would s include such rigorous training? Jack sucks. Shouldn't teeth, claws, and eight feet of furry terror be enough to defend myself with? Men are stupid. Well them, and the whole being a werewolf, and having to fight other supernaturals that require this kind of training. Oh hell, that hurts. Why is Beth squishing me against the wall?*

When she cleared out of her internal fog of complaining, she found herself staring over the back of Beth's head. They had made it to the twelfth floor landing, and her friend was pressing her into the wall. She drew breath to cuss her friend out, but something about her friend's rigid stance put her on edge. A tall man with russet hair fading to white walked down the stairs. Kama could feel the tension rolling off of Beth and could hear her heart beat loud and fast. Kama watched the man walk toward them; his muscles rippled and moved with sinewy grace. His cinnamon brown eyes looked over them carefully as he stepped down onto the landing with them. He wore mountain hiking boots, faded jeans and a dark green button down shirt. He wore no jewelry, but she could see that he had a black tattoo curling around his forearm.

"Good afternoon, Ladies."

"Sir," Beth said.

Kama tried to speak, but Beth pushed her further back against the wall in an unusual defensive posture, protecting her from the stranger. He paused just a moment and made direct eye contact with Kama. His lips curled into a warm smile, and she could feel the laughter well up inside him. She thought him pretty charming, but her friend acted like he would kill them. She watched Beth's head swivel and watch him as he walked past them and down the stairs.

He stopped and gazed back again at Kama. His eyes drank in every feature of her face, and he smiled even more broadly as he turned and continued his journey down the stairs. Beth continued to block her until the man had walked far enough down the steps that they could no longer hear his footsteps fall. With a deep sigh, Beth moved away from Kama and sagged against the wall.

*She looks like she is about to be violently ill. Why is she having this reaction? Not like he cussed us out or tried to hit us or something. Oh, I bet he's Loup. Is she freaking out because he's Loup, too? Seems to be a bit of an overreaction, if you ask me.*

Kama watched Beth compose herself and stand upright; even still, she trembled.

"What is wrong with you?" Kama asked "Why did that old man get you so upset? He smiled, but it wasn't like creepy molester smile or anything. Not to mention, we could have easily taken him on."

Beth looked at her like she had lost her mind.

"My dear friend, the only Loup who live to be so old are those warrior who are so incredibly powerful that nothing has been able to kill them," Beth said. "I wonder what he was doing in your building."

Kama looked at Beth as she put in the added afterthought. It only took about two seconds for her panic response to kick in. The answer assaulted her as she remembered where she had seen the same tattoo before. She began to run the last few flights of stairs, taking them two at a time.

"Oh shit," she said. "My mom."

"Kama," Beth yelled running up after her. "What is going on?"

"My mom has the same mark on her neck. I have never seen anyone else with the same mark – he must have been here for her," Kama said.

She flung the door open on the stairwell and began to run down the hall. Fear made her movements feel like slow motion. The hallway stretched into an impossibly long corridor. She didn't notice Beth behind her until she reached the door to her home and dropped her keys. Beth picked them up, unlocked and opened it for her.

"Thanks. My hands were shaking too much."

"No problem. So, when did you find out about your mom?" Beth asked.

"Just last night. After the big fight I had with my brother. Remember I told you about it? I can't believe that someone from her pack would get here so quickly."

"I wonder why the Alpha came. I mean, did you see the size and power of that man? I wonder if she ran away or something. Why did she never tell you?"

Kama ignored Beth's questions and pushed by her to get inside the house. She didn't realized how nervous she had been until relief filled her.

Thank god, no blood. Where is my mother?

She opened her mouth to call out for Brenna, but a small strangled sounding sob from the kitchen caught her attention. Kama pushed the door open and felt her heart jump when she saw her mother in a crumpled heap on the floor. She rushed to her side, shocked as the tear stricken face raised to meet her. Brenna looked pale and distraught. She tried to talk to Kama, but no sound came from her mouth.

"Mom," Kama cried. "Mama, what happened? Are you okay?"

She offered comfort, because her mother being flustered didn't register in Kama's mind. Brenna DeKosse, was the woman who had engaged in a multicultural relationship in a world destined to hate interracial parings; she was the woman started a catering company when it wasn't popular to be a female chef; and above all, she had made sure her dark-skinned children were accepted into the best private school Manhattan had to offer, against the wishes of the board. What could that man possibly have said to make someone as strong as her mother fall into a crying heap?

*I've never seen her cry, and I've lived with her for seventeen and a half years. Oh hell, this is a disaster.*

Her mother nodded and took a few moments to gather herself. Kama waited for her to be able to speak; knowing something terrible would come from her mouth. She steeled herself to hear the worst.

*Okay, so if she tells me she has to leave and go back to this Pack, we will work with it. Although if she had to go back wouldn't old dude, have just taken her? He didn't look mean. Well, he did stare and smile a lot, but old men tend to look and smile all the time. I wish she would just talk to me about this.*

"It's okay, Darling. Just a shock to me system is all," Brenna said.

Kama heard the brogue and sighed.

*Crap, her accent is out full. She is stressed and freaked out, so not a good sign.*

Brenna stood and walked to the sink to get a cloth. Kama would have laughed under any other circumstance, because her mother then noticed Beth and jumped into hostess mode.

"Hello, Dear. It's so nice to see you again. Would you like something to eat or drink?"

"No, thank you, Mrs. DeKosse," Beth said.

"Mama, who is he?" Kama asked.

Her mother faced her, and Kama noted the color returned to her face and relaxed. As she stared at Brenna, she mentally replayed the features of the man who had passed her on the stairs. Her eyes went round as she noticed the similarities. Especially the cinnamon brown colored eyes.

"He is my grandfather," Kama ventured.

At the same time, Brenna answered, "My father."

They stared at each other for a moment, and Kama didn't know what to say. She hadn't thought about her mother's parents for a very long time. At a young age, she had learned not to ask about them because it caused her mother pain. Now, those unasked questions led to more than she could have ever imagined.

*Huh, guess Jack isn't to blame after all. We do have werewolves in my family.*

Kama almost wanted to laugh at the inane reprieve Jack had just gotten, but she feared her laughter would launch into full blown hysteria, and she knew more serious matters had to be dealt with first.

"I'll leave you two. I'm sure there is a lot to talk about," Beth said.

Kama had almost forgotten her friend was there, because she had remained silent through their exchange. As she watched Beth speed off through the door, she was curious as to why her friend would run out like fire was under her feet. Something more was happening, and Kama wasn't sure if she face anything else.

*I wonder if she's going to the Park to tell them about my family. No, she wouldn't do that- she would at least let me tell them what I found out myself. Unless she thinks my grandfather will cause a war or something. Well, he can't make me fight against them. I'm only a cub there; it's not like I have any status or anything. Dang, this all just got really complicated.*

Kama took a deep breath and expelled it. She watched her mother drag out pots and pans and get ready to cook. She knew her mother needed to calm down. The irreverent we're going to eat good tonight thought flickered through her head.

"So, about the talk we were supposed to have later? I think it might be better to have it now," Kama said.

Brenna nodded as she brought out various vegetables and a wicked looking knife that she wielded with rapid skill. Kama watched her julienne the onions before she started to ask questions.

"Apparently there is a lot more going on here than I thought."

"Aye, I guess so."

The steady chop, chop, chop, swish rhythm also calmed Kama. She had grown up in the kitchen with her mother cooking. She fell into routine, washing carrots, kale, and squash, and then set it aside for her mother to chop.

"Okay, so you are Loup and since my grandfather wears the same Claw, he is too. Is your whole family werewolves?"

The knife never stopped moving, but Brenna gave Kama a bemused look.

"Dear, I'm not Loup, only my father and brother."

"But you are marked."

"Aye, all Loup and their bloodlines have them."

"Really, the only people I have seen with a Claw are Loup."

Brenna paused and looked at Kama. She watched her mother's head tilt as a realization struck her.

"That girl, Beth - the new friend of yours - she's Loup, isn't she?"

"Well yea, Mom. She's been helping me adjust to all this stuff."

Brenna pursed her lips and didn't say anything; however, the sounds of chopping got louder and fiercer with every second.

"I think, you had better explain to me just how long this has been going on and just who the hell you have been hanging out with."

Kama put down a head of cabbage and looked at her mother questioningly.

*Wait a minute. She's mad at me? I have not heard that tone of voice since I was six. What has gotten into her?*

"Okay, seventeen days ago when I went running in Central Park, I walked into drug deal. Those details are rather blurry, but I was attacked and learned I am a werewolf. The local Loup pack saved me, and I have been working with them ever since. Beth has been a great friend and source of information, so I can make sense of all of this, because my own family neglected to fill me in on such things."

Kama stared at her mother while she said her piece. She hadn't wanted to sound hostile, but by the end of her short speech, she couldn't help but to feel bitter.

"Seventeen days? You have known for so long, but you never said anything," Brenna said.

Kama watched emotions play over her mother's face in a rapid pace. She went back to washing vegetables so she had something to do. The conversation had raised the tension level in the kitchen, which all the chopping in the world couldn't erase.

"Funny, you had seventeen years and never mentioned anything. What should I have said, Mama? I didn't know anything about this life; I didn't even know this life existed. Did you really expect me to come home and tell you?"

"I'm sorry, Love," Brenna said. "I am truly sorry you had to go through such an ordeal with no help."

"I did have help, Mom. My pack helped me through it, and I'm learning about being Loup and everything now."

"Your pack?"

Kama looked at her mother in shock. Brenna had all but spit out the word "pack" as if it were an obscenity.

"Yes, my pack- you know the people who saved my life? The ones who kept me from going insane when I couldn't control myself? Yes, Mother. My. Pack."

"But they are mongrels."

"Mongrels? What are you talking about?"

"That pack is just a random group of people who happen to be Loup, but they have no idea of their origins or family lines," Brenna said.

"I guess so. Are you saying your group was different?"

Brenna's back stiffened so much, Kama thought it might crack. The kind of action usually preceded a telling off.

"Yes. I come from a pack that can trace our lineage back to one of the originals. And for that matter, Dear, so do you."

"What's the big deal, Mom?" Kama asked.

"The big deal is that our pack has years of tradition, knowledge, and customs. That mongrel group has nothing to offer you."

Kama broke eye contract from their fierce stare-down as a loud and frantic knock sounded at the door. She opened the door to find Beth standing there, panting hard.

"Your grandfather went to see the Alpha at the park."

"Okay."

"He wants you," Beth said.

"What are you talking about?" Kama asked.

She ushered Beth inside and shut the door. Kama noted her mother had yet to look at her friend; instead, she went back into the kitchen. Kama heard dishes clanking and knew her mother was putting together a snack tray.

"He wants to take you with him back up north," Beth said. "And because you are still a cub, you have no choice, no say in the matter."

Kama felt her panic rise at the notion of being carried off. She enjoyed being a city girl and being cloistered in a rural area would suffocate her. Not to mention, she had some serious issues about marrying a cousin. Kama scowl as her mind went through the courtesy of giving her vivid imagery of every worst case scenario she could come up with.

"No," Kama said.

Beth's pale face told Kama more words would be said, and she got the feeling she wouldn't like them. She felt an urgent need to sit and went into the living area.

"So, what happened? I mean, didn't you just leave here?"

"Your grandfather went to the Park, to announce himself and all to our Alpha, and demanded you be handed over to him," Beth said. "He wants to leave tomorrow."

A tray clattered loudly to the floor, and two sets of eyes turned to find

Brenna in the doorway, never having heard her push the door from the kitchen open. Her drawn face made her eyes look huge. Kama went over and helped her pick the food up off the floor. She caressed her mother's arm.

"It's okay, Mom," Kama said.

"Oh Blessed Goddess," Brenna whispered. "I had no idea he would move so quickly."

Kama finished picking up the scraps, when her mother's words, finally sunk in.

"You knew he was going to take me?" she asked.

"Well, yes. He is your family, and he wants you trained properly before anyone gets hurt. After that fight with your brother last night, I thought it would be best."

"You are my family, Mama. I don't want to leave," Kama said.

She sat on the floor with her mother, until Beth cleared her throat. All eyes upon her, made Beth look around nervously and she shifted from foot to foot uneasily.

"I think there might be a way Kama can stay…"

##

Bright and early the next morning, Kama walked with determination towards the Park. It had been a long night, and her head wanted to pound as the enormity of what she was doing caught up with her.

*Right, because I have any other options in this case. Either I do this, or I pack up my stuff and head to Nowhere, Michigan, and live with people I don't know.*

She strode into the cabin, went down into the tunnels, and straight into Jack's office.

*Well, he doesn't look surprised to see me. I wonder why not. No one besides me, Mom and Beth knows about our plan. Maybe he asked the sentries to send me to him as soon as I arrived. Oh my, what is he doing here?*

Both Jack and her grandfather stood as she entered, and Kama smiled at them. They greeted her, and Jack motioned for her to sit down. She glanced at her watch and remained standing.

*6:11 a.m. on the dot. Okay, here goes everything.*

Kama took the stance she had been practicing every day in combat class for the last few weeks. She stood firm and made her declaration.

"Alpha, I hereby request taking my Rite of Passage today."

Stunned silence filled the room, and her grandfather's face took on the unhealthy red flush of fury. Kama tried not to giggle at Jack's look of shock. She waited out the eerie silence, for him to respond.

*Wow, I haven't seen a look so intense since he found out I'm seventeen and a half. Hmmm, that didn't turn out so well. Maybe I shouldn't be too amused.*

To Jack's credit, he didn't stay stunned long. Kama figured protocol demanded an answer, and he gave it. His voice started off quiet, but grew stronger and more firm with each word.

"Cub, do you stand prepared and ready for the Challenge?"

"Aye sir."

"Your Rite is guided by Luna herself. Why do assume you are prepared?"

"Life comes with twists and turns that no one can predict. Learning I am Loup has only opened my eyes to new possibilities, and I feel the time has come for me to join the ranks of my brethren as an adult."

Kama tried not to expel a deep breath.

*What the hell kind of question is that? Beth said he might ask me if I have been trained enough- but prepared is a way different question. Sheesh, Jack, don't you want me here?*

"Will you accept your Challenge with full mind, body, and spirit?"

"I resolve to be guided like the curving fullness of the moon," Kama said.

As the last timbre of her words faded, Kama felt a rush of something pass over, around, and through her. Instinctively, she tilted her head back and howled with pure and perfect pitch. She heard Jack, and then her grandfather join her song. Kama let her wolf take over, and her sound wound through intricate riffs and trills, making it wholly theirs. As the howling song died down, she felt buoyed and energized; she looked intently at Jack. He returned her gaze in amazement, and with a respect she had never seen from him before. Then he pushed her with two fingers against her chest. Kama didn't smile, but she wanted to.

*My stance is sure, Jack; I know what I am doing.*

"Go to Lorna, and let her know you will take your ritual this evening," Jack said.

Kama gave a careful nod to both men and walked with confidence out of the room. As the door shut, she exhaled a shaky breath and when her legs would support her again, she made her way to Lorna's workroom. She told Lorna about her upcoming Rite, she then sat in the large ornate circle in the center of the floor.

"Let's find out what Luna has in store for you."

Kama waited patiently, happy for a still moment before the chaos that was sure to ensue. As she let her mind wander, she reviewed once more how she had gotten there.

##

"I think there might be a way Kama can stay," Beth had said. "But it is risky, and I'm not sure that you are ready for this."

"What is it?" Kama asked. "I'm not really one to live in the woods, so I'm willing to try just about anything. Well, I mean aside from being jumped-in gang style or whatever."

"Well, the only reason your grandfather can claim you is because you are still a cub. We have a Rite of Passage in our Pack. You have to successfully complete it and then swear loyalty to our Alpha, before you are seen as an adult," Beth said. "Just be warned, most of the time it includes a first kill."

"What does this kill entail? I don't have to kill people, do I?" Kama asked.

"Actually, your First Kill is part of a ritual," Beth said. "It signifies your transition from youth to adulthood. There are specifics that must be met and ritual words and preparations. You have to declare it before our Alpha, and then pass whatever task is set before you."

Kama noticed her mother watching Beth, while she explained everything. The look on her mother's face had gone from nasty, through irritated, and landed on downright furious. She wondered if her mother would throw things at Beth, or maybe even smack her with the tray containing the snacks. Beth's gaze brought her back to the situation at hand and Kama nodded as she thought her way through her options. They were pitiful: go live in Northern Michigan, or try to do some ritual which may or may not involve killing someone or being killed yourself.

"My options suck. Well then, I guess I need to prepare for this Rite of Passage thing," Kama said.

She paused a moment while she tried to figure out all of the logistics in her head.

'This is so much more than just wanting to stay in New York. This is about my family, friends, and Jack. I don't see where I have any other choice. This man may be my mother's father, but I have never met him. He is not the Grandpa I know.' Kama thought.

"It seems like it is the only option I have to stay here," Kama said aloud.

"No," Brenna said. "You do not know what you are saying."

The ferocious intonation caused Kama and Beth to snap their attention to her. Brenna had set the snack tray on a coffee table and stood facing the girls, red faced. Kama watched her mother try to calm herself, confused at the outburst. Brenna sucked in deep breaths of air.

"Mama, it is the only chance I have to stay here," Kama said. "You can't possibly want me to leave and go who knows where."

"No, I do not, but I don't want you hurt. Living up with your Grandda willna be so bad," Brenna said. "I would rather have you in Michigan and safe, than running around with a pack of mongrels."

"Are you kidding me? I'm not going to live up in the middle of nowhere and give up my life," Kama said. "And who says I am going to be hurt? Beth said each test is different. Maybe mine will be eating fast food."

Kama tried to cajole her mother into a lighter mood, but Brenna stood there and gave her a look as if the decision were already made. Kama almost expected her mother to start packing up her belongings.

"You canna possibly take on your First Kill; you are not ready," Brenna said.

Her words were strong and the capital F and K were punctuated in her speech. Kama could hear them clearly and wondered just what her mother knew about Loup Rites. It occurred to her, in that moment, that her mother knew a lot more than she was telling.

"Tis better for you to be safe up there, until you learn enough to do it. You aren't ready now."

"Our Rite of Passage is always geared for each person, Mrs. DeKosse," Beth said.

"So, you are the Pack Shaman?" Brenna scoffed. "I hate to break up your plans, but I happen to know more about real Loup life than either of you. These Rites are not something to be taken lightly. There is a lot of training involved."

"No, I am lower rank in our pack, but Kama has had weeks of training already," Beth said. "Not to mention, most of it is getting your mind in the right place."

"And that should be easy. I have been training at being calm and collected since I began singing on stage," Kama said.

"I dinna think you girls understand..." Brenna started.

"Not for nothing, but I passed my Rite of Passage, Mrs. DeKosse," Beth said. "It wasn't easy, but I did it. Kama is much more aggressive than I am. She is strong enough to do this."

Kama noticed Beth's volume dropped considerably, as if the memory pained her. She wanted very much to ask what Beth had gone through, but common sense told her perhaps another time would be better. She had more important things to figure out. Quite frankly, if she couldn't sell her mother on the idea, how would she be able to convince Jack?

"Mama, please," Kama pled. "This is the one shot I do have to stay here."

Brenna sighed and as her shoulders drooped, Kama knew she had relented. Kama wanted her to give verbal consent, but instead, her mother gathered the empty tray and walked back into the sanctuary of her kitchen.

"Okay," Beth said "Aside from your mother looking like she wants to skin me, I think it went well. Now, let's see what I can remember to tell you so you can be prepared as much as possible."

"Yea, somehow I don't think you are going to be welcome here for a while," Kama said. "Too bad, I think my brother has the hots for you. What do I need to know?"

"Your brother doesn't notice I'm even here," Beth said. "He stays in his room most of the time, playing crap he tries to pass off as New Age music."

"Are you blind? He is forever peeking out at you whenever he is home. Before you started coming around, he would be home for dinner and then go back out with his loser friends. Not to mention, he thinks he is a thug. New Age anything isn't his style. He's playing it to impress you."

"Wow, I never would have thought he might be interested," Beth said. "What are we doing? We are not talking about me going on a date with your brother. Let's focus on what is really important."

"What?"

"You need to be able to adapt to very quickly. I can't give you specifics, because your test will be different from mine. I do know being calm helped me out," Beth said. "For as long as it lasted."

"Your Rite went well, eh?"

"I'm trying not to tell you much about mine, so you don't plan on my events happening to you."

Kama looked at Beth for a moment and then burst out laughing. She figured her friend thought hysterics had finally kicked in. Reality seemed much more absurd to her.

"Huge, fast changes I will be forced to adjust to?" Kama asked. "What do you think I have been doing ever since I changed for the first time? Somehow, I don't think this will be much of a problem."

Beth smiled at her and Kama shook her head.

"Well, you might as well stay the night and ply me with words of wisdom."

"With your mother hating me, is that wise?"

"I want some Loup company tonight, just in case any questions pop up at midnight or something," Kama said. "Besides, if I am going to change the course of my life tomorrow, I deserve at least one girls' night."

Beth had stayed, and sheer nerves kept Kama awake half the night. When she woke from a slumber she didn't remember falling into, she squinted at the clock. She had exactly one hour before sunrise, so Kama stood and stretched.

"Care for a bite to eat?" Kama asked.

She noted Beth looked more exhausted than she.

"No, my stomach is far too jumpy."

"Okay, well I'm going to grab a snack and then head out," Kama said.

She walked out of her room to the scents of a full breakfast, a peace treaty before she went off. Her mother hovered anxiously while she ate, saying little, but continued to keep her plate full until Kama pushed away.

"I'll be back soon, Mama."

As Kama started to walk towards the door, Brenna grabbed her and held her close. Unshed tears graced both their eyes, but Kama wrapped her courage around her mother in a tight embrace and a champion's smile. Her mother released her and stroked her cheek.

"I know you will. I love you."

Kama hugged her mother again, and then strode out the door. Never once did she allow herself to think her plan would be anything other than successful. And precisely as the sun rose, she opened the door to Jack's office and demanded to take her Rite of Passage.

# CHAPTER Fifteen

Jack sat in his office and stared at the clock.

*It's 8:00 p.m. already. Where did the night go? At some point, I am going to learn how to balance my schedules better. And I haven't seen Kama since she started her new regime with The Judge. Damn, I miss her. Of the course, there is still the problem of not being able to date without her being Challenged. Okay, let's crank out another hour or two and then head home for the night. I think Carla said something about a business meeting tomorrow, and I should probably review the files.*

Just as he had made up his mind to stop letting his mind wander and do some work, a knock sounded at his door. Before he could make any response, it opened and a cloud of smoke preceded The Judge as he walked in.

"Well, Boy, glad to see you are still here."

*Damn, I hate it when he calls me 'Boy'. I understand he's like a thousand years old, but does he really have to make me feel fifteen all over again?*

Jack watched him stroll over to the cabinet and grab the scotch.

"So, the Gal is coming along well. Aturus is impressed with her; I haven't heard him say anything nice about a cub in a long time," The Judge said.

"Really? I didn't think he could be impressed by anyone."

"Well, it has been a while. The Gal has natural fighting ability and enough sense that her sass doesn't always get her in trouble."

"Sass without trouble? Is that possible for a female?" Jack asked. "Maybe Aturus is going soft?"

The Judge barked a smoker's laugh and poured two glasses of scotch. Jack took one with a smile and sipped in contentment.

"Probably best not to challenge his assessment skills; you know he is looking for an excuse to give you another special class."

"Oh for the love of the Great Mother, not another one of those," Jack said with a shudder. "So, where do you think she should be placed when you're done terrorizing her?"

"The Kid's group should be a challenge for her. I think she'll be a damn good warrior once she figures out she belongs here. She's damn stubborn enough to be a warrior," The Judge said.

Jack shrugged. Placing Kama in Aturus' quadrant wouldn't have been his first choice, but she would be a great warrior. His Pack had the distinction of being regimented; he had four Betas working underneath him, almost unheard of in the Loup world, but necessary for the smooth running of an eight hundred acre park.

When Jack had taken over ten years prior, the park had been segmented into two dozen packs, each with their own Alpha. However, his military training and skill had changed the haphazard nature of the park. His own Alpha became intimidated by Jack's prowess and Challenged him, to no avail. Once he took over, he reorganized his pack and soon found others were willing to follow him.

More and more Loup abdicated to his pack and the stability it offered. Civil war erupted soon after, as the other Alphas felt threatened by his growing numbers. In the end, seven held ground in Central Park. Jack called a council to figure out a way they could either work together or at least co-exist.

He had proposed coming up with some sort of guidelines to live under so there could be peace. The proposal had resulted in one Alpha assassinating another and Jack killing the assassin as a warning to the rest.

He had been particularly brutal to drive his point home. He was then left with four leaders: Aturus, Lorna, Gabe, and The Judge. To his surprise, The Judge had taken him aside.

"The way I see it, Boy, is you have got the training to unify the whole park. Offer these others positions of power in their own sections, but you stay arbitrator over it all. With your knowledge, you can have this park become the most powerful pack in miles and running like a well-oiled machine. If not, we're going to have a bloody massacre."

He had proposed the idea the next day at their meeting. Jack outlined his plans to take the pack from a group who happened all to be Loup, to a pack of highly trained Loup. No one besides The Judge looked thrilled with the proposal, but they all accepted it and their new roles as park Betas.

The next five years proved to be some of the most difficult for Jack. He still had to run his own business, else Twist Industries would have gone down the drain and Carla would have killed him. In addition, he had to moderate the park and prove he had the right to. The work had been it worth it though; his pack stood eighty strong and as well run as any military corps.

"Reliving the past?"

The sound of The Judge's grating voice shook Jack out of his memories. It had been a long road to stabilize the park.

*And just what does this have to do with Kama? Except a relationship with her could threaten what I have worked so hard to establish. Why is this all so hard? It seems like at every turn we are being forced apart. Maybe now she's accepted being Loup, things will calm down and - who knows? - maybe by the time she is no longer a cub, she will be strong enough to stand for her place.*

A cloud of smoke in his face brought Jack back to the question asked of him.

"Yea, a bit. Seems like things are finally smoothing out," Jack said.

"Just like the old days, before all this posturing nonsense got in the way of being a pack," The Judge said. "You've done good, Boy."

"A compliment?" Jack asked. "Are you dying or something, Old Man?"

"Anyhow, thought you might like to know another Alpha entered the park about ten minutes ago. Probably headed down here to see you," The Judge said. "One of my boys told me."

"What?"

"You stood there being all maudlin. I couldn't interrupt your moping, but your guest should be here…"

A knock on the door sounded as The Judge finished his scotch.

"…about now. Right then, I'll leave you to your meeting."

The Judge opened the door and walked out, leaving ample room for Gabe and the strange Alpha to enter. Jack looked over his visitor and a mall headache started. From his stance, Jack could tell this meeting had purpose, and one he wouldn't like. He nodded at Gabe, who left the office and shut the door.

"Welcome to Central Park," Jack said. "Can I offer you a drink?"

"Scotch, neat. Thank you."

Jack's grabbed the bottle, which The Judge had left on the cabinet, and poured two drinks. He knew he would need another one.

"So, other than a good drink, how about we skip the pleasantries and get right down to why you are here?"

Jack handed the man his drink and after mutual nods, they each took a swallow.

"I like a man who doesn't mince words," the man said. "I am Angus McBride, and I am here to take my granddaughter back to her rightful family pack."

*Great, a Purist Alpha to boot.*

He gave Angus a long look and took another drink.

"Okay, as long as you understand any member of my pack has a choice," Jack said.

"This won't even be necessary. My granddaughter is still a cub, so she doesn't have adult rights yet," Angus said. "At least, it is my understanding your pack has the same rules as mine."

"Who is your granddaughter?"

Jack knew the answer even as he asked the question. He didn't want it to be true but had to hear it nonetheless.

"Kamaria DeKosse."

Jack finished his drink and resisted downing the rest of the bottle.

"Have you told her you plan to take her?"

"I have spoken with my daughter, and she understands," Angus said. "As it's night, we won't be leaving until the morning."

Angus finished his own drink and stood.

"I'll summon her and have her get ready to leave," Jack said.

His mind spun furiously at how to keep Kama there and came up with nothing. Cubs had no rights, and this seemed to be universal. While the Central Park pack didn't acknowledge family rights, this Alpha came from a Purist group, and Jack couldn't justify a war with them over one cub. No matter who she might be. His wolf growled at him.

"I would like to leave early, though. Is six too early to meet you?" Angus asked.

"No, six will be fine," Jack said. "Would you care for a meal? It's not often I get to meet another Alpha."

Damn, stupid protocol. I would rather kill him and keep Kama here. Maybe I'll get him drunk enough to forget? What do I do now? Goddess, this is such a mess. Blessed Mother, please help us. Oh great, he's accepting. Go dine with the man, and then give him our mate. You, Jack, are an idiot.

##

The next morning at six sharp, Angus sat in his office again. Jack sighed and called Kama's cell phone.

*Well, this is weird, I got her voicemail. I don't think I have heard it before. Okay, so this buys me a bit of time.*

"Kama, this is Jack. Please give me a call."

"You allow them to call you by your first name?" Angus asked.

"On the off chance someone else gets her messages, I don't want her to have to answer odd questions by referring to myself as her Alpha," Jack said. "Things have to work differently here; we can't be as open as you."

"That makes sense. Well, now we wait."

Jack didn't have to wait as long as he would have thought or liked. At 6:11 a.m. on the dot, Kama marched through his door. She spoke before he could even greet her.

"Alpha, I hereby request taking my Rite of Passage today and join this pack as a full adult."

Jack knew he looked stunned. Nothing could have prepared him for those words coming out of her mouth.

*What did she just say? Her Rite, what? Who the hell told her about the Rite? She's been Loup for, what, a month? And hell, it's close to a new moon. I need a drink. Oh right, let's not forget her grandfather is sitting across the desk from me, and right now he looks like he wants to kill me.*

Jack watched Angus' face flush a furious red, which prompted him to reply to Kama.

"Cub, do you stand prepared and ready for the Challenge?"

"Aye, sir."

"Your Rite is guided by Luna herself, why do assume you are prepared for this challenge?"

"Life comes with twists and turns that no one can predict. Learning I am Loup has only opened my eyes to new possibilities, and I feel the time has come for me to join the ranks of my brethren as an adult."

Jack stared into her eyes and couldn't help but feel pride when she didn't flinch.

"Will you accept your Challenge with full mind, body, and spirit?"

"I resolve to be guided like the curving fullness of the moon," Kama said.

Jack felt her words sink into the core of him and the Spirits roll through the room. As he watched, she tilted her head back and howled. He joined her without another thought. His wolf took immediate control and laced his song through his mates'. In the fuzzy distance, Jack heard another howl and realized Angus had stood witness to her demand as well.

*She is amazing, and if she lives through this Rite, I am going to kill her. Great Mother, I love her. Please keep her safe.*

Jack smiled at her and without warning, poked her hard in the chest with two fingers. Part of him prayed she would topple, but his wolf knew better and smirked in his head. Kama stood firm before him with an amused smirk of her own, and he mentally sighed.

"Go to Lorna, and let her know you will take your ritual this evening," Jack said.

The door shut with finality, and Jack wanted to close his eyes and bang his head on his desk. Instead, he had to face a very irate, Purist grandfather.

"You canna be thinking to let her take her Rite."

"It is her choice; she demanded to take it," Jack said. "The rules in our Den state whenever a cub feels they are ready, they can petition to take their Rite."

"She's only known about being Loup for a month," Angus said. "And of all nights, it is nearly a new moon. The child will get herself killed. Let me take her and train her."

Jack wanted to send Kama with him, for her own safety, but had no choice.

"Unless your rules are different, you know once the demand is made and Spirits accept it, we have no choice but to see it through," Jack said. "As it appears you will be here a while longer, we might as well get some breakfast."

And when I am out, I am going to find out who put this damn stupid notion in her head and kill them.

##

*This has to be the longest day of my life. Not only have I had to entertain Angus McBride, I am driving myself crazy hoping and praying the Spirits take into account she only Changed six weeks ago. I suppose the one benefit is Angus has had twelve hours to get a good look at our Den. He seems impressed that we are not some snarling pack of untrained curs. Though I am not sure I shouldn't be insulted…*

The door opened and interrupted his thoughts. Jack looked in irritation at the person who walked through the door.

"Lorna said she is ready to prepare Kama for her Rite."

Jack stared at the Omega, who looked at the floor, and had a thought.

"You told her about the Rite, didn't you?"

"She wanted to stay and asked for help. It was the only way I knew, Sir."

Jack didn't think twice about backhanding the Omega to the floor. As he watched her lay there with a bruise swelling over her eye, he hoped she would get up so he could vent his frustration. She didn't, so he settled for snarling at her.

"Don't step above your station ever again."

*Get a grip, Jack. You are not going to beat your Omega because you are scared.*

He didn't say anything to the girl, but walked out of the office and toward Lorna's workshop. Before Lorna joined as one of his Betas, Jack had never heard of a Pack Witch. She had explained that during the Civil War, her Alpha had been grievously wounded. When she went to his dying side, he had given her all the knowledge that had been given to him from his Purist mate. The transfer left her with a lot of half bits and understanding from the Purist traditions. As they formed their pack, she often relied on the guidance from Spirits in important matters. Since his reign as Alpha, Lorna had consulted them each time a cub wanted to take their Rite of Passage. Jack couldn't deny that each Rite seemed to be well suited for each cub, even if he didn't understand how it all worked.

*Okay, calm down, Twist. There is no reason to go into the room looking all upset. It will only cause questions. Go in the room and act like the Alpha.*

Jack watched carefully as Lorna prepared Kama for receiving the Spirits. No cub had tried a First Kill so ill-prepared, at least not one from his pack. He loved the woman and was terrified he would lose her in this insane attempt. Lorna handed Kama her Kuba, and Jack looked at it. The Kuba, a dagger carved from a piece of wood, had been a long held tradition of the Loup. Jack had been made aware of it and its significance from The Judge. Ever since he had found out about them, Kubas had played an important role in each cub's Rite of Passage.

*Hmmm, she worked quickly on her Kuba. Most cubs take at least a week to carve it. Smells like cypress wood, a nice hardwood if I remember correctly. She even put some Celtic symbols on it. Dammit, she could have at least waited until a full moon to do this. Did the stupid Omega not even bother to let her know she would be at her weakest during the new moon? Okay, Lorna's calling the Spirits.*

He watched the Spirits spiral around, in and out of her and was curious when an ecstatic smile play across her lips. With a finger dipped in wolfsbane oil, Lorna drew a rune, on her forehead and said some words in a language that Jack had never been able to decipher.

*You would think after ten years this would be old hat, but I still find it fascinating.*

Jack watched the oil imprint illuminate. It never ceased to amaze him how the Spirits worked. The rune gave the people in the room vision through Kama's eyes as she went through her trial. Lorna gave a low, keening growl and poured three drops of oil in a bowl. The water rippled with each added drop; but as it stilled, a picture formed, revealing an old apartment building with a clear view of its address. Lorna then released the Spirits, and Kama glowed with residual power.

"The Spirits have chosen for you. You have until the set of the moon and rise of the sun to complete the mission," Jack said.

He made Kama repeat the address three times and then waited for her to ask for further clarification. He could see her eyes searching his for clues, but if she didn't ask, he couldn't offer advice. Instead of saying anything, Kama bowed to the group and walked out of the room.

*What is she doing? She should at least be asking questions at this point. Oh hell, unless she hasn't been told she could. Why is she doing this? She has to know she's not prepared. Well, all I can do at this point is watch and try not to make an ass of myself. What the hell?*

"Of all the daft things," Angus exploded. "She's taking a cab?"

Jack stood there with a stunned group of fellow watchers. Kama had actually taken a cab to her Challenge. Granted, nothing in the rules specifically objected to taking a cab to a destination, but no one ever had. Then again, no one in his pack had ever requested taking their First Kill after having only changed six weeks prior.

*Hell, this is what happens when you take your Rite so damn unprepared.*

"Well, the Gal has guts. I don't what she plans to kill it with," The Judge said. "She should be real interesting to watch."

The other Betas didn't comment, and Jack tried hard not to let his mouth hang open, since she hadn't bothered to take any sort of weapon when she left the Den. Jack steeled himself for the eventuality that she would die, because he couldn't foresee any way she would survive the ordeal. Angus kept shooting him steely barbs, clearly unhappy, as he had come to the conclusion his granddaughter would perish over her foolishness. With a mental sigh, Jack sat back for the long haul.

*Well at least she didn't stop for a bite to eat. I sure thought she would stop at Coppola's when she walked by. I'm surprised she didn't walk into someone as she stared at the building. Ah. She is there.*

He watched Kama walk in the door like she belonged there and go up the stairs. She paused for a moment at the door, but then opened it. She stepped inside and the vision went dim.

"Why isn't she using her Vision?" Aturus snarled.

"Because she's been Loup for six weeks and doesn't know better," Lorna said.

*Shut the hell up and let her fight. Crap, I need a drink. Would it look odd if I stepped out? What if she gets killed going through the door? Oh hell, just be done already.*

Kama looked around the apartment, much to the dismay of the Betas. They made groaning noises as she inspected furniture and pieces of old paper. The group quieted as an older man entered the room she was in, and they saw that he looked startled. Jack groaned in his head.

*Crap, isn't that the professor she had the special audition with? He looks like what she described in one of her many rants about not being successful.*

"Wonder what makes him so special?" Lorna asked. "He looks like a simple enough kill for her."

"Except we know it's never that easy," Jack said.

He wanted to howl with frustration; he knew how hard this would be for her. He watched Kama look around and realized she had no idea the old man was a vampire. He groused for just a moment about not being able to hear.

*The Spirits allow us to see, but not hear what is going on. It doesn't seem fair.*

The group watched her talk with the vampire, not recognizing the danger. Something tipped her off because the room shifted into startling clarity as her Vision was activated. A few of the Betas chuckled as she took a step back.

"She must be getting a real nose full being so close to that thing," Aturus said.

"She could just kill it and be done," Lorna said.

Jack wondered when a cub's Rite of Passage had become like a sporting event. Normally, he wouldn't have minded comments from the Betas, but not this time, not when so much could be lost.

*Hell, Kama keep your eyes open. You do not know this man, no matter what you think.*

"Did she just close her eyes? For the love of the Goddess," Aturus said.

Jack almost smiled; at least someone else had a hard time with her lack of tactics. The others in the room leaned forward, while Lorna cursed about needing sound. Jack recognized the strong tension that rolled through the room. Apparently, he wasn't the only one nervous. Angus snarled and began to pace.

"She should just kill him and be done with it," Angus said. "This is what happens when you send an unprepared child in to commit suicide."

"She asked for her Rite," Jack said.

"I canna believe you would let her do this," Angus said.

"I didn't let her do anything," Jack said. "She asked for the Rite and once the Goddess accepted her petition, she had the right to proceed forward."

"You should have tried to contact her family once you learned of her Loup heritage," Angus said.

The words were growled, and Jack supposed the tone signified Angus's fear, but still didn't appreciate it. He looked at Angus as a pointed reminder of whose territory they were on.

"We didn't know of her family heritage," Jack said.

"She didn't even know," Aturus said.

Angus opened his mouth to make a retort. With a loud sigh, Lorna stood up and admonished the group.

"Gentlemen, lower your hackles and your voices. We are trying to see what happens," she said.

From the looks she gave everyone, smacks were about to be handed out, and Jack really didn't want her to smack a visiting Alpha across the snout to keep him quiet.

"You are right of course, Lorna," Jack said. "We will continue to watch in silence."

The silence lasted for a few more moments until the vampire vanished from view. That was, until Kama turned her head to look at his hand upon her shoulder and almost everyone in the room groaned.

"Didn't you teach her anything?" Angus asked in a surly voice.

"I know I taught her never to put her back to the enemy," Aturus said.

Jack watched with a dry throat as Kama flinched and stepped away, turning to face the vampire but continued to stand there. He held out a sheaf of paper, and Kama took it. She looked over it, with shaking hands, and then placed it reverently on a nearby desk.

The breathing in the room had gotten loud, and Jack realized this Rite had been the most intense any of them had witnessed in a very long time.

*Maybe all cubs should take their Rites sooner rather than later. Well, only if we want to lose some of them. Some really do need the time to acclimate and get used to the lifestyle. But it is possible we allow too many of them to take advantage of being a cub, instead of forcing them to be responsible sooner. Come on Kama, just kill it and come home. Why is this taking so long? What did he just offer her?*

Just when Jack wanted anything to break the stifling tension in the room, Kama acted. She reached into her coat, took out her Kuba in a smooth motion, and buried it in his chest. The vampire had no real warning and looked shocked to see the wooden hilt protruding from his body.

"It's about bloody time," Angus said as the Betas all whooped.

"I knew the girl would make a great warrior. I bet she played with him, just to test him out," Aturus said.

Jack felt bile rise as she just stood there and stared at the tree the vampire had become. The cycle of life required that the stolen essence make life again. Because the instrument of destruction was wood, it only stood to reason that a tree would grow. From the size of this one, Jack judged it to be about 150 years old. The older the vampire the more mature the tree.

*Wow, her Rite had some serious repercussions to it. Then again maybe she needed the very clear message to choose one life. She would have had an extremely hard time trying to balance being Loup and a professional singer. She's going to be mad at me.*

They watched Kama look around and as something startled her, she grabbed the hilt of her Kuba, broke it off, and left. Jack looked up at the clock.

"Only two hours," he said.

"Well, the Gal is special," The Judge said.

Only then did Jack realize he had spoken aloud. They watched as Kama returned to them, on foot, and waited for her to come and present herself. The others stood as she entered the room, looking a bit shocked but none the worse for her ordeal. Jack resisted the urge to pull her into a tight embrace. Instead, he concluded the formalities.

"Welcome back," Jack said. "Do you bring proof of your kill?"

She pulled her Kuba from her pocket and handed it to him. Jack accepted it and turned it over in his hand. At least two new inches of wood were found on the jagged edge where she had ripped it from the tree.

*Nicely done. I wonder if she will be upset that she will have to carve it over again. We don't normally use our Kubas as weapons, which she might have known if she had been prepared. Okay, down Jack. she is safe and right here. Be done with it so we can see her sometime tonight.*

Jack leaned back his head and howled; Aturus, Gabe, The Judge, and Lorna joined him and after a few moments, Angus's voice mixed in with the chord, adding a new base note. Kama united the howls, her musicality apparent as they sounded more like a blended song.

"The Goddess has accepted this First Kill and proclaims it Done," Lorna said.

Jack put his hand on Kama's shoulder and looked into her eyes, which were a swirling mix of Loup gold and her human chocolate brown.

"By the laws of this Pack, you are now an adult, and we welcome you."

"It's done?" Kama asked.

Her whisper seemed to carry through the whole room.

"Yes."

The Beta's surrounded her, offering their congratulations as they all accepted her into their pack. Jack took the opportunity to fade into the background and stood by in quiet contemplation as her grandfather talked to her.

*Of course, he would extend the offer that she come and visit his pack. She's mine now. Back off.*

Lorna ushered Kama and Angus out of the room and then returned as the final stages of business took place.

"Who will vouch for a proper First Kill?" Jack asked.

All four Betas took a step forward.

"Does anyone contest Kama's being accepted as an adult in our pack?"

Jack looked at each face and accepted each negative nod.

"Then I announce her to have earned full rights and responsibilities as an adult member of our pack and full access to our Den and protection."

Jack took a knife from his belt and made a shallow cut across his thumb. He smeared a drop of blood onto the jagged blade of Kama's Kuba and then handed it to Gabe. After each Beta had added a drop of blood, Jack took her Kuba back.

"We are all agreed."

With his dismissal, all of the Betas left. Angus was waiting in the hallway, and Jack motioned for him to come back in.

"I would like for her to visit," Angus said. "You mongrels are not what I expected, decent even, but I would like for her to know her family."

"Of course it will be her choice, but I look forward to perhaps a new understanding between our packs," Jack said.

"We shall see," Angus said. "It is hard to overcome years of bias, but I have learned a lot coming here and I think it might be worth working on."

"It will challenge us as well. Maybe your granddaughter can be the vehicle to end some of the crazy rumors and bring some semblance of understanding."

Angus thought for a moment and nodded. He looked as if he had more to say.

"I'll take my leave tonight."

"Safe travels."

The men clasped hands and shook once. They left the workroom and Jack guided him to Kama's party before returning to his office. Jack sat at his desk and picked up the phone. He looked at the receiver for a moment, and then punched in some numbers.

"I need an apartment on 79th West sketched," he said.

After listening on the other end for a minute, he smiled.

"Most of the stuff can go up on the auction block in Europe as soon as it can be shipped. However, I want all of the papers brought to me."

He sat alone in the dark for a few moments more and then headed home.

*Damn, this has been the longest day I have ever had. I went from almost losing her to her family to having her risk her life to going up against her biggest dream. I'm sure her Rite was harder on her than on me, but damn if it didn't end up being a test for me to keep calm. I'll give her a few hours to enjoy her party with her new pack mates, but afterwards she is all mine.*

His wolf howled its consent.

## CHAPTER Sixteen

Kama looked at the tree standing before her; it mocked her, damning her actions by its very presence. She couldn't believe she had done it.

*It looks so harmless for something that used to be an evil bloodsucking fiend. Dammit, I can't believe this is the creature who rejected me for my audition. Then again I suppose he would know good opera, being the one who composed the original and all. Stupid jerk he cost me everything. It almost seems right I destroyed him like he destroyed my dreams. Then again, now I don't have any dreams.*

Her anger carried her through the shakes which threatened to pull her to her knees. In the midst of her pacing, Kama's keen ears picked up a new wail and her wolf prodded her into action.

*Police sirens, I'm sure the loud yell had a neighbor calling the cops. Good thing they didn't bother to come and see what all the noise was about. Rather sad really, people have really checked out of caring. Neighbors should be more concerned with that is going on around them. Though, I can't imagine that a vampire would want neighbors all up in his business unless he was preparing to eat them. Right, get moving before the caring officers escort you into a jail cell.*

She made it down the stairs and outside without encountering anyone. To her surprise, the police cars flew by her and didn't stop as they headed toward their destination. As she walked the few short blocks toward the Park, nothing seemed different in the City. She had almost expected some huge changes or palpable variance from the Universe proclaiming she had done well, but the hustle and bustle still carried on as it had hours before. Looking at the clock on her cell phone, she realized two hours had passed.

*Wow, it felt so quick. No time to spend thinking and mulling things over. Then again I suppose two hours is a good amount of time to have spent there. I wondered if he entranced me or something. But if he had, I doubt I would be walking out here in the city and him standing there as a big tree. What the heck is with the tree thing anyhow? I thought they were supposed to be dust.*

Kama shook her head at no one in particular as her thoughts forced physical reactions as she worked through what had just happened. Her mind tumbled and tripped as she tried to recall all the events which had happened during the previous two hours. It all started with a slip of paper...

##

After leaving Lorna's workroom, Kama wrote down the address she had seen in her vision on a piece of paper. She hadn't been sure where the address was and rather than waste time, she had hopped in a cab and gone across town. She was almost amused that it was actually only two blocks away from the West side of the park. She had easily found the old building described and walked in the unlocked door. She found it clean, polished and very quiet. Kama walked up the three flights of stairs as quiet as she could.

*So this is it. After this point my life changes forever. I cannot believe I am here to kill a vampire. I mean really, so I just walk in and stake it and then I'm done? This is going to suck, the last time I met up with a vampire I got my butt kicked. Okay, prepare for a serious fight. They are evil, ugly nasty things and should be killed. Odd thing to do for a Rite of Passage, it's something we would do anyhow. Shoot, kids in Africa have to memorize their lineage since the beginning of time not being able to eat or drink until they are successful. At least this will be done after today and then I can do something else.*

As she cleared the top of the staircase she noted only one door. The hallway had opulent décor accented by low lights. She stood in front of the door and stared at it. She knew both Jack and Beth had passed, but wondered all the same if she could. In her moment of panic an image of her mother sprang to mind. It had been before her first concert at Julliard, and she had gotten stage fright. Her mother took her aside and explained why Kama would not fail.

*'Tis not in your nature lovely, and to doubt yourself is the worse form of failure possible. Now be a proper DeKosse and go do us proud.*

# Enter the Moon

Kama smiled at the lingering rant that had followed but the point stuck home, and buoyed by the memory she squared her shoulders and turned the handle as slow as she could.

*I guess this would be it. At least I don't have to worry about making a mistake. Who knew vampires left their doors unlocked? Huh, I never would have expected them to live so lavishly, I wonder what happens with all of this stuff afterwards.*

She tried not to make noise as she peered inside, and nothing moved. With no more excuses to hide behind, except her nerves, Kama took a deep breath and entered. The room stood dim with only one small lamp providing scant light. As Kama looked around, she noted despite papers scattered all over an antique roll top desk in disarray, it felt comfortable and lived in. The room acted as a study and living room together but the richness of the furniture brought her to a stop.

The settee, chairs and lounge were from what she thought to be from the Baroque period. The twisted columns on the legs and delicate 'S' scrolls through the pieces were an indicator. She admired the soft glow of the polished wood and moved closer.

She looked closer at the papers and saw they were compositions. She started to pick one up when a slight noise from the room off to the corner made her freeze in place, papers in hand. An older man came out of the door and when he saw her he looked as startled as she did. To Kama's surprise and relief, Signor Ristori stood before her.

*Oh thank goodness, I am here to save him from some evil vampire. This makes things so much easier. Heck, he might even decide to take me on as a student after this.*

She looked again at him to make sure her eyes didn't play some sort of trick on her and mentally breathed a sigh of relief. He squinted at her in the wan light and then pushed his glasses up on his face and stared at her. Kama looked at him in confusion; he didn't seem to recognize her for a moment.

*Hell, were my songs so abysmal at my audition that I'm not even memorable?*

"What do you want? I have nothing here of value," he said. Then he peered at her, looking her over very carefully.

"Oh, I know you, Miss DeKosse, isn't it?"

"Yes, Signor Ristori," she said.

He watched her for a moment more, and then moved to sit in a large chair. He grabbed a pipe and lit it. He looked at her all the while and Kama didn't know what to do. A tingling thrill went through her because something didn't feel right anymore. The walls seemed to close in on her as she began to assess her situation.

*Why wouldn't he recognize me? Hell, after all he ruined my chance to study with him. So should I tell him I am here to kill a vampire out to get him or what? Probably not, then he would think I am just some jaded wanna be star.*

"Did we have an appointment I forgot about?" he asked her and then mused to himself "No, of course not, we wouldn't have an appointment at my house. What are you doing here, my dear?"

Kama stood there for a moment trying desperately to think of a good excuse, not only why she would be there, but also as to why she would be in his home without invitation. Her attention kept being pulled away from her, as her nostrils flared at the rancid smell permeating the room. Despite the scent of acrid smoke from the pipe, the smell of death came through clearly. The smell resembled a flesh wound rotting away with disease and sickness, like something on its way to death but fought against the natural conclusion. She knew the vampire must be getting close, and she tried again to think of an excuse.

"Well Professor, it's rather hard to explain."

Taking a deep breath, and fighting the urge to gag afterwards, she closed her eyes for a moment and with concentration forced the energy to flow. The smell of death closed in on her and she knew she only had moment.

*After I save him from being chomped on I can try to explain my eyes being all yellow. He shouldn't care by then.*

She blinked her eyes to shift and then looked around the apartment with her Loup vision. She hoped just maybe the professor would not notice the shift of her eyes from human to lupine. She prayed the dim lighting would act as a cover.

*Then again, how many people actually could recognize wolf eyes? I mean if I all of a sudden had cat eyes, the oval pupils would give it away. Come on Kama, focus.*

With a slow sweeping motion, she looked around the room, letting her nose guide her gaze until finally she caught sight of a sickly trailing aura. The aura oozed and pulsed with pustules of greenish- grey colors looking sickly and very rotten. It took a few moments for Kama to realize the smell and the aura had led her in a circle. Signor Ristori stood in front of her and to her stunned horror, the aura and smell emanated from him. In shock, her vision shifted back to human as her concentration faltered. She found him staring at her with a look she couldn't read.

"You have come for me then," he said. "I certainly never figured you for Loup. I've not seen many werewolves in the Fine Arts."

"I guess we are even, since I would have not figured you to be evil," she said.

He took another puff from his pipe and Kama noticed he never exhaled. The smoke wafted from the corners of his mouth and nose in controlled curls.

*Right, he doesn't breathe so the smoke wouldn't actually go into his lungs. I wondered if he tried to perfect the allusion of smoking. So tobacco must really be addictive if he still does it after he is dead.*

Her wolf growled in her ear, snapping her back on track. Kama realized her Rite of Passage had just gotten harder and she needed to stay focused.

"Evil? My dear, I may be vampire but I am most certainly not evil," he said.

"You murder people and drink their blood. Don't tell me you survive on rodents or animals because I will not believe it for one second," she said and was glad find herself becoming angry.

*This is what rejected me? He is an evil dead thing and he judged me? And now sits there calm like I am not here to kill him. Jerk.*

"No, I do not eat animals," he said.

She watched him as he returned to sit in his chair with a chuckle and no apparent care for his own safety. The calm almost unnerved her.

"I am careful with whom I choose to dine. There are some criminals, some transients, but mostly I content myself with those who would prostitute others."

"You still kill people," she said.

"Only those who would harm or abuse others," he said. "Really, Darling Girl, how evil can I be? I work to advance the Arts. I have worked with some of the greatest composers and trained young talent. Does that sound evil to you?"

Kama furrowed her brow, but raised her Kuba. Her wolf urged her to kill him and be done with it. Her logic got stuck in his argument of promoting the arts.

*He is a vampire but look at all of the good he has done over the years. I mean Julliard has relied on him for years to promote the best and brightest. Perhaps vampires have a choice too? Maybe he didn't even want to be turned and did what he could to make the best of the situation. But, he just admitted to killing people. Why does he get to judge who should live?*

Kama raised the Kuba further.

"Okay, I see you are intent on this but will you hear me out?" Signore Ristori asked.

"Hear you out for what?"

"Well it is obvious you feel justified in your quest because I didn't accept you as a student."

Kama faltered for a moment.

*So is this driven by revenge? Is this part of the test, to be able to tell who is evil and who is not? Am I supposed to rid the world of this vampire because he is evil or am I supposed to learn how to tell the difference between murders and those who kill to survive? No, that can't be right - he kills. Then again, here I am justifying killing him.*

"Did you ever stop to think I just couldn't accept you?"

"I have the talent," Kama said. "I have been working towards this since the age of seven. Why couldn't you?"

"Because most Loup kill vampires with no provocation. When you first came into your audition, you made me nervous. I couldn't even concentrate on your audition piece because of the fear I felt toward you. How could I possibly work with someone who made me tremble? At first I thought you chose that piece to mock me, but now I realize you had no idea of the pain that particular work would bring me," he said and paused for a moment. "Your technique was flawless and your rendition of the piece impressive but I couldn't take the chance that you would kill me over a criticism."

Kama looked at him skeptically. The wolf nagged at her to be done with it all. The girl wanted to accept the reason.

*It means I am good enough, just this whole werewolf thing screwing up my plans, again.*

"But maybe now because we both know the truth, we can make a new agreement."

Kama's heart leapt, he would take her on as a student. Then her mind began its own slow and seductive dance of rationalizations. If she worked with him she would be able to control him, she would be able to curtail any activities he did and as long as they worked together he wouldn't be tempted to feed on any one because she would be there. She thought of the heights she could reach under his tutelage; no doubt he only worked with the best and her dreams could all be realized.

"Lost in thoughts of the glory that can be, *carne dolce*? " Signore Ristori asked.

He had walked so softly toward her, she hadn't heard him move. As he murmured the endearment, Kama's head snapped up and she realized that he had flanked her. Upset she let her guard down, even for just a second; Kama whirled on him with a calm face. Her lips rolled in and she nibbled her bottom lip, in an old habit of thinking. The phrase meant "sweet meat" and it sent a shudder through her. She put her hand up defensively.

"I have not decided anything yet."

"Come now, we both know this is what you deserve. You have the talent and drive. I have the connections to see you through. But perhaps you need something special yes? I can see you cannot be swayed by the ordinary. I see, you know you deserve better."

Kama stood in indecision, watching Ristori.

*Would he be this calm if he were evil? He should be afraid I'm going to kill him. What is he doing?*

Ristori moved towards his roll top desk and after a moment of rifling through the papers pulled out an old document and held it out to her. She took it and glanced over it. The notes were cramped and scrawled so tiny it made her dizzy, and then she saw the signatures. She closed her eyes, only to snap them open when his hand touched her shoulder. She fought down the waves of revulsion and nausea as he touched her.

"What you see here is an original Ristori and Vivaldi document. By all means take it and look it over. The last piece we worked together on before the sickness took him; the final Vivaldi opera. We were going to produce it together, a brand new opera to grab firm my hold on the musical world. It has never been heard, now it would be yours," he offered her. "Just as people relate Luciano Pavarotti and Mirella Freni with *La Bohème*, they will know you for this. It will be yours, and everyone who sings it after, will be compared to you."

Kama found her mind churning. He had just offered her more than her goals had ever been. A new and unknown opera from a classical great was rare, almost unheard of and almost a guarantee that it would shoot her into instant fame and stardom.

"It will be yours, Kamaria. You know what an opportunity this is. You will rise to the ranks of virtuoso quickly and no one will be able to touch you," he said. "Together, we can be great, just think of the possibilities my dear one. We will rise to the top and stay there, forever."

His voice continued on melodically, twisting and winding. His words rose and fell in a seductive cadence. She placed the score on the desk to her left. Kama turned to face him. Signor Ristori's face held a pleasant smile, assured of her acceptance. She buried his Kuba into his chest with no wasted monologue or motion. Dispassionately she watched shock cover his face as the wooden hilt buried itself into his chest. Kama stepped back, not being sure what would happen and dropped her hand off her Kuba. She left the intricately carved wood deep in his chest.

*Oh God, I just stabbed a man. No, not just a man, one of the greatest vocal teachers at Julliard. No Kama, we just killed a vampire put it into perspective.*

She flinched as a sound of agony poured out of his mouth and filled the room. Ristori twisted and writhed as his chest exploded out as a sapling emerged and tried to anchor into the floor. The harsh sound cut off just as sudden as it started when a thick branch split his skull, as his enchanted and stolen blood moved from him into the wood of her Kuba and again reanimated what had once been alive. Ristori's split face turned grey as it aged and decayed. His bones snapped and crumbled as they hit the floor around the tree and soon nothing of the man was left. As Kama watched a fine mist of ash surrounded the small sapling buried into hardwood floors of the apartment. She stood there stunned at what had just happened and when she when able she took a deep breath.

*My Kuba, where is it? It has my prints on it. Okay Kama grab it and let's go.*

As sirens jostled her into motion, Kama grabbed the hilt of the Kuba. It stayed firmly in the heart of the tree, despite how hard she pulled. In desperation, she pulled down and a loud crack rewarded her efforts. She looked around the place, and left, locking the door behind her. She moved down the stairs and out the side door before she took a breath.

"Excuse me."

Kama stepped back from the slight impact and stood ready. Until she realized the other person had already moved away and down the street. Lost in her own thoughts she ceased to notice her surroundings and had walked into someone else as equally occupied in thought.

*Wow, that really happened. I would have thought there would have more give and take but I just did it. I didn't even think.*

But she had thought and those thoughts tumbled around her head as she walked back to Central Park. Back to where she would have to explain her actions and show her proof.

*But I don't have any proof.*

Thrusting her hands into her pocket she felt the jagged edges of her Kuba.

*Well I can show them this; it should prove I killed him. I mean, it's not like I could have taken the whole tree. Well maybe, I am pretty strong now. Never mind I have my Kuba, although I certainly could have taken the score. Dammit, it would have been proof too. Except I could have taken it and just left him alive. Well undead, well whatever he could have gone about his way. Oh.*

Realization began to dawn on her the whole Rite was more complex than she had thought originally.

*There is no other proof I would have except my Kuba. Anything else could mean I let him live. They already knew I would be tempted by him; they just gave me the choice. Either kill the evil thing or lie to my Pack. I'm sure the whole Rite was designed to offer me what I wanted and see how I reacted. Sheesh and I thought it easy.*

A sudden sobering thought made her stand still. She thought about what Ristori had offered her and couldn't imagine he didn't promise them the same thing to his other progeny.

*But where are they? I mean he works with a lot of students, and the last I knew most of them went to work in Europe. Right, they would have but instead of fame they found themselves being a snack. I bet if I look, the majority of his students have accidents. He was selling my dreams, like I had a choice. But there never could have had that option. Jack wouldn't be able to trust me, the pack wouldn't trust me, heck I wouldn't even trust me if I sold out.*

The truth crashed in over her head like ice water, awakening her to reality. Ristori had been evil and she would have never been able to control or affect the fact he would always be evil. Thoughts swirled faster in her head and drowned her with internal ramblings. The fact remained he would have used and discarded her, like he had done with the so many others that had come before her. He would not have brought her glory, there were only his evil whims and no her plans for greatness.

*Only his survival mattered. He would have offered me anything for it but he happened to have the one thing he knew I wanted. It wasn't so easy after all. I just killed off my chance for superstardom. Quite frankly, I just killed off being anything but Loup. It seems unfair what I had planned to do my whole life just got snatched away from me, and for what? I turn hairy, growl and shift.*

She bit back tears as the unfairness of it all coursed through her and she grieved her loss of her dreams. To her surprise, her wolf mourned too. Kama pulled herself back into her professional shell as the Park came into view. All in all, she had expected the whole thing to take longer, but she couldn't help but feel relieved at the task being finished. She strode with much purpose back to the castle, not faltering nor stopping to talk to anyone. She walked down the narrow stairs, through the now short tunnels and into Jack's office.

She paused in the doorway before her Elders, who rose at her entrance and then walked in front of Jack's desk. The Judge, Aturus, Gabe and Lorna all looked at her with a look she couldn't decipher.

*Hell if I know what they want. I killed the damn thing. Quite frankly I'm too tired to care and my brain hurts. If there is more to this test it might just kill me.*

Jack had a look on his face she had never seen before and didn't know how to interpret. Her Grandfather stood next to Jack with a small smile on his face.

"Welcome back," Jack said. "Do you bring proof of your kill?"

Kama reached back into her pocket and pulled out the Kuba. It the bright light of his office she could see colored threads caught in the jagged edges of the blade.

*I almost expected to see blood. But why would there be?*

To Kama's surprise, no one else in the room looked surprised to see the Kuba.

*I guess if you come back then it means you have made it? Odd, I would think everyone would want to see proof that I killed him and didn't take the easy way out. Dang I wish I would have nabbed that score.*

Jack leaned back his head and howled; Aturus, Gabe, The Judge and Lorna joined him and after a few moments Angus' voice joined the chord. Angus had added a new base note and Kama took the howl from discord to harmony again and with a rush, energy and a balance passed over and through her; soothing her frayed nerves, calming her.

"The Goddess has accepted this First Kill and proclaim it Done," Lorna said.

Jack put his hand on Kama's shoulder and looked into her eyes. His eyes were a swirling mix of Loup and his human olive.

"By the laws of this Pack you are now an adult and we welcome you."

"It's done?" Kama asked.

Her whisper seemed to carry through the whole room.

"Yes."

The Beta's surrounded her, offering congratulations and words Kama didn't hear in the rush of emotion that flooded and overwhelmed her. She wanted to be in Jack's arms and celebrating but she knew it would have to wait until they had some privacy. In fact, she felt he held back too much.

*Sure, he gave me an official welcome and hug. But I could have gotten a warmer hug from my brother and he hates me right now. Sheesh, he better have some really good plans for later. Then again I am assuming there is a later; we haven't spent any time alone since this whole being Loup thing came up.*

Kama noticed Angus approach her with slow careful steps, and the other Loup in the room moved back to give them some space and privacy. She looked into his eyes, reading the shifting emotions he carried.

"Ye did well lass," Angus said. "You have done your family proud. You have carried on the MacBride tradition of excelling early."

His voice was gruff with emotion and his eyes held a glimmer. Kama steeled herself for what she knew would come next. She took a silent breath.

"Thank you Grandpa," she said.

He took her hand with a smile at the term, which she had never called him before. While he held her hand, he pressed something smooth and warm into her palm.

"I am proud you are my granddaughter, very proud you are Loup. Even more, proud you are Luna's Warrior in every aspect. You are always welcome," Angus said in a low husky voice.

"Thank you," she said.

Much to his surprise and even some of Kama's, she impulsively hugged him tight. She looked at the gift he had given her, an ornately carved wooden hair pin. It fit in the palm of her hand; smooth and worn with age, but a beautiful piece with a classic beauty. It was one long slender piece of wooden with Celtic carvings in the eye and Kama quickly pulled her hair out of its bind and used the pin to secure a messy bun in place.

"It belonged to my mother and now is yours. Always remember we are your family," Angus said. "I hope in time you will come and visit. I know you haven't had the chance until now, but I am hoping that will soon be rectified."

Kama heard the catch in his voice and gave him a reassuring smile.

"I plan to get to know all of my family," she said. "Thank you for the lovely gift. I will be in touch soon; there is much we need to talk about."

Heavy emotions quieted the room, until Lorna cleared her throat.

"Well, shall we celebrate?" Lorna asked. "Our girl just became a Woman."

"Come on, Gal, the rest of your pack is in The Lounge waiting to hear if you bit it or not," The Judge said. "Get going."

Kama walked out of Jack's office, and Angus followed her, but no one else. She graced him with a smile.

"I need to call my mom and let her know I am okay," she said.

"Of course," Angus said.

Kama walked a few paces down the tunnel for a bit of privacy and dialed.

"Hello?" Brenna asked.

"Hi, Mama."

"Oh, thank the Great Mother," Brenna said.

The words were whispered, but the brogue came out loud and clear. Kama smiled.

*Some things are so predictable.*

"I need to finish up a few things, and I'll be late tonight," Kama said.

"Okay, I'll wait for you."

"No, Mama, it will be a while. They are throwing me a party, and after my ordeal, I want to celebrate with my Pack" Kama said. "We can talk tomorrow."

"I love you."

"Love you, too."

Kama paused in the hall after she hung up her phone. She waited until her emotions were back in check and then looked at Angus standing in the hall, staring at the closed door. No one had followed her out yet.

*So, why are they staying behind closed doors and talking about me? They said I passed, is there anything else to discuss? I guess I should head to The Lounge. I wonder who is going to be there. Beth should be, and Karl, because we patrol together. Maybe a few of the other crazies that The Judge has me walk around the park with.*

She heard the party long before she reached it - a drum beat thrummed low and steady. She could tell it was already in full swing, and lot of energy pulsed through the room. To Kama's surprise, more Loup than she could remember ever seeing at the Park packed the room full. To her relief, she spotted Beth holding up a wall in the corner and went to join her.

"Who are all these people?"

"Our pack mates," Beth said. "We love to party, for whatever reason possible. But I will say, I have never seen this many all at once. I think they are curious about you."

"Curious about me? What for? I've been here for weeks and have never met half of them. They can't be that interested."

A cloud of smoke in her face let her know The Judge had materialized near her.

"Hell, Gal. You made it through your Rite after only being here a few weeks. Most cubs take at least a year. You are the new superstar, the new one to watch."

"That sounds rather foreboding."

Kama turned towards the husky voice to ask more questions and got a mouthful of smoke for her troubles. She coughed, watching the old coot smile at her.

"Go meet your people. There is plenty of time to ask questions."

Kama grimaced as he nudged her away from the wall and grabbed Beth's hand to pull her along.

"Trust me, they don't want to meet me; they already know who I am, and most of them don't care for me," Beth said.

"I don't care," Kama said. "You are my best friend."

She walked through the middle of the room and over to a snack table. She filled her plate and waited for Beth to do the same. They made a point to find a small table toward the center of the room. The girls sat and Kama looked around, making eye contact and smiling when smiled at.

"This is going to take some time to get used to," Kama said. "Why didn't they show any interest before?"

"They've learned not to get too close until the new cub passes their Rite," Beth said.

"Why?"

"You might have failed."

Kama shook her head as she ate her appetite in full drive. When she noticed Beth nodding along to the music, she dragged her friend out to the floor where others were dancing. She let the tension flow from her as she celebrated her success.

*Well, I certainly couldn't have seen this coming. People actually want to know who I am, which might not be a good thing, but damn, these people can party.*

She continued to enjoy her party for a few more hours, and then made her own excuses to leave. Beth offered to walk her home, but Kama smiled and declined. Not three steps out of the park, she found Jack's car waiting for her. She scowled when she found it empty.

*Where the hell is he? Just send a car? That is crap. Then again, I have been in there for hours. Well, at least we're going to his place.*

Kama walked up to Jack's house and rang the doorbell. He answered the door and stepped aside so she could enter. She had made it up the foyer steps and into his den, before he grabbed her from behind, holding her tightly in his embrace. Kama didn't settle for a mere hug and pulled him into a passionate kiss. Her hand splayed over his chest as she tried to touch all of him. She needed to assure herself that the Rite was really over and she was actually there with Jack. When they came up for air, she returned the smile he gave her.

"You were fantastic," he said. "Scared me out of my mind, but you handled it well."

Kama led him by the hand to the couch and sat with him.

"I'm glad you think so," she said. "I was terrified and angry, not to mention a little bit tempted."

"Tempted?" Jack asked. "About what?"

"Well, this great lost opera just sat there on his desk, and now it's going to be destroyed or whatever. But dammit, it will never be mine," Kama said.

Kama smiled at him and moved to snuggle in his lap. She didn't understand why her statement had brought a chuckle from him. She reveled in his touch and enjoyed being there with him. She kissed him again and then lay her head against his chest, letting the rhythmic beat drum away the tension of the day. He stroked her hair, and she moved closer.

"I'm glad it's done," she said.

"As am I," Jack said. "You did well, I am more proud of you than you will know."

Kama looked up into his eyes and smiled at him.

"I love you, Jack."

"I love you, Kamaria."

Kama didn't know what else would happen, but she looked forward to it.

*The rough part is behind me. I just have to go home and explain this all to my mom, make good on my promise to meet my werewolf family in Michigan, and keep my relationship a secret for another five months. No problem, right? Then again, I finally have adult status, and I have Jack. Who knew being a werewolf would make my life so complete?*

# ABOUT THE AUTHOR

*Jennifer Fisch-Ferguson has been writing and publishing fantasy stories since 2003. Publishing credits include short fiction, writing contests and novels.*

*She attended the Eastern Michigan University and graduated with a B.A in African American History and promptly went to work with AmeriCorps on a literary initiative. She went to the University of Michigan and got her Master's degree in Public Administration in 2008 and while she finished writing her thesis, also got a Masters in English – Composition and Rhetoric in 2009. She recently is working on her PhD at Michigan State University in the field of Writing and Rhetoric. She has been teaching collegiate and community writing classes since 2003 and loves the variety and inspiration her students bring.*

*She currently is finishing her trilogy and dutiful writes on her blog space about her journey.*

*She lives in the Midwest with two amazing sons, one coffee supplying mate and acts as staff-in-residence to one cranky cat.*

- See more at: http://warriorsofluna.com